KATHLEEN FULLER

"Fuller brings us compelling characters who stay in our hearts long after we've read the book. It's always a treat to dive into one of her novels."

—Beth Wiseman, bestselling author

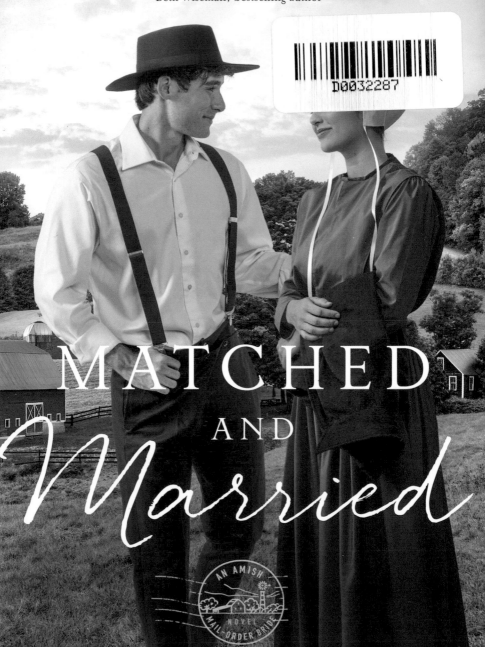

MATCHED
AND
Married

AN AMISH
NOVEL
MAIL-ORDER BRIDE

ACCLAIM FOR KATHLEEN FULLER

"This is a cute story of two sets of twins learning to grow up and be adults on their own terms and finding love along the way. It is another start of a great series."

—*PARKERSBURG NEWS AND SENTINEL* ON *A DOUBLE DOSE OF LOVE*

"Fuller (*The Innkeeper's Bride*) launches her Amish Mail-Order Brides series with the sweet story of love blooming between two pairs of twins . . . Faith and forgiveness form the backbone of this story, and the vulnerable sibling relationships are sure to tug at readers' heartstrings. This innocent romance is a treat."

—*PUBLISHERS WEEKLY*

"Sign me up for a one-way ticket to Maple Falls. If you love small towns, charming characters, and sweet, swoony romance, *Hooked on You* is your next favorite read. Kathleen Fuller has knit one wonderful story yet again."

—JENNY B. JONES, AWARD-WINNING AUTHOR OF *A KATIE PARKER PRODUCTION* AND *THE HOLIDAY HUSBAND*

"The quaint Arkansas town of Maple Falls could use a little sprucing up, and as it turns out, Riley and Hayden are the perfect pair for the job. What neither of them is counting on, of course, is that their hearts may receive some long overdue TLC in the process. Kathleen Fuller has knit together a lovable cast of characters and placed them in a setting so rich and dear you may find yourself hankering for a walk down Main Street on a warm summer's evening. I loved every minute of my time in Maple Falls, and I can't wait to return to visit the friends I made there."

—BETHANY TURNER, AWARD-WINNING AUTHOR OF *HADLEY BECKETT'S NEXT DISH* AND *PLOT TWIST*, ON *HOOKED ON YOU*

"A sweet, refreshing tale of idyllic small-town life, family, and unexpected romance, *Hooked on You* is the perfect read to cozy up with on a rainy day."

—MELISSA FERGUSON, MULTI-AWARD-WINNING AUTHOR OF *THE CUL-DE-SAC WAR*

"A charming story of new beginnings, family ties, love, friendship, laughter and the beauty of small towns. Fuller invites you into Maple Falls and greets you with a cast of characters who will steal your heart, make you want to stay, and entice you to visit again."

—KATHERINE REAY, BESTSELLING AUTHOR OF *THE PRINTED LETTER BOOKSHOP* AND *OF LITERATURE AND LATTES*, ON *HOOKED ON YOU*

"Fuller cements her reputation [as] a top practitioner of Amish fiction with this moving, perceptive collection."

—*PUBLISHERS WEEKLY* ON *AMISH GENERATIONS*

"Fuller brings us compelling characters who stay in our hearts long after we've read the book. It's always a treat to dive into one of her novels."

—BETH WISEMAN, BESTSELLING AUTHOR OF *HEARTS IN HARMONY*, ON *THE INNKEEPER'S BRIDE*

"A beautiful Amish romance with plenty of twists and turns and a completely satisfying, happy ending. Kathleen Fuller is a gifted storyteller."

—JENNIFER BECKSTRAND, AUTHOR OF *HOME ON HUCKLEBERRY HILL*, ON *THE INNKEEPER'S BRIDE*

"I always enjoy a Kathleen Fuller book, especially her Amish stories. *The Innkeeper's Bride* did not disappoint! From the moment Selah and Levi meet each other to the last scene in the book, this was a story that tugged at my emotions. The story deals with several heavy issues such as mental illness and family conflicts, while still maintaining humor and couples falling in love, both old and new. When Selah finds work at the inn Levi is starting up with his family, they clash on everything but realize they have feelings for each other. My heart hurt for Selah as she held her secrets close and pushed everyone away. But in the end, God's grace and love, along with some misguided Birch Creek matchmakers stirring up mischief, brings them together. Weddings at a beautiful country inn? What's not to love? Readers of Amish fiction will enjoy this wintertime story of redemption and hope set against the backdrop of a beautiful inn that brings people together."

—LENORA WORTH, AUTHOR OF *THEIR AMISH REUNION*

"A warm romance that will tug at the hearts of readers, this is a new favorite."

—*The Parkersburg News & Sentinel* on *The Teacher's Bride*

"Fuller's appealing Amish romance deals with some serious issues, including depression, yet it also offers funny and endearing moments."

—*Booklist* on *The Teacher's Bride*

"Kathleen Fuller's *The Teacher's Bride* is a heartwarming story of unexpected romance woven with fun and engaging characters who come to life on every page. Once you open the book, you won't put it down until you've reached the end."

—Amy Clipston, bestselling author of *A Seat by the Hearth*

"Kathleen Fuller's characters leap off the page with subtle power as she uses both wit and wisdom to entertain! Refreshingly honest and charming, Kathy's writing reflects a master's touch when it comes to intricate plotting and a satisfying and inspirational ending full of good cheer!"

—Kelly Long, national bestselling author, on *The Teacher's Bride*

"Kathleen Fuller is a master storyteller, and fans will absolutely fall in love with Ruby and Christian in *The Teacher's Bride*."

—Ruth Reid, bestselling author of *A Miracle of Hope*

"*The Teacher's Bride* features characters who know what it's like to be different, to not fit in. What they don't know is that's what makes them so loveable. Kathleen Fuller has written a sweet, oftentimes humorous, romance that reminds readers that the perfect match might be right in front of their noses. She handles the difficult topic of depression with a deft touch. Readers of Amish fiction won't want to miss this delightful story."

—Kelly Irvin, bestselling author of the Every Amish Season series

"Kathleen Fuller is a talented and gifted author, and she doesn't disappoint in *The Teacher's Bride*. The story will captivate you from the first page to the last with Ruby, Christian, and other engaging characters. You'll laugh, gasp, and wonder what will happen next. You won't want to miss reading this heart-warming Amish story of mishaps, faith, love, forgiveness, and friendship."

—MOLLY JEBBER, SPEAKER AND AWARD-WINNING AUTHOR OF *GRACE'S FORGIVENESS* AND THE AMISH KEEPSAKE POCKET QUILT SERIES

"Enthusiasts of Fuller's sweet Amish romances will savor this new anthology."

—*LIBRARY JOURNAL* ON *AN AMISH FAMILY*

"These four sweet stories are full of hope and promise along with misunderstandings and reconciliation. True love does prevail, but not without prayer, introspection, and humility. A must-read for fans of Amish romance."

—*RT BOOK REVIEWS*, 4 STARS, ON *AN AMISH FAMILY*

MATCHED
AND
Married

OTHER BOOKS BY KATHLEEN FULLER

THE AMISH MAIL-ORDER BRIDE NOVELS
A Double Dose of Love
Matched and Married
Love in Plain Sight (available May 2022)

THE MAPLE FALLS ROMANCE NOVELS
Hooked on You
Much Ado About a Latte (available January 2022)

THE AMISH BRIDES OF BIRCH CREEK NOVELS
The Teacher's Bride
The Farmer's Bride
The Innkeeper's Bride

THE AMISH LETTERS NOVELS
Written in Love
The Promise of a Letter
Words from the Heart

THE AMISH OF BIRCH CREEK NOVELS
A Reluctant Bride
An Unbroken Heart
A Love Made New

THE MIDDLEFIELD AMISH NOVELS
A Faith of Her Own

THE MIDDLEFIELD FAMILY NOVELS
Treasuring Emma
Faithful to Laura
Letters to Katie

THE HEARTS OF MIDDLEFIELD NOVELS
A Man of His Word
An Honest Love
A Hand to Hold

STORY COLLECTIONS
An Amish Family
Amish Generations

STORIES
A Miracle for Miriam included in *An Amish Christmas*
A Place of His Own included in *An Amish Gathering*
What the Heart Sees included in *An Amish Love*
A Perfect Match included in *An Amish Wedding*
Flowers for Rachael included in *An Amish Garden*
A Gift for Anne Marie included in *An Amish Second Christmas*
A Heart Full of Love included in *An Amish Cradle*
A Bid for Love included in *An Amish Market*
A Quiet Love included in *An Amish Harvest*
Building Faith included in *An Amish Home*
Lakeside Love included in *An Amish Summer*
The Treasured Book included in *An Amish Heirloom*
What Love Built included in *An Amish Homecoming*
A Chance to Remember included in *An Amish Reunion*

Melting Hearts included in *An Amish Christmas Bakery*
Reeling in Love included in *An Amish Picnic*
Wreathed in Love included in *An Amish Christmas Wedding*
Love's Solid Foundation included in *An Amish Barn Raising*
A Lesson on Love included in *An Amish Schoolroom*

MATCHED
AND
Married

An Amish Mail-Order Bride Novel

KATHLEEN FULLER

ZONDERVAN

Matched and Married

Copyright © 2021 by Kathleen Fuller

Requests for information should be addressed to:
Zondervan, *3900 Sparks Dr. SE, Grand Rapids, Michigan 49546*

Library of Congress Cataloging-in-Publication Data
Names: Fuller, Kathleen, author.
Title: Matched and married / Kathleen Fuller.
Description: Grand Rapids, Michigan : Zondervan, [2021] | Series: An Amish mail-order
brides novel ; 2 | Summary: "She has no plans of getting married. Marriage couldn't be
further from his mind. But can an Amish community with love on the brain bring two
reluctant lovebirds together?"-- Provided by publisher.
Identifiers: LCCN 2021013323 (print) | LCCN 2021013324 (ebook) | ISBN 9780310358961
(trade paper) | ISBN 9780310358978 (ebook) | ISBN 9780310358985 (downloadable
audio)
Subjects: GSAFD: Christian fiction. | Love stories.
Classification: LCC PS3606.U553 M38 2021 (print) | LCC PS3606.U553 (ebook) | DDC
813/.6--dc23
LC record available at https://lccn.loc.gov/2021013323
LC ebook record available at https://lccn.loc.gov/2021013324

Scripture quotations are taken from the New King James Version®. Copyright © 1982 by
Thomas Nelson. Used by permission. All rights reserved.

Apple cider vinegar home remedy in chapter 17 from Devon Miller, *Home Remedies from
Amish Country*, rev. ed., Millersburg, OH: Abana Books, 2001.

Zondervan titles may be purchased in bulk for educational, business, fundraising, or sales
promotional use. For information, please email SpecialMarkets@Zondervan.com.

Printed in the United States of America

21 22 23 24 25   LSC   10 9 8 7 6 5 4 3 2 1

To James. I love you.

Glossary

ab im kopp: crazy in the head
aenti: aunt
appleditlich: delicious
boppli: baby
bruder: brother
bu/buwe: boy/boys
daed: dad
danki: thank you
Deitsch: Amish language
dummkopf: stupid
familye: family
frau: wife
geh: go
grosskinner: grandchildren
grossmutter: grandmother
grossvatter: grandfather
gut: good
Gute morgen: good morning

Glossary

Gute nacht: good night

haus: house

kapp: white hat worn by Amish women

kinn/kinner: child/children

mamm: mom

maedel/maed: young woman/young women

mann: man

mei: my

mutter: mother

nee: no

nix: nothing

onkel: uncle

Ordnung: written and unwritten rules in an Amish district

rumspringa: running-around period when a teenager turns sixteen years old

schwester: sister

sohn: son

vatter: father

ya: yes

yer/yerself: your/yourself

yung: young

Family Tree

THE YODER FAMILY (HOLMES COUNTY)
Doris m. John

Margaret   June   Ruth Wanda

THE BONTRAGER FAMILY
Thomas m. Miriam

Owen   Ezra   Jessie   Elam

THE STOLL FAMILY
Delilah

Loren

THE YODER FAMILY (BIRCH CREEK)
Freemont m. Mary

Seth m. Martha	Ira m. Nina	Karen m. Adam Chupp	Ivy m. Noah Schlabach	Judah

OTHER CHARACTERS
Cevilla and Richard Thompson

Lester

Rhoda Troyer

Aden Troyer

Chapter 1

SALT CREEK, OHIO

*F*orbidden . . .
 The word repeated in her mind, but it didn't stop Margaret Yoder from placing a pair of faded skinny jeans on the bed in front of her. The jeans joined a red crop top and a light sweater in bright pink along with a makeup bag filled with lipstick, eye shadow, and mascara. Four-inch-high wedge sandals were on the floor. All looked out of place in her simply furnished room, the prohibited clothing clashing with the faded quilt on her twin bed.

She touched one of the clips on her *kapp*. All she had to do was remove it and her English transformation would start. And once it started, she knew from experience it wouldn't stop. But this time, changing out of her Amish clothes and into her English clothes would not only be forbidden by the *Ordnung*, but also considered a broken promise to God. In spite of knowing that, she was still tempted.

She glanced at the battery-operated alarm clock on her

1

bedside table. It was almost 8:00 p.m. If she was going to break that promise, she needed to do it now. Still, she hesitated. This wasn't the first time she'd broken her vow, and she was still paying the consequences of that terrible choice. *Why can't I learn my lesson?*

If she had, she would have run away earlier that afternoon when a crimson-red sedan screeched to a stop in front of her parents' driveway, nearly scaring her out of her skin. The passenger window rolled down, and a young woman in her early twenties leaned out the window. "Hey, girl!" she drawled.

Margaret recognized her right away. "Hi, Alexis," she said, dread filling her.

Dylan, Alexis's cousin, peered around her from the driver's seat. "Been a long time, Maggie."

Not long enough. Margaret had looked around, glad that her father was out in the field cutting hay with her three brothers-in-law, while her mother and sisters were inside baking pies for tomorrow's church service they were hosting. She dashed to the car but didn't get too close, as if being near the vehicle would pull her into the vortex of her former life.

"There's a party at Jessica's tonight," Alexis said. "You should come with us. We can pick you up at the usual spot."

"I don't do that anymore," Margaret said, lowering her voice and hoping none of her nosy neighbors were watching this exchange. "I thought everyone knew that." Everyone meaning the English friends she used to have during her *rumspringa*, which had ended a little more than a year ago, when she joined the church right before visiting her aunt and uncle in Birch Creek.

"We figured you might change your mind." Alexis lit a

cigarette with a bright-pink lighter. She blew a smoke circle in Margaret's direction. "Like you did before."

Dread turned to nausea as she waved off the smoke, remembering the days when she and Alexis would see who could make a flawless smoke ring. Picking up smoking, even though she'd only smoked around her English friends, was another regret among many. Enough to last a lifetime.

Dylan leaned over the steering wheel and leered at her. "I'm digging the *Little House on the Prairie* look, Maggie. I don't think I've ever seen you so . . . covered." He gave her a knowing wink.

Margaret recoiled, her cheeks blazing as she remembered one particular party where she and Dylan had gotten close. Too close. But as usual when she saw him, her heart leapt a little. He was still handsome with thick blond hair, caramel-colored eyes, and muscles that didn't quit. She'd always been gullible when it came to good-looking men, and she was the only Amish woman she knew who thought English men were better looking than most of the Amish ones. Dylan was particularly gorgeous and well built, and despite herself, she was still attracted to him. But it was a shallow attraction. The personality underneath his sublime surface was revolting. *I must remember who he really is.*

She stepped away from the car. "I'm not interested." Hopefully, he would realize she wasn't just talking about going to a party.

Alexis leaned farther out the window, the tight-fitting tank top she wore barely covering what it was supposed to. "Are you sure you don't want to go? Remember all the fun we used to have?"

The uneasiness in the pit of Margaret's stomach grew. That was the problem. She did remember—in vivid detail—everything she had done during her *rumspringa*, and it filled her with shame.

At first, she vowed not to go crazy like some of her peers had when they reached sixteen—the usual age of permitted freedom. But it hadn't taken long for her to succumb. Finally, she made her decision, determined to be a meek Amish woman like her mother and three older sisters. Like her *mamm* had always wanted her to be.

Yet she had to admit that a small part of her still missed the English world. At least parts of it. Attending parties had been an opportunity to be with the friends she'd made during her time in that world. There were good times when she snuck out for sleepovers with those friends. They'd have long talks in the middle of the night while they consumed junk food and had the TV on in the background. They mostly talked about boys and sometimes about the future, which Margaret had always been unsure about. She never brought up with anyone her hesitation to join the Amish church, especially the party girls she hung out with.

"Just think about it," Alexis begged. "Please?"

Against her better judgment, Margaret nodded once. She told herself she agreed so they would leave, but she was already thinking about the many times she used to sneak out of the house. She was an expert at it, and until that day eleven months ago, her parents and the rest of the community had never known that she was an excellent escape artist. After the humiliation of confessing and asking forgiveness in front of the church for rebelling, she vowed she would never rebel again. But here she was, thinking about doing exactly that.

"Awesome." Dylan grinned as he sat back in his seat and shifted the car into drive. "We'll pick you up at the usual spot around nine." Before Margaret could respond, he and Alexis sped off.

Now she stood in her bedroom several hours later, seriously

tempted to betray her vow to the church and her own personal promise. Again. After three years of living with one foot in the English world and one foot in her Amish community—and due in no small part to her parents' strong encouragement—she had finally decided to join the church. And for the most part she hadn't regretted that decision. During her *rumspringa* she was far from God, and being a part of the church had drawn her closer to him. Yet she also couldn't deny that, at times, the English world still pulled at her.

Margaret looked at the letter lying next to the English outfit. She knew the contents, having read them as soon as Alexis and Dylan left. If the outfit represented her past, the letter symbolized her present.

Dear Margaret,

Thank you so much for the lovely pressed flower picture you sent me. I have it displayed in my bedroom on the dresser. The yellow, blue, and pink wildflowers are so beautiful, and the frame is remarkably simple and pretty. It looks like something I would buy in a store!

Doris said that she told you about the mail-order bride advertisement that someone from our community put in the paper. We still don't know who put in the ad, but it certainly has had some repercussions. Some good—we've had one double wedding already. Do you remember the Bontrager family, the one with all the boys? The oldest twins got married. Then their oldest son also married, but not to a woman in Birch Creek. The downside is that now we have an overabundance of single females! That isn't all due to the advertisement, though. We've had four more families move to Birch Creek since you last visited, all who had mostly daughters. Of course, we still have a few bachelors left, but the tables have certainly turned.

I hope someday we'll find out who put the ad in the paper. Of course, the two main suspects are Cevilla and Delilah, our local matchmakers, although no one will mention it within their hearing. But they seemed as puzzled as the rest of us, so they might not be involved. It would be nice to know the truth, but the culprit might always be a mystery.

I hope you're doing well. Know that you're always welcome for another visit. I miss you—it was nice to have another woman in the house now that Karen and Ivy are married and settled in with their own families. Feel free to come to Birch Creek anytime. You can stay as long as you like!

Love,

Aenti Mary

Margaret already knew about the ad her aunt mentioned. Her mother had shown it to her almost two months ago: "Looking for marriage, ladies? Single Amish men available in Birch Creek, Ohio." The advertisement, which was so small and had been crammed in the corner of a local Holmes County area newspaper, was easy enough to overlook. Apparently, people liked to scour the newspaper, because some of her peers had seen the advertisement too. Her married friends, knowing that she had relatives in Birch Creek, had teased her about packing her bags and moving there, where she would have her pick of husbands.

Like that would ever happen. She enjoyed the time she spent in Birch Creek, and not just because she liked being with *Aenti*

Mary. She had also made friends with Nina Stoll, now Nina Yoder since she had married Mary's son, Ira. Her visit to the community happened before the advertisement hit the paper, and she'd seen firsthand that the single men far outnumbered the single women, with her being the only single woman in town. She had to admit she enjoyed the attention of the young men, even if it was limited to one singing at her uncle's house and a few flirtatious conversations after church. She hadn't seen anyone who piqued her interest, and when she returned to Salt Creek, she hadn't given any of the Birch Creek men a second thought.

But from almost the moment Margaret was baptized, her mother had been dropping hints as big as anvils that she needed to get married like her three older sisters, June, Ruth, and Wanda. She'd mentioned it just this morning, as Margaret helped her and her sisters prepare the pie shells for baking. "Marriage is the best thing for you," *Mamm* said with an emphatic nod. "You're at the right age to get married." As usual, her sisters backed up their mother's words with looks of silent approval. All four were a united front and had been since Margaret could remember. And of course, all three of them were married by the time they were twenty—the same age Margaret was now.

But it was what they left unsaid that stuck in Margaret's craw. Marriage would make her an acceptable member of the community and redeem some of the embarrassment her family had experienced due to Margaret's latest indiscretion. Better yet, she would become someone else's problem.

She clenched her fists and shifted her gaze to her English outfit. If her family thought she was so imperfect and such a failure, she might as well prove them right.

Nee. She gave her head a hard shake. She didn't join the church because of her family—she joined because she wanted to be Amish. As much as she would like to forget about the pressure she felt from her family to be as perfect as possible, doing something against the *Ordnung*, and her own personal principles, wasn't the way to do that. Going back to her English life, even for one night, wasn't an option anymore.

Quickly she grabbed the illicit clothing and placed it in a flat plastic bin under her single bed, shoving the box to the very back until she heard the plastic hit the wall. She had to get rid of the clothing, but only when she was sure *Mamm* and *Daed* wouldn't catch her. If they did, that would open up another can of worms that she wouldn't be able to put back. Until she could throw out the clothing unhindered, it would stay under the bed.

She sat on the edge of her mattress, stunned by how close she had come to making another huge mistake. Her shoulders slumped. She thought God had changed the rebellious part of her heart. And maybe since she'd ultimately changed her mind, she had indeed made a little progress. Very little, but she would take what she could get.

Margaret stood and started to pace, biting her fingernail. She'd made the right decision, but she still had problems to deal with. Being at odds with her mother all the time, for one. That wasn't going to change anytime soon. She was still the black sheep of her family too. *Mamm* had never pressured Margaret's sisters to get married. In fact, she cried at every single one of their weddings. Margaret reckoned her mother would squeal with joy once Margaret finally tied the knot.

Then there was the problem of Alexis and Dylan. She couldn't be sure they wouldn't show up at her house again, and she could only hope they wouldn't come any closer than their usual meeting spot down the road when they came to pick up her tonight. She wouldn't be there, and she figured their desire to party would keep them from waiting too long. Dylan's leering had made her uncomfortable, and she knew from experience that he was a man who always got what he wanted. Alexis asked her to join them, but she could see Dylan showing up alone next time. Would she be able to resist him if he did? She wasn't so sure.

She shuddered and picked up her aunt's letter. A thought occurred to her. She did miss her aunt and uncle and cousins, and she would love to see Nina again. *Maybe I do have an escape.*

Decision made, she went downstairs and found *Mamm* and *Daed* in the living room. Her father had his feet up on an old tufted stool that had been in the family for two generations, his hands folded over his stomach as he softly snored. *Mamm* was sitting in her chair near the gas-powered lamp, darning a pair of his socks. When Margaret entered the room, her mother lifted her gaze and peered over her reading glasses. "Shh," she said, gesturing to *Daed* with a lift of her finger. "He's sleeping."

Margaret nodded and walked over to *Mamm*. She sat down on the floor at her mother's feet and looked up at her. She'd been told over the years how much she favored her mother in every way except for height and temperament. While Margaret was petite, barely five feet tall, her mother was at least five foot six, just like her other three daughters. Margaret was lively, *Mamm* staid. Margaret was adventurous. Her mother was a homebody. All the qualities *Mamm* possessed were also passed down to her sisters. She couldn't be more opposite from the women in her family.

Perhaps that was part of the reason she'd been so drawn to the English world. Among her friends she could just be Margaret, instead of the troublesome daughter and sister. Yet just thinking about how close she'd come to going out tonight scared her and strengthened her resolve.

"*Mamm*," she said, keeping her voice low so she wouldn't wake up her father. "I'm going to visit *Aenti* Mary and *Onkel* Freemont for a while."

Mamm set the sock down in her lap, her expression almost unreadable except for a quick lift of her brow. "I've suggested that to you several times. Since you haven't caught the eye of any of our eligible young men in this district, you need to look elsewhere." She eyed her suspiciously. "What made you change your mind?"

"Oh, *nix* in particular." She bit the inside of her cheek at the fib, then told *Mamm* about her aunt's letter. "I miss Nina too," she added. "I thought it would be a nice time to visit."

"It's harvest time."

Oops. How had she forgotten about that? She knew how busy everyone was this time of the year. Yesterday she went out to pick buckets of blueberries from the bushes her father had planted years ago, and tomorrow she'd planned to put up blueberry jelly and pie filling. She glanced down at her lap, resisting the urge to argue with *Mamm* even though she was desperate to leave. *Meek and mild, remember?* "I'll wait until after the harvest then."

"*Nee, nee.* Your *schwesters* and I can take care of all that. Miriam is old enough to help."

Her oldest sister's daughter was almost five, and she had helped with canning last year, mostly sorting out the fruits and vegetables and handing them to June to prepare. Not only did Margaret not have a close relationship with her sisters but she also didn't feel accepted by their families, including her four young nieces and nephews. They had all kept their distance from her since she was sixteen, and in hindsight she didn't blame them. She didn't exactly set a good example, and they were vindicated when she had broken the *Ordnung* so soon. But she had always helped out with the harvest, even during her *rumspringa*. "Are you sure you don't need *mei* help?"

"This is more important."

"Visiting *aenti*?"

"*Nee*. I'm talking about you getting married. You're twenty years old already," *Mamm* said in her quiet but firm way. "You've put off your duty long enough."

Margaret held in a sigh, knowing she would get a quick but cutting look from her mother if she heard it. On the outside, Doris Yoder was a humble, soft-spoken wife and mother who embodied the Amish way of life. But when her buttons were pushed, she could devastate the strongest of men with one facial expression.

But tonight, Margaret was prepared to appease her mother. "You're right. It has been long enough," she said, being vague on purpose and letting her mother think she was agreeing that she needed to find a husband.

Doris set the sock on the side table next to her chair. "Are you sure this isn't just an excuse to rebel against the *Ordnung* again? How do I know you're not planning to take off to the English world like you did last year?"

Margaret flinched. She deserved this censure, even though it hurt. She wanted to be a compliant Amish woman, but she didn't want to lose who she was in the process. "It was only one time," she said, hanging her head. "I only went to one party and came right home." How was she supposed to have known her father would be up in the middle of the night with a gallbladder attack? He had his gallbladder removed shortly after that, and while she was glad he wasn't in pain anymore, she couldn't help but feel a little resentful that a tiny human organ had been her downfall. The party was a bust, and she'd felt guilty the moment she left her house. But apparently not guilty enough, because she had just considered sneaking out again.

She met her mother's disapproving eyes. "I promise the only place I'm going is to *Aenti* Mary's."

"I'm sure she will let me know if you don't show up." *Mamm* sniffed. "Hopefully, you'll be able to find a suitable Amish man while you're there. Men don't want rebellious wives, but perhaps there is one desperate man in Birch Creek who would be willing to set you straight."

The idea of any man setting her straight, desperate or not, didn't sit well with her. But she swallowed that thought and didn't respond.

Suddenly another idea occurred to her, and although it made her stomach twist, she didn't dismiss it out of hand. What if she did seriously consider marriage? Being married would ensure she wouldn't go back to her rebellious ways. To do so would mean deceiving her husband, and she would never do that. She had done some shameful things in her past, but betrayal was a line she would never cross.

Despite herself, she continued to entertain the notion. The men in Birch Creek didn't know about her past. She wasn't sure if any of the young men in Salt Creek knew the extent of it either, other than her one indiscretion that she had to publicly confess.

There were a few who had dipped their toes into the English world, but their paths had never crossed with Margaret's. Still, there would be a higher chance for them to find out. In Birch Creek, she would be able to start anew. Eventually her old life wouldn't have the hold over her that it did now. And this was the opportunity she needed—a new start in her life, and in her heart.

She snapped back to reality. What was she thinking? The last thing she needed was a husband, regardless of what her mother and sisters thought. Marriage wasn't for her, and it wouldn't be until she could get her brain and heart in line. She still had a lot of changing and maturing to do before she could even think about being an Amish man's wife.

"I'll help you pack." *Mamm* rose from her chair.

At the same time, her father snorted as his eyes flew open. "Pack? Pack for what?"

"Margaret is going to Birch Creek tomorrow," *Mamm* said, a slight smile on her face.

"You are?" *Daed* sat up and yawned. "That's nice. Give Freemont *mei* regards." He rose from the couch and arched his back. "I'm heading for bed."

Margaret watched her father leave, feeling disappointed. He hadn't asked how long she would be gone, but she wasn't surprised by that. He wasn't demonstrative with his daughters and had left the child raising to *Mamm*, which she'd been more than happy to do . . . at least with their first three daughters.

"Have you arranged for a taxi to pick you up in the morning?" *Mamm* said, walking toward the stairs that led to Margaret's room and the other bedroom on the second floor.

"I just now decided to *geh*, *Mamm*." She moved to stand in front of her mother. "I haven't even written *Aenti* Mary that I'm coming yet."

"I'm sure you can call her in the morning and let her know. Then you can catch the afternoon bus to Ashtabula." She stepped around Margaret and started up the stairs.

Margaret paused. Was her mother that eager to get rid of her? The last time she visited Birch Creek, *Mamm* had been glad she was seeing family, but she hadn't acted like she wanted Margaret gone. Then again, this visit was all about getting Margaret married off. *And getting me out of her hair.*

Taking in a big breath, she headed up the stairs. She'd break it to her mother later when she got back from Birch Creek that it wasn't the right time for her to get married. This visit was about taking a break from the pressure at home, both from her family and her so-called English friends. During this visit she would spend time with her aunt, uncle, cousins, and friends only. Seeking out a husband was out of the question, something she would make clear to any man who came within five yards. No, make that ten. She couldn't afford misunderstandings, and she would make sure there weren't any.

"Owen, that's your fifth yawn in a row."

Owen slammed his mouth closed and shot his brother Ezra an annoyed look. He picked up his cold meatloaf sandwich from the lunch his *mamm* had made for him and his father and brothers. The others had finished eating already, but he and Ezra were lagging behind. "I didn't know you were counting," he said, irritated.

"How could I not?" Ezra smirked. "You've done more yawning than eating."

Putting down his sandwich, Owen said, "I've had a few things on *mei* mind, and I didn't get a *gut* night's sleep last night." He took a swig of his glass of cold tea. They were eating lunch on the back patio, surrounded by the land and livestock of their family farm. Behind the large house were acres of corn, two types of peas, three types of beans, regular size and cherry tomatoes, and a variety of greens, all ready for harvest. The potatoes, beets, parsnips, and carrots needed more time in the ground. Then there was his mother's garden, which was filled with all sorts of vegetables, and on the side of the barn, the parcel of pastureland for their herds of cattle, sheep, and a few pigs his younger brothers raised.

"Let me guess," Ezra said, pushing up the brim of his yellow straw hat. "You're thinking about irrigation or installing solar panels or taking a plumb line and making sure all the rows of corn are perfectly straight."

"Very funny." Ezra wasn't the wiseacre their younger brother Jesse was, but that never stopped him from cracking a joke or two. Owen looked at his sandwich. "If you gotta know, I was pondering whether or not to harvest the salsify." He bit into the meatloaf, which had been left over from last night. His mother made great meatloaf, but Owen preferred to eat it cold.

"Then I guessed correctly." Ezra smirked. "You were thinking about work."

"What else am I supposed to think about? Today's a workday."

"Every day is a workday for you." Before Owen could protest, Ezra added, "Except the Lord's Day. At least you rest then. A little."

Rolling his eyes, Owen ignored Ezra and polished off the rest of his sandwich. While all the Bontragers worked hard, he had developed a reputation for being a workaholic. It was an exaggeration, of course. Sure, he was the first one up and doing the chores and the last one making sure all the animals were snug and safe before turning in. But that was just him being conscientious. And what did it matter if he was the one who had designed the garden this year and had diagrammed all the crops they planted, including the new one he wanted to try? He never missed a livestock auction either, but those were more fun than work. He loved farming, and he believed that a job worth doing was a job worth doing well. Their farm was thriving, and he wanted to keep it that way.

Their father, Thomas, who had come from a long line of farmers, hadn't always been prosperous. Owen's parents and his eleven siblings used to live in Fredericktown, and farming hadn't been a successful vocation for them until they moved to Birch Creek, when his only sister, Phoebe, married Jalon, a local man who was also a farmer. The new farm they established here had flourished. And while Owen was young back then—when times were lean—he could still remember how tense everyone was . . . and how hungry he had been. That wasn't something he'd ever forget.

"While we're on the subject of work," Ezra said, polishing his apple with his napkin, "I gotta admit I thought you were a little *ab im kopp* for planting that salsafee stuff. But it looks like it's coming along just fine."

Pleased by Ezra's comment, Owen smiled. "You mean salsify." When he had decided to try growing the plant from seed after seeing it at a garden show in Akron last year, he wasn't sure if it would grow. Now he wasn't sure what he was going to do with it. He'd never heard of salsify, which was a reed-type plant that was pre-pared similarly to mashed potatoes or turnips. It wasn't the nicest looking vegetable, but it was useful. "Turns out salsify loves Birch Creek soil. I'm going to end up with more than I can give away."

"That's a *gut* problem to have." Ezra eased his long legs from underneath one of the three picnic tables spaced out on the patio. He picked up his plate and plastic glass, then pointed to Owen's. "Are you finished?"

Owen nodded and handed Ezra his plate, keeping his tea glass. His mind still on the salsify, he decided to harvest a few and take them over to Freemont and Mary Yoder's. Mary was a good cook, and if the bishop and his wife gave their stamp of approval to the vegetable, he would start harvesting in earnest and give the crop away.

He drummed his fingers against the table. Maybe he would take some to the farmers market that was held every Monday just outside of Birch Creek, if he had enough left over. The market had become more popular in recent years, according to Ezra. He was in charge of selling their vegetables and *Mamm*'s homemade bread and cinnamon rolls, with their younger brothers' help when they weren't in school.

There was a time when Owen was the youngest son working on the farm, in the shadow of his older brothers. But over the last year, things had changed. His three older brothers Devon, Zeb, and Zeke had left to start their own businesses—Devon was a roofer in Fredericktown, and Zeb and Zeke owned a horse farm a few miles away. All three had gotten married, which was a shock to Owen since all the men in the community had given up on marriage due to the lack of prospects in their town. Zeke and

Zeb, who were identical twins, had even married another pair of identical twins, courtesy of a stupid ad someone in the district placed in a Holmes County newspaper, which had to have been a practical joke. Regardless, the ad had contributed to two of his brothers marrying, while Devon had married a woman back in Fredericktown, surprising their whole family. He didn't think any of his family would want to go back there. He certainly didn't.

After the advertisement had been in the paper for a while, a tidal wave of women started showing up in Birch Creek. A few of them, like the Keim sisters, moved to the community with their families and were unaware of the bachelor ad. But there were at least five women that had arrived in Birch Creek with the express interest of getting married, and they took up residence at Stoll's Inn. One woman, Katharine, even lived with Delilah Stoll and her son, Loren, the owners of the inn.

Owen thought the whole advertising for a bride thing was ridiculous, and he had no idea if his brothers and two friends who were of dating age were actually dating anyone, since it was typical for Amish youth to keep their dating lives a secret. Besides, he was too focused on his work here, along with reading books on horticulture and farming, to pay attention to anyone else's social activities. Dating and romance had never been something he seriously considered, and he didn't see that changing anytime soon. Maybe someday. Getting married was the natural progression of Amish life. But for him, marriage was a far-off future prospect. Dating took time, and right now his time was at a premium.

He blinked and realized he'd been woolgathering longer than he intended to. He stood, drained the tea from his glass, and took it inside the kitchen to find the room empty. *Mamm*, who spent most her time in the kitchen, had left for her usual Wednesday afternoon visit with Rhoda Troyer. He placed the glass in the sink and then walked toward the barn. Along the way, he saw that Ezra, Nelson, Perry, and Jesse were back in the field harvesting green beans. He went out and joined them.

For the rest of the afternoon he picked green beans, the hot summer sun beating down on his back and the top of his head, the heat penetrating through his straw hat. Sweat ran down his face, but he didn't mind. He never shied away from hard work unless it was schoolwork. He always liked reading and didn't mind learning some math, but the worst part about being in school was that he had to sit still. That had been torture, and he'd never been so happy when he turned fourteen, finished his last year of school, and left his school days behind.

He and his siblings hauled several bushels of beans to the gardening shed. Tomorrow, the youngest would go through the beans and divide them—two-thirds would be for sale and the other third would be snapped, washed, and canned for their family's use. When his brothers went inside to wash up for supper, he strolled to the cow barn. As he neared, he heard the sound of streams of milk hitting metal pails.

"Do you need any help?" Owen asked, looking at his youngest brothers—Elam, who was eight, and the twins, Moses and Mahlon, who were eleven. *Daed* stood nearby, supervising their work as they milked their three dairy cows. Most of the milk was used by their family, but Ezra would take a few bottles to sell at the Middlefield market.

"We've got it all under control," *Daed* said, casting a glance at his youngest sons. "Don't we, *buwe*?"

"*Ya!*" the twins said at the same time, with Elam's affirmation coming a second later. "I'm almost done filling *mei* bucket," Elam added.

Owen nodded but hung back for a few minutes in case they needed assistance. He yawned again and looked at his hands, seeing the dirt that gathered in the creases of his palms and had collected underneath his fingernails. It would take a good scrubbing to get it all off, but he didn't mind. Just like he didn't mind a hard day's work outside surrounded by the fruits, or in today's case, vegetables, of his family's labors. The times in Fredericktown when there wasn't enough for the family to eat had made an impression on him and an even stronger one on his older brothers.

Because the Bontragers had experienced both lack and abundance, not a single member of the family took their current good fortune for granted. Even the little ones, who didn't remember anything, knew that their prosperity could change at any time. But even in hard times, God was there. "And my God shall supply all your need according to His riches in glory by Christ Jesus." That was his father's favorite verse, one his mother had embroidered on a cloth, put in a frame, and hung on the wall in the kitchen for everyone in the family to see. There wasn't a meal that went by that Owen didn't see that verse, and he believed it to be true.

When he realized his brothers and father didn't need help with the milking, he turned around and headed for the house, ready to get the dirt off his hands and to dig into whatever delicious meal his mother had made. Life was good, and he was satisfied. He had the farm, his family, and his faith. He smiled. Those three things were all he needed.

Chapter 2

Rhoda Troyer waved to her friend Mary Yoder as Mary climbed into her buggy to head back home. Rhoda smiled and crossed her thin arms over her chest. A few brown leaves floated from the three trees in her front yard, and she leaned against the doorjamb. Another fall. Another season without Emmanuel. She pressed her lips together, then turned and went inside.

The house, which had once been occupied by her husband and two boys, was now empty except for her. Her sons, Sol and Aden, were married and had their own families, and she derived great joy from them and her grandchildren. Sol and Aden's upbringing had been difficult, to say the least, and she praised God that he had healed them of their childhood wounds and that they had married two lovely and kindhearted women. They were also wise and affectionate fathers. Two things Emmanuel wasn't.

She went into the kitchen and filled up the kettle for another cup of peppermint tea. She drank the beverage several times a day, as it was the only thing that settled her stomach. Indigestion and nausea were nearly lifelong companions ever since she had met Emmanuel Troyer when she was sixteen. She should have listened to her stomach—and her intuition—back then. But he had charmed her, and she thought he was not only handsome, but also smart and driven. Her father had abandoned their family shortly after Rhoda was born, and she was convinced that Emmanuel, with his serious demeanor and single-minded devotion to God, would be a faithful husband and father. When he moved to Birch Creek and became the bishop, she thought he had God's favor upon him. And because of that, she ignored the warning signs that her husband wasn't the good man he seemed to be.

A chill ran through her, as it usually did when she remembered the past. The kettle whistled, and she put a peppermint-flavored tea bag in her mug, then poured the hot water over it. As the tea steeped, she tried to push the past out of her mind. Emmanuel was gone and had been for years. She had no idea where he was, and she hadn't heard a word from him since he'd been exposed as a thief. For years she insisted he would return, while her sons had believed the opposite. She was unwilling to give up, but each year hanging onto that faith became harder and harder.

Rhoda picked up the mug and sat down at the table. She was grateful for her friends, especially Mary Yoder and Naomi Beiler. Naomi had also experienced her own marital troubles, but her husband, Bartholomew, returned to her, and Rhoda had hoped Emmanuel would do the same. If he was brave enough to come back, that would mean he'd changed. He would have atoned before God and would be eager to repent in front of the church and ask everyone for forgiveness, because not only had he sinned against God and his family, he had also sinned against the congregation.

But after years of silence, she was beginning to believe her husband would never return and make things right. She knew God could perform miracles, and that's what it would take for Emmanuel to realize the magnitude of what he had done. She hadn't lost faith in God but in her husband—a man she once thought was closer to God than anyone.

A knock sounded at the kitchen door, surprising her. She wasn't expecting anyone tonight. Her sons' families never knocked, and she never minded them bursting right in, especially the grandchildren. Although she had enjoyed Mary's visit a short while ago, her thoughts about Emmanuel had soured her mood, and she wasn't interested in being around anyone right now. She considered not answering the door and then changed her mind. She might not want company, but she wasn't about to be rude either.

She was surprised a second time when she opened the door and saw Loren Stoll standing there, holding a wicker basket. "Hi, Rhoda," he said, averting his gaze for a second before looking at her again. "*Mamm* asked me to bring this over. She would have come herself, but she's had a cold for a few days and didn't want to pass it on to you."

Opening the door wider, Rhoda motioned for him to come inside. "Let me take that from you," she said, accepting the basket when he handed it to her.

"It's just a loaf of white bread, some peanut butter spread, homemade butter, and elderberry jam." Loren half grinned. "*Mamm* is always making too much, and she thought you might like some of the extras."

Rhoda's bad mood lifted a little. "She's right, I do like all those foods. Delilah is so kind."

"That she is. She's always making sure everyone is taken care of." Rather than turn to leave, Loren stood there a bit longer, and suddenly he started looking around the kitchen as he shifted from one foot to the other.

"Would you like some tea?" Rhoda asked, realizing she was being a poor hostess. Then again, she'd never had a widowed man in her house before. Loren, along with his mother and his son, Levi, owned and operated Stoll's Inn, a bed-and-breakfast that had been busy almost from the first time they opened nearly two years ago. Right now, it housed several single women who had answered the recent newspaper ad for bachelors. She couldn't imagine who would have done such a foolish thing, but the advertisement had yielded three marriages. Perhaps the ad wasn't so foolish after all.

"I'm afraid I'll have to decline," he said, now looking at her. "I need to get back to the inn. It's *mei* evening to man the front desk, which will be an easy, if unpleasant, task. We haven't had a vacancy in several months, and I don't like turning away people in need."

"I understand." She set the basket down on the table and walked to the back door, opening it for him. "*Danki* for coming over. Please thank Delilah for me. I'll pray she gets over her cold quickly."

"I know she'll appreciate that." He smiled.

She felt something flutter in her stomach, and for once it was a pleasant feeling. As she met Loren's gaze, she realized he was an attractive man, something she'd never paid attention to before. Like his son, Levi, he had sandy-blond hair, although his was threaded with plenty of silver, and clear blue eyes. He stood several inches taller than her, which wasn't much since she was on the short side. He was also clean-shaven, something that was unusual at his age but made sense due to his being a widower. She'd known him and his family for a while and had crossed his path many times, but for some reason, she couldn't look away from him as he stood in her home.

"I guess I better go. I wouldn't be surprised if *Mamm* was working up front. Even with a cold she's hard to keep pinned down." He started to leave, then turned around. "Uh, Rhoda?"

"*Ya?*"

"Do you need any help around here? I know Sol and Aden take *gut* care of you. But if there's a job that needs doing, like cutting firewood or cleaning out the barn, I'd be happy to do that for you."

Her cheeks warmed, and like the flittering in her stomach, it felt nice. But there was nothing for him to do. Her sons made sure she didn't want for a single thing. "I can't think of anything now, but thank you."

"Oh." He glanced at his feet. "Well, the offer stands if you change your mind."

"I'll remember that." She smiled, and when he looked at her, his expression matched hers.

"See you later, Rhoda." He opened the back door.

"*Gut* bye, Loren."

After he left, she closed the door behind him, then put her hand over her stomach, still marveling at her giddy emotions. How long had it been since she felt like this? Far too long. She basked in the warmth of sensations she couldn't define but allowed herself to enjoy, then she brought herself up short. Was she wrong to have these feelings? She didn't know if Emmanuel was alive or dead, and she was still a married woman as long as that question remained unanswered. How could she even be thinking about another man, never mind that she was actually attracted to him?

But am I supposed to be alone forever?

The sour pain in her stomach returned, and she picked up her tea, which had cooled down enough for her to take a long drink. She had to regain her senses. Loren was just being nice, and of course biblical, since Christians were supposed to look after widows, even though no one was sure if she was a widow or not.

But she was alone . . . and lonely. She couldn't deny that.

Then again, maybe loneliness was her penance for standing by while Emmanuel committed so many sins. She couldn't count how many times during the years she had almost intervened when Emmanuel was cruelly disciplining their sons. But she always remembered what he'd said the first time she caught him treating them so horribly. "If you ever interfere with *mei* decisions, you will get twice the discipline as the *buwe*." Even now her blood ran cold as she remembered the ice in his eyes and the menacing tone of his words. She had been scared of Emmanuel that day and made sure she stayed in line ever since.

Yet she had also hated her cowardice. Her fear overran her instinct to protect her boys, and they paid the price. They said they forgave her, but she couldn't forgive herself. She would have to pay whatever penance God gave her, and she would pay it for the rest of her life. *It's what I deserve.*

Thursday afternoon, Margaret stepped off the bus at the station in Ashtabula, a book under her arm and her purse slung over her shoulder. The bus had only been half full, and she noticed she was the only Amish passenger. The mid-September wind whirled around some of the dry brown leaves that had fallen from the trees, and one settled on the toe of her black sneaker. She shook it off, then went to get her suitcase, which was stowed underneath the bus in the luggage compartment.

Yesterday morning she had followed *Mamm*'s suggestion and called her aunt, who was thrilled about Margaret's visit—of course she didn't mind that she was coming at the last minute. She couldn't get a ticket yesterday afternoon or this morning, like her mother had wanted her to, and had to settle for arriving in the afternoon. Again, Margaret couldn't help but feel like she was being rushed out of the house. June and Wanda came over right before she left, and they barely told her goodbye. And right before she got into the taxi, her mother told her not to be in a hurry to come back. *Gee. Thanks.*

She inhaled a deep breath. Regardless of her mother's motives and behavior, now that she was away from her family and Salt Creek, she felt freer than she had in a long time. In Birch Creek she wouldn't have to worry about upsetting her parents or wonder if any of her English friends would show up with more temptations. For the next few weeks, she could relax and enjoy time with family and friends who wouldn't judge her or try to get her to turn her back on her commitment to her faith.

As she waited for her suitcase, she wondered who was going to pick her up. She hoped it would be Nina, although that was unlikely. When she had called her friend and firmed up plans for

Margaret to visit, she'd sounded exhausted. Margaret knew Nina liked helping Ira with the farmwork, and harvest time had to be even harder for Freemont's family, whose farm was larger than her father's. More than likely, *Aenti* Mary had booked a taxi for her, although she didn't mention it when they talked last night. Maybe it slipped her mind. Margaret wouldn't be surprised. Harvest time was busy for everyone.

"Here you are, ma'am."

She turned around and took her dark-brown suitcase out of the bus driver's hand and gave her the tip she had stashed in her jacket pocket. With her book in one hand and her luggage in the other, she walked to the parking lot and waited for her ride. She glanced around and watched as one by one the other passengers had either left in their own cars that were parked in the station parking lot or had been picked up by other drivers and taxis. Before long, all the other passengers were gone, their rides having picked them up. She frowned. Surely *Aenti* Mary hadn't forgotten about her?

Then a dark-blue sedan pulled up alongside the curb in front of her. Instead of the driver getting out, the back door opened and a wiry Amish man exited the car. He regarded her for a second, then walked over to her. "Hello. Are you Margaret Yoder?"

She paused, not recognizing him. "I am."

"Oh *gut*. I was worried you might have called another taxi. I'm Owen Bontrager. Your *aenti* asked if I wouldn't mind picking you up for her."

Her guard immediately went up. Had her mother talked to *Aenti* Mary behind her back, telling her that Margaret was here on a husband hunt? She wouldn't put it past her. She was familiar with the Bontragers, and not just because her aunt had mentioned them in her most recent letter. When she had attended the singing with Nina, her friend told her that all the young men who were of dating age were there, including several Bontragers. But she didn't remember this brother.

"I'm sorry we're late," he continued, gesturing to the car behind him. "I stopped by to give your aunt and uncle some extra seeds I had from my salsify plants. The crop isn't quite ready to harvest, but I thought Freemont might like to try growing some himself."

She had no idea what salsify was or why he was telling her this story, but she nodded anyway, not wanting to be rude.

"Turned out Mary was right in the middle of canning tomato sauce and had lost track of time. Since Freemont and Judah had gone to the diner for lunch and hadn't returned yet, she asked me if I could *geh* get you, since she didn't want you to have to ride in the taxi alone." He glanced at her suitcase. "Can I help you with your luggage?"

This all seemed innocent enough, and she wasn't surprised her aunt didn't want her riding by herself. When she handed him her suitcase, he took it and then gave her a quick smile, revealing front teeth that overlapped each other.

"How was your trip?" he asked as he took the bag from her.

"*Gut.*" She tried not to fall into the habit she usually had of evaluating a man's physical attributes at first sight, but she couldn't help it. For sure, Owen wasn't in Dylan's ballpark when it came to good looks. He was too thin for one thing. And those teeth . . .

She gave her brain a mental shake. Good looks didn't make a good man. Dylan was a prime example.

"Glad to hear it," he said. "I'll put this in the trunk for you."

29

For the first time, Margaret fully met his gaze. *Whoa*. His teeth might not be perfect, but his eyes sure were. Or more accurately, the thick black eyelashes that rimmed them. She thought about her own sparse ones. That wasn't fair. A man shouldn't have better eyelashes than a woman.

Margaret blinked more than was necessary as Owen walked over to the trunk, which the driver had already unlocked. He put her luggage inside, then shut the lid. He opened the car door and got into the back seat behind the driver.

Realizing she was dawdling, not to mention overthinking her lack of eyelashes, she hurried to the front passenger door and opened it. She was about to sit down when she saw a box filled with magazines on the front seat, along with another overfilled box on the floor.

"I'm sorry." The driver, an older woman with short salt-and-pepper hair, gestured to the boxes. "I moved these from the trunk so you would have enough room for your luggage. I was on my way to donate these to our local elementary school for their art classes when your aunt called. I hope you don't mind sitting in the back."

"Not at all." Margaret smiled at the woman, who seemed genuinely apologetic. She closed the door, then opened the back door and slid onto the seat. She set her purse and book in her lap and glanced at Owen. To her surprise, he also had a book with him, and he was already reading it.

"Ready to go?" the driver said.

"Yep," Owen said, not lifting his gaze from the book. Then, as if he'd had a second thought, he looked up and said, "Thanks, Peggy."

"Any time." She adjusted the rearview mirror. "I think a lot of your family, and the Yoders too. I'm glad I could help you guys out."

As Peggy guided her car out of the parking lot, Margaret stared straight ahead, feeling awkward and unfriendly. It was easier to be reserved back home since her public confession, mostly because she was still ashamed of her behavior. But she discovered being aloof wasn't easy. She liked being friendly with everyone and hadn't realized that she wasn't supposed to be too sociable with men until her sisters had pointed it out to her, with a good dose of disgust.

"You're too forward," June had said one day when Margaret was fourteen and was seen chatting with one of the Miller brothers after church.

"What does that mean?" Margaret asked as she climbed into the front of the buggy.

"You stood close to Timothy." Ruth, her second oldest sister, chimed in.

"So?" She'd had to since his cousin Merlin, who was standing next to him, started yelling at his younger brother to stop picking the bark off the Hershbergers' tree, the family that had hosted church that morning. Timothy was telling her that he'd gone to a Cleveland Indians baseball game and saw a grand slam home run. He could always tell a good story, and Margaret was delighted by his lively description of the event. "I couldn't hear what he was saying. Did you know he saw a grand slam—"

"And you giggled too much." Wanda sniffed and lifted her chin.

"He's funny."

"You always giggle too much."

Margaret crossed her arms over her chest, vexed by their criticism. Why did her sisters have to be so boring? And judgmental? *They're just jealous. They wish they were as pretty as I am.*

She cringed at the memory, embarrassed she'd been so prideful. It didn't matter that she was young at the time and that her sisters constantly irritated her. Truth be told, she was pretty, especially compared to her plain-faced sisters, although that had been in doubt when she was younger and was more interested in climbing trees and fishing than she was in boys. That didn't mean she should be arrogant about her beauty, or worse, use her looks to her advantage—something she had done more than once during her *rumspringa*. Her cheeks heated even though the temperature in the car was comfortable.

She glanced at Owen, hoping he didn't notice she was flush with shame. Fortunately, he seemed engrossed in his book. He turned the page, and from the pictures, it looked like he was reading about plants or gardens. Then she remembered that his family owned a farm, so it made sense he would read such a book. She wracked her brain trying to figure out why she couldn't place him. Then again, would she have noticed him in the first place? She recalled that his older brothers were quite good-looking, and other than his eyes, Owen definitely wasn't.

There she was, judging him again. *I'm just as bad as my schwesters.* No, she was worse, because she was shallow. Why else would she be evaluating his looks?

She settled back against the seat, trying to shift her thoughts but failing spectacularly. If her mother and aunt were in cahoots to match her with Owen, they'd clearly picked the wrong man. He was more interested in reading than he was in her. Which was a little ego bruising now that she thought about it. She was used to men wanting to talk to her, not ignoring her. But shouldn't she be glad that he would rather read than pay her a single second of attention?

Margaret grabbed her own book and yanked it open, making a second attempt to distract herself from her contradicting musings. Two weeks ago, she went to the library and saw the book, which was a quick reference guide to herbal medicine, sitting on a display table. On a lark, she'd looked through it, then checked it out. While she had always enjoyed picking and pressing wildflowers, and had recently started framing them as art, learning about natural medicine was new to her.

She ended up being engrossed in the different uses of the herbs she and her mother often planted in the garden, and she also read about some new varieties she'd never heard of, such as Gentian lutea, a yellow flowered plant that is native to Europe and good for indigestion. After reading the small volume, she had wanted to find out more about herbal medicine, so she returned the book and bought a copy for herself using the library's computer since the manual was only available for purchase online.

But as she turned to the page on the uses of dandelion root, she couldn't focus on the entry. Instead she glanced at Owen again, who turned another page in his book. Unable to stand the silence anymore she remembered what he'd said when he picked her up. "What's salsify?"

He turned, his eyes widening as if the question surprised him. "It's a root vegetable, similar to a turnip or potato in consistency. It doesn't look anything like a turnip or potato, though, because it's long and thin and resembles tree roots."

That didn't sound very appetizing. "What does it taste like?"

"Well, depends on who you ask. Some people say it tastes like oysters."

"Ew. Why would anyone want to eat a plant that tastes like that?"

The corner of his mouth lifted slightly. "You realize some people like oysters, *ya?* Anyway, not everyone thinks it tastes like that. Some folks say it's like eating a mild artichoke. Others say it doesn't taste like much of anything, which is why they like to use it in dishes that have stronger flavors. You can mash it, stew it, and put it in soups. It's very versatile."

She wasn't a fan of artichokes either, but to each his own. "What made you decide to plant it?"

"I like trying new things. Last year I experimented with Bodacious corn."

"And?"

"Best corn I ever ate. We planted double the crop this year—it was so popular at the farmers market. I reckon it will be again this season too." He went back to reading his book.

As he continued to read, she looked at him again. Deep-black hair, close to the color of charcoal, curled over his ears and at the nape of his neck. His straw hat was pushed back from his forehead, but her gaze skimmed straight down to his eyelashes again.

Suddenly he turned to her, lifting a questioning eyebrow.

Oh *nee*. She'd been caught. Quickly she picked up her book and held it in front of him. "I, too, like to read about plants." Oh, for goodness' sake, she sounded nuts. She set the book back down and smoothed the part in the middle of her hair. "I mean, I like reading about herbal medicine. Which is what I'm doing. Right now." She snapped her eyes to the page, hoping she looked casual, but knowing that yet again she was failing.

"Herbal medicine," he said. "Sounds interesting."

Her gaze flew to his, and all promises of being quiet and unnoticeable flew out the window. "I find it fascinating how many important uses a simple plant has." She gestured to the book. "This has a lot of recipes to heal whatever ails you, from bone spurs to sweaty feet."

He rubbed his chin. "Sweaty feet, huh? A few of *mei bruders* could use some help in that department." Then he added, "I think *Mamm* has a few herbal recipes she uses, and I know *Daed* has a handwritten notebook of animal and farm remedies that have been passed down through our family."

"Really? *Mamm* was never much for home remedies, but she swears by her wild cherry cough syrup."

"Is it easy to make?"

Margaret paused. She didn't know because her mother had never shared it with her. She had given a copy of the recipe to all her sisters after they got married, though, but Margaret wasn't about to admit that to Owen. Wait, she wasn't even supposed to be talking to him. "Pretty easy," she said in a clipped tone, irritated with herself for dropping her resolve so easily, and with her mother for being so . . . herself. She picked up the book again. "If you don't mind, I'd like to finish this chapter."

A confused expression crossed his face as he nodded. "Sure. I'm almost finished with this one too."

She started to ask him what the chapter was about, but she pressed her lips together and stared at the dandelion picture in front of her. She wasn't sure how much time had passed before

Peggy turned into the Yoders' driveway, but when she looked up from the book, which was still open to the dandelion page, and saw the familiar house, the tension that had been gripping her shoulders eased. Her aunt and uncle's place wasn't her home, but when she visited them, it sure did feel like it.

Not that she visited often. Other than last year, she and her family had traveled to Birch Creek one other time, well before her uncle had become the bishop. Things had been different in the district back then. Even at her young age, she'd felt the unease in the air, and she remembered her father made a comment as they went back home that he wished his brother would move back to Salt Creek.

"It's not like Freemont's farm is worth anything," he murmured when their taxi passed the Summit County line. *Daed* didn't like to ride on buses, and even though it was more expensive to hire a van for their family's ride to and from her uncle's, to him it was worth spending the extra money. "I doubt it ever will be."

But as she stepped out of the car and surveyed *Onkel* Freemont's home and the farmland surrounding it, she was glad her uncle had proved her father wrong. The farm had changed a lot over the years, something that struck her the last time she was here. Instead of failing crops, thin livestock, and a house in need of repair, she could see how God had blessed the fruits of her uncle's labor. Several acres of corn swayed in the breeze. Yellow, purple, and crimson mums, bright and voluminous, filled pots on the front porch, and plump cows chomped on the grass in the large pasture on the other side of the house. She breathed in the crisp fall air, detecting a light hint of chimney smoke, and smiled. *I'm so happy to be here*.

"Margaret!" *Aenti* Mary flew out of the house and hurried down the few porch steps. Without a misstep, she rushed toward her. Margaret met her halfway, and suddenly she was caught up in her aunt's welcoming embrace.

"I'm so glad to see you." Releasing her, *Aenti* Mary stepped back and gave Margaret a once-over. "I'm sorry I wasn't able to meet you at the bus station. Thankfully, Owen was able to help me out."

Margaret turned around to see him bringing her suitcase toward her as Peggy drove away. She'd been so caught up in her happiness that she'd forgotten her luggage. Thankfully, Owen hadn't.

"*Danki*, Owen." *Aenti* Mary reached into the pocket of her tomato-stained apron. "Here's the fare—"

He held up his hand. "That's okay. I took care of it."

"I can't let you do that." When Owen refused to accept the money, she put the bills back in her pocket. "At least come inside and I'll fix you a cup of coffee. I have some cinnamon snickerdoodles I picked up from Carolyn's bakery yesterday."

He shook his head. "*Danki*, but I need to get back to the farm while there's still some daylight left." He turned to Margaret. "Nice to meet you."

"You too," she said, but as soon as the words left her mouth, he had already started to walk away. He seemed to be in a hurry to get back to whatever work he had to get back to. Although she wasn't at fault, she couldn't help but feel a niggle of guilt that he had to take time off to come pick her up. "Owen?"

He paused but didn't turn around. Instead he glanced over his shoulder. "*Ya?*"

"*Danki* for riding to the Yoders with me. Oh, and for getting *mei* suitcase."

He gave her a slight smile and a quick wave, then rushed over to his buggy, which was parked in the driveway close to her aunt's house.

"You and I can have those snickerdoodles then," *Aenti* Mary said, putting her arm around Margaret's shoulders. "I know they're your favorite."

She grinned, her mouth watering at the thought of the sweet dough covered in cinnamon sugar. *Aenti* Carolyn was her father's and *Onkel* Freemont's sister, and knowing she had baked the cookies herself made Margaret more eager to try them. *Aenti* Carolyn's baking skills were legendary in their family, and snickerdoodles were one of her specialties. "Is she still working at the bakery?" Margaret asked, referring to *Aenti* Carolyn's business. "I thought she retired after having Junior."

"She did, but when she heard you were coming for a visit, she wanted to make these special for you."

Her heart warmed. When was the last time her mother, or anyone, had done something special for her? Surely there had been times while she was growing up, but not lately.

She heard the sound of Owen's buggy pulling out of the driveway and fought the urge to turn around and watch him leave. Despite her vow to remain aloof—and her knowing for sure that she wouldn't be interested in any man in Birch Creek—she found herself intrigued by Owen, and she told herself that being intrigued wasn't the same as being interested. He was different from most of the men she'd ever met, and that included the English ones. Other than some small talk about plants, something they both were interested in, he had basically ignored her—and she wasn't used to being ignored by the opposite sex.

"Margaret?"

Thankfully, her aunt's voice pulled her out of her thoughts. Intrigued or not, she didn't need to think about Owen. "That was nice of *Aenti* Carolyn. I'll have to pay her a visit soon and thank her for the treats."

"I'm sure she'll love that. Just know that Junior is a handful, so she'll probably be spending most of the time chasing him down instead of visiting."

"How old is he now?"

"Two, and he's very, very busy. Atlee and Carolyn often joke that God allowed them a rambunctious child so late in life to keep them in shape."

Margaret chuckled. *Aenti* Carolyn had married Atlee, who was a widower and didn't have any children, when she was in her late forties and he in his early fifties. No one had been more surprised than they were about Junior's impending arrival.

As they walked to the house, *Aenti* Mary said, "I hope you didn't mind that Owen picked you up." She dipped her head. "I was elbow deep in tomato sauce and had more simmering on the stove, so I couldn't just leave. I didn't want you to have to ride all the way from the bus station by yourself."

"That's what Owen said, but I would have been fine alone, *Aenti*."

"Oh, I know. But it's always *gut* to have company, and I know how much you enjoy conversation. Owen is a nice *yung mann*, and of course I can't say enough *gut* things about his *familye*. I knew you two would get along well."

Margaret wouldn't exactly describe her and Owen's interaction that way, but at least he was cordial to her. She held in a disappointed sigh. So, her aunt did have an ulterior motive when she sent him to fetch her. "*Aenti*," Margaret said, her guard back up. "Did *Mamm* talk to you before I left?"

"About what?"

"About . . ." She didn't want to say out loud that her mother was eager to get rid of her by marrying her off. "About anything."

"*Nee*. I haven't talked to Doris in at least two weeks. Maybe three." *Aenti* Mary's brow creased. "Why do you ask?"

She really doesn't know. She was just being thoughtful. Relieved that her aunt wasn't colluding with her mother behind her back, Margaret said, "Oh, I just wondered if you and *Mamm* had talked before I left, that's all. I thought she might have called you since I know how close you two are." Then to make sure *Aenti* Mary didn't ask any more questions, she quickened her steps. "I can't wait to try *Aenti* Carolyn's snickerdoodles." Then she added, "But I'm sure they're not as *gut* as yours." Which wasn't exactly true, but *Aenti* Mary's baking was almost on par with *Aenti* Carolyn's. Except for her donuts. Those had always been awful.

"Oh, I don't know about that." But *Aenti* Mary smiled, clearly pleased with Margaret's kind words, although she would never outright acknowledge them. Compliments weren't handed out very often, at least not in her own family. They were seen as a source of pride, and the last thing Margaret needed was to be more prideful. She had to learn more humility, particularly when it came to her thoughts about herself. Her list of failings was endless, and it would serve her well to keep that at the forefront of her mind, instead of pondering about how curious she was about Owen Bontrager.

By the time she and her aunt went inside the house, Margaret had put him out of her mind . . . hopefully for good.

Chapter 3

S *he sure is pretty . . .*

Owen blinked, then gripped Apollo's reins as he made his way back to the farm, his thoughts focused on Margaret. When was the last time he'd noticed a woman's looks? He couldn't recall, even with the influx of women who had arrived in Birch Creek since the mail-order bride ad ran in the paper. Surely he would have paid more than scant attention to at least one of the young women, wouldn't he? But he genuinely couldn't remember any of their faces—not well enough for them to make an impression on him.

But Margaret definitely had.

When he arrived at Mary's with the salsify seeds, she had explained who Margaret was and that she had previously been to Birch Creek for a visit. That jogged Owen's memory, but for some reason he had no idea what she looked like. Now that he'd seen her, he couldn't understand why he didn't remember her . . . unless he'd had his head in the clouds, like he normally did.

As he continued to head home, he vaguely remembered hearing Devon and Zeke mention Margaret more than a year ago when they returned from the singing at the Yoders, an event he hadn't bothered to attend because he wanted to clean out the sheep barn instead. At the time, he hadn't thought his decision strange because Nina would have been the only single woman in attendance, or so he believed. Nina was nice but not his type at all, and as it turned out, she was head over heels for Ira anyway. Besides, he didn't need to go to the Yoders to sing hymns and eat snacks with his brothers and the three other single young men in the district. Even when his brothers had returned and Devon and Zeke started blabbing on about Margaret, he had tuned them out.

But how had he missed seeing Margaret after that? She would have attended church at least once. Then again, why would he pay attention to the female side of the congregation when he knew everyone? Maybe he had just overlooked her. She was a petite woman—a little taller than her cousin Ivy, who was the shortest adult in the district. He was a little less than average height but seemed much taller when he stood in front of her. Since she was so small, he may not have seen her. Now he couldn't stop seeing her in his mind. Or thinking about her. Like how big her brown eyes were. She had a slightly sloped nose and smooth, lightly tanned skin. Then there was her perfectly shaped mouth . . .

His face heated despite the cool air filtering through the buggy as Apollo trotted at a brisk clip. He tightened his hold on the reins. Mary had trusted him to accompany Margaret to the Yoders', and here he was thinking about how pretty she was. Thankfully, he'd brought a book to distract him, or he would have stared at her the whole way home. It didn't work since he couldn't remember what he'd read, even though he scanned the page three times. Finally, he gave up and started turning the pages in case she noticed he wasn't really reading.

His grip relaxed. Just because he thought she was pretty didn't mean anything. And once they started talking, he was able to shift his thoughts to plants, something he was always open to discussing. He enjoyed their conversation and would have liked to continue it, but she surprised him by cutting things off and returning to her book. She might be pretty and interested in plants, but she was an odd bird. One that he would do well not to ponder further. Before long, Ezra or Nelson or even some of the other single guys in the district would start vying for her attention anyway. He didn't have time for such foolishness, even if he did have the inclination. Which he didn't. *I definitely don't.*

He shoved Margaret out of his mind as he neared his driveway. After he parked the buggy and released Apollo into the horse pasture for a late-afternoon snack, he yawned and headed straight for his garden. He'd noticed this morning that weeds had started to sprout, and since this was his personal garden patch and the one he liked to experiment with, he made sure to keep it as unspoiled as possible.

Owen knelt on the ground and started weeding around a row of mint plants. It didn't take long to tidy up the garden, and after he finished, he started working on other farm chores, which never seemed to end. He spent the rest of the afternoon harvesting carrots alongside Elam, who was a chatterbox. By the time the two of them finished picking as many carrots as they could, Owen's ears were sore. They'd not only worked up a sweat but also a big appetite.

During suppertime, he ate two plates of chicken and biscuits, an extra serving of green beans, and a huge helping of cherry gelatin salad, while the rest of his family chatted about the day. As soon as he finished eating, he turned to *Daed*. "May I be excused? I wanted to give Apollo a brushing before I turn in for the night." He stifled a yawn. He was tired from the long day, but he wouldn't rest until he had brushed Apollo clean.

Daed frowned a little, then nodded. "You may."

Owen took his dish and glass to the counter and set them by the sink. Then he went outside to the barn. He grabbed a currycomb and started to brush Apollo, yawning freely this time. As he ran the comb over Apollo's gleaming black coat, Margaret popped into his mind again. When he was busy working earlier in the day, he'd managed not to think about her. But now that he was doing an important but mindless task, he suddenly couldn't stop thinking about her again. He picked up the pace, moving the currycomb faster.

"I think he's well brushed," *Daed* said, entering the horse's stall. "Don't you?"

Owen stopped and looked at the horse, who hadn't really needed the brushing in the first place. But even if he hadn't used Apollo as a distraction from Margaret, he probably would have brushed him a few times before going to bed, as was his habit. A man's horse was an investment, and Owen had bought Apollo two years ago and treated him well.

"*Ya*. I guess he is." Owen hung the currycomb back on the hook near the stall door.

"Have you got a minute?" *Daed* gestured with his head to the main area of the barn.

"Sure." When he'd first walked into the barn after supper, he noticed it needed a quick sweeping and had planned to do that before he went back inside. He took down the push broom leaning against the barn wall and started to sweep. He and *Daed* could talk while he worked.

Daed held up his hand. "The sweeping can wait until tomorrow."

Owen paused, then put the broom back where he found it as his father walked over to a pile of square hay bales that were there for the express purpose of sitting down, not that Owen ever used them. As Owen lowered himself onto a bale, he tried not to yawn. That was the thing about yawning—sometimes once a person started, it was hard to stop. He didn't need to be yawning in front of his father. Owen couldn't read his expression, but he had the feeling whatever *Daed* was going to tell him was serious. He rarely spoke to him alone like this.

"We need to talk about last spring," *Daed* said.

Uh-oh. Owen's gut twisted.

"I know what happened."

The words started to rush out of Owen's mouth. "I promise that's the first time. The only time. I've never fallen asleep while plowing before, and there was no harm done. The horses stopped as soon as I let go of the reins—Wait. How did you know?"

"Elam told me." *Daed* crossed his arms over his chest. "He was scared something bad had happened to you when he saw you hit the ground."

"I was fine," he mumbled, but he still felt as guilty as he had when he looked up and saw his youngest brother hovering over him, his eyes wild with worry. Owen still wasn't sure what happened, other than he'd been extremely tired that day, having spent the previous several days working from dawn until past dusk digging up his garden by hand. The draft horses could plow the field by themselves, and even with the bumpy ride as the plow drove through and overturned the cold dirt, he had managed to doze off, let go of the reins, and hit the ground, waking up immediately. He told Elam not to say anything, but the eight-year-old clearly hadn't listened to him.

"Thank God you weren't hurt . . . or worse." *Daed* uncrossed his arms, but his expression remained grim. "If you weren't feeling *gut* you should have said something instead of working through it."

"I was tired, not sick." He tempered his tone, knowing his next question could be construed as being belligerent. "Why are you bringing this up now? Did Elam just tell you?"

Shaking his head, *Daed* said, "He told me that afternoon. The reason I didn't say anything is that I suspected there was a problem, but I wanted to see if it was worth addressing. After this summer, and now with the harvest in full swing, I'm convinced that there is."

Owen didn't like the sound of this. "What problem?"

"I'm worried about you, *sohn*"—he held up his hand—"and before you say anything else, listen to me. I was going to have this conversation with you when the time was right, and in *mei* mind, that time is now." Determination was in his eyes. "I'd like for you to take over the farm when I retire."

Owen almost fell off the hay bale. He'd expected his father to give him a lecture on being irresponsible. Instead he was talking about Owen taking over the family business. Which made sense to Owen—he was the one who was the most interested in the day-to-day business and work of the farm. But he hadn't expected his father to tell him that so soon, and not on the heels of being angry with him for falling asleep at the plow. Then he realized the full implication of what his father was telling him. "Are you retiring?"

"Not for a while. There are still a few years left in these old bones. The work is in *mei* blood, just like it was in *mei vatter*'s. I can see it's in yours, too, *sohn*. You're the first one up working and usually the last one to turn in for the night. You took initiative with the Bodacious corn, and now you're growing the salsify. Working hard and being innovative are key qualities of a *gut* farmer. The older *buwe* didn't have the same love for the land that you do, and neither do the younger ones, although I think Elam might grow into it. Devon was never interested in farming, but he's an excellent roofer and is happy doing construction. When Zeb and Zeke struck out on their own and started a horse farm, I wasn't that surprised, just concerned they were putting their cart before the horse, pun intended. At least in Zeke's case I knew the decision was more impulsive than anything else."

"He's not as reckless anymore," Owen pointed out. "Since he married Darla, he's settled down a lot."

"She's a *gut* influence on him, that's for sure. There's an English saying that behind every *gut* man is a *gut* woman, and I believe that to be true." He leaned back, his hands moving from his knees to the hay bale. "That's been the case with your *mamm*. I couldn't ask for a better *frau*, and she's a wonderful *mutter* to you and your *bruders* and *schwester*."

Owen nodded, surprised his father was getting a little emotional. "Are you sure *nix* is wrong?" he asked.

"Other than *mei kinner* growing up faster than I'm ready for, *nee*." He shook his head, his expression wistful. "You'll know what I mean when you're a *vatter*."

That wasn't about to happen anytime soon. But knowing that his parents were eager for more grandchildren, he didn't say the words out loud. So far, his sister, Phoebe, who was the oldest, had been the only one to have children—Malachi and Hannah. Owen was sure that was going to change soon enough now that his three older brothers were married. He'd let them fulfill *Mamm* and *Daed*'s hankering for more *grosskinner*.

"While we're on the subject of family, that leads me to something else I wanted to talk about. Well, more like your *mutter* and I have been talking about this, and she's asked me to bring it up to you."

Now Owen was starting to get confused. First his father talked about the plow incident, then he told him he was letting him take over the farm when the time arrived. Now he was bringing up another subject that apparently concerned his mother. "I don't understand."

"Your *mamm* has been worried for a while now that you might be a little too single-minded when it comes to work. At first, I dismissed the idea, but now it's clear that she's right. It's not just that you work hard—which I appreciate—but you don't do much else other than that."

"The farm involves a lot of attention and a lot of work."

Daed tugged at his long beard, giving Owen a reproving look. "*Nee* one knows that more than I do."

Owen nodded, casting his gaze downward. "I didn't mean anything by that."

"I know." He sighed. "Guess I should just stop beating around the bush. *Sohn*, you need a vacation."

His head jerked up. "What?" He couldn't believe what he was hearing. "It's the middle of harvest season."

"And we have plenty of hands in this *familye* to make sure everything gets done. In fact, I need the twins and Elam to pitch in more. And since you refused to *geh* on vacation with us the last three years—"

"Because someone had to feed the animals."

"Jalon, Adam, and Malachi would have taken care of that," *Daed* pointed out, referring to his son-in-law, cousin by marriage, and grandson. "But you simply wouldn't budge. Don't get me wrong. I would never begrudge a hard day's work. But *sohn*, you put in more than your fair share. It's time you took a break."

None of what his father said made sense. Usually parents admonished their children to work harder so as not to be slothful. Then again, Owen had never been lazy when it came to farmwork, so he'd never been scolded for that. School had been a different matter altogether. He'd enjoyed reading, but only books he wanted to read, not assigned material that always ended up being boring. Sitting still at a desk was torture when he'd rather have been outside. He learned more at home and on his own than he had ever learned in school, although he was well aware that was his own fault. He almost failed a grade more than once, and his performance—or rather lack of—had gotten him grounded several times during his school years.

But school was different from farming, and he wanted to give 100 percent to that endeavor. Make that 110 percent. He more than made up for his lack of effort in school. In fact, he couldn't imagine doing anything else but farming. "I don't need to take a break. And I can't sit around while everyone else is working."

"We're not asking you to. Isn't there a hobby you've wanted to try? Or something new you wanted to learn?"

"*Ya.* I want to learn how to grow better crops." He thought about Margaret again, and how she was learning herbal medicine. "I also thought about adding extra herbs to the garden next year, so I was going to start planning that soon." That idea had just popped into his mind, but it was a good one. If he grew enough special herbs just for medicinal purposes, Ezra and the younger boys could sell them at the market next year . . .

"When was the last time you sat by yourself and just prayed?" *Daed* asked. "Or took a nap?"

"Sunday." He hadn't napped, but he definitely had prayed. What about, he couldn't recall, but probably something about the farm. Wow, he really was single-minded, wasn't he? But that didn't mean he needed to take off during the harvest, the most important time of the year for the farm and family.

"Then why did I see you in the toolshed that afternoon?" *Daed* raised a brow.

Oops. "I thought about reorganizing it. But I didn't. I was just thinking about it."

"That's still work, Owen."

"Thinking is work?"

"In your case, *ya*. Even God rested from his labors, but you never do. Overwork causes a lot of problems. Sickness for one. Then there's exhaustion, which I think is your biggest trouble."

"I get plenty of sleep—"

"You fell asleep plowing. Think about that for a minute."

He stilled, his father's words sinking in. He had dismissed the plow incident, but he probably shouldn't have. "I guess I could cut back on work a little. And I promise I'll take a vacation this winter. Wherever you and *Mamm* decide to take the *familye*, I'll *geh* with you." Uneasiness ran through him as he made the promise. Even though vacation was months in the future, he didn't like the idea of leaving the farm. What if something happened, like a fire? That was a real possibility. A fire had taken out a lot of Freemont Yoder's farm two years ago, and they had rebuilt, but that had set the Yoders back a lot. Then there were the animals. One of them might get sick while he was gone—

"Owen." His father snapped his fingers in front of him. "I can see those wheels spinning. You're reconsidering vacation, aren't you?"

His father knew him better than he knew himself. Scary. "*Ya*," he mumbled.

"That does it." *Daed* slapped his hands on his knees, then rose to his feet. "As of tonight, Owen, you're on a one-week vacation. Enjoy sleeping in tomorrow."

Owen's mouth dropped. "Really?"

"Really."

"But what am I supposed to do?"

"Well, your *mamm* would suggest getting to know some of the young women in the district. You have your pick of them now, thanks to that *ab im kopp* advertisement." He chuckled, shaking his head. "I really thought your *mamm* put that in the paper. I know she was worried about how you *kinner* were going to find *fraus*. She promises she didn't have anything to do with the advertisement, and she's always simply trusted that God would provide all of you *buwe* with *gut* Amish women. Looks like her prayers have been answered. Three of our *sohns* are married."

"Only eight more to *geh*," Owen mumbled.

"God willing. But you're making it difficult on yourself, you know. You can't meet someone if you're here all the time."

"I'm not here all the time. I *geh* to church, to the auctions, the farmers markets . . ." He paused. Other than an occasional trip to Schrock's Grocery for garden supplies, or to Barton if he couldn't find what he needed at Schrock's, he couldn't recall the last time he'd gone somewhere that didn't have to do with his job. Except for today. "I even picked up Margaret Yoder this afternoon from the bus station." There. That should make his case.

"Oh really?" *Daed*'s eyes twinkled. "Your *mamm* will be happy to hear that."

"I was just picking her up as a favor to Mary," he said quickly, not wanting his parents to get the wrong idea. "She was busy canning tomato sauce and asked me to help her out."

"And you were only too willing to oblige," *Daed* teased. "See? You're off to a *gut* start. You talked to a *maedel*."

Owen didn't reply. There was nothing humorous about this situation.

"Thank goodness this is all settled. It's been weighing on *mei* mind for a while." He grinned. "Enjoy your vacation." Then he walked out of the barn.

Owen shot up from the hay bale and ran after *Daed*, who was halfway to the house. "I can't stop work for a whole week. That's impossible."

Daed leveled his gaze. "And that, *mei sohn*, is why you need this vacation." He turned and kept walking. When he reached the house, he opened the screen door, then let it shut behind him.

End of conversation.

Dusk had descended while he and his father talked in the barn, and tiny twinkling lights appeared in the light-purple streaked sky. As if on cue, all of his brothers poured out of the house and started on the evening chores, going off in threes and pairs to bring in the sheep, lock up the pasture gates, settle the horses in for the night, and all the other chores that were necessary to keep the farm running smoothly.

He turned and followed Ezra and Nelson into the barn where Apollo and the other three horses were kept, intending to sweep the floor as planned. His vacation didn't start until tomorrow, and he fully intended to plead his case one more time with his parents when he went inside. But when he entered the barn, Ezra and Nelson blocked his way.

"*Daed* said you were on vacation." Ezra put his hands on his waist, an amused expression on his face.

"He also said you wouldn't listen and would try to work anyway." Nelson imitated his brother, looking almost like his twin since Nelson's last growth spurt had brought them within less than an inch of each other in height.

"I wish I was on vacation," Ezra said. "Talk about lucky."

"Wanna trade?" Owen said weakly.

"In a heartbeat. But that's not going to wash with *Daed* and *Mamm*."

"I know." Owen took a step back. He was at the point of no return. Any pleading he did with *Mamm* and *Daed* would fall on deaf ears. Worse, *Mamm* would probably give him pointers about finding a woman. He shuddered at the thought. "*Geh* on and finish up the chores," he said, giving up. "I won't follow you."

"Promise?" Nelson tapped the toe of his work boot on the floor, which still needed sweeping.

"Promise." Unable to do anything else, Owen trudged toward the house, still trying to absorb everything his father had said. Being in charge of the farm was something he'd prayed for, and under any other circumstances, he would celebrate that answered prayer. Instead he walked into the kitchen, went to the sink, and washed his hands, at a loss since he wasn't joining his brothers as they completed the chores they had all done every night since he could remember.

Mamm was cutting slices of chocolate cake for dessert, glasses of milk already poured and ready for everyone when they came inside and washed up again. "Ready for your piece, Owen?"

"I can do that for you, *Mamm*." It wouldn't be the first time he'd helped her with the nightly dessert or with some of the housework. He didn't ascribe to certain chores for women and certain ones for men, although he knew there were things men and women were particularly suited for. Cutting cake was an equal opportunity task. At least it would give him something to do.

"*Nee*." *Mamm* grinned. "*Yer* on vacation, remember?"

Owen groaned. "I can't even cut a piece of cake?"

"Not for the next week. No work outside or inside." She handed him a fresh slice. "What a lucky *yung mann* you are, free from chores and jobs for seven whole days. Enjoy your cake."

He took the dessert from her, ignoring her light laughter as he sat down. His whole family thought this was hilarious, and he didn't appreciate that one bit. Staring at the cake, he thought about his options. He could defy his parents, but that was something he had never done before and couldn't bring himself to do now. Except for school, he had always been a rule follower, and even when he had been grounded, he didn't complain because he deserved the discipline.

The only other option he had was to accept that he was now officially on vacation. Oddly enough, that acceptance sparked his appetite, and he dug into the cake. He was nearly finished when the back kitchen door opened and his brothers stampeded inside.

"All of you wash up," *Mamm* yelled as they rushed out of the kitchen to the three bathrooms in the house. Owen swallowed the last bite of his piece, then rinsed the dish and his empty glass and put them in the sink. He didn't want to be around his brothers right now. They would probably goad him with questions, tease him for being on vacation, or pout that they would have to work while he was loafing. There was nothing left for him to do but to go upstairs to his bedroom.

As the oldest son still at home, he finally had his own room after his married brothers had moved out. But instead of getting ready for bed, he paced the floor. He'd been exhausted at supper, but now he was wide-awake. How was he supposed to sleep when he'd never been in this position before? Who would tend his garden? Who would make sure all the vegetables were harvested, even the little scrawny ones his younger brothers thought weren't worth the hassle? Who would follow up after them and make sure the compost pile behind the barn was turned over on a regular basis? His father could do that, but he hadn't needed to in a long time. Not when Owen was there to make sure all the work was done correctly.

Owen fell back on the bed, annoyed. One thing he wasn't going to do was look for a date.

First, he needed to know a woman before he would ask her out, and one or two dates would go nowhere. Once this ridiculous vacation was over, he would be busier than ever. The salsify would be ready for harvest, his garden patch would need attention, and soon he'd have to get started on planning for next season. There wouldn't be any time to get to know someone, even if he was interested.

Out of the blue, Margaret came to mind. He shook his head. Even if he was inclined to get to know a woman, she would be the last one he'd seek out. Unlike the other *maed* in Birch Creek, she was a visitor. Eventually she would go back to Salt Creek, where she lived, and that would be it. A long-distance relationship was beyond out of the question. He couldn't imagine a single circumstance where he would agree to such a thing.

At the high risk of disappointing his mother, he vowed that dating was off the table, which was an easy decision to make. He still had to figure out how to spend his time over the next seven days in a way that didn't involve work, and that would be far more difficult. But he had to find something to keep him occupied. Because if he didn't, his father might extend his vacation—and he didn't think he could handle that. Being forced to take a week off was torture enough.

By suppertime, Margaret already felt more at home than she did in her own house back in Salt Creek. *Aenti* Mary had invited the entire family over for supper, including Seth and his wife, Martha, his sisters, Ivy and Karen and their husbands, Noah and Adam, along with their children. And of course Ira and Nina. As soon as Nina walked through the door, Margaret gave her a big hug.

"I'm so glad to see you," she said, squeezing Nina tight. Unlike Margaret, Nina was solidly built and several inches taller. Margaret enjoyed being engulfed in her friend's soft embrace.

"Me too." Nina stepped back and grinned. "I've missed you so much."

Supper was a lively time, with everyone talking and eating the delicious meal *Aenti* Mary had prepared. The fried squash blossoms, baked chicken turnovers covered in white gravy, chow-chow, and bountiful garden salad were scrumptious, and her aunt had topped off the meal with a lemon pie piled high with lightly browned meringue. Margaret, who tried not to overeat too often, had seconds of everything.

After supper she helped Nina, Martha, and Mary clean the kitchen, while Karen and Ivy watched the children. Karen and Adam had two boys and Ivy and Noah one girl, all of them under three years old. Then she and Nina walked onto the spacious back deck that Freemont and Judah had built over the summer. They sat down across from each other on white plastic lawn chairs, and as the fading sunlight yielded to dusk, they started to talk.

"Is everything all right with you?" Nina tugged her navy-blue sweater closer to her body. Now that the sun was almost past the horizon, the temperature had dipped, and a slight chill hung in the air.

Margaret was a little stunned by the question. "*Ya . . .*" Of course, that wasn't the truth, even though her mood had perked up considerably since arriving in Birch Creek. Knowing Nina would see straight through any deceptions, she regrouped. "Actually, things aren't okay. Far from it."

Unlike Margaret, Nina didn't seem surprised by her response. "I figured."

"You did?"

"Your sudden visit is the first clue. Actually, it's the second. When I read your last letter, I could tell you weren't your usual self."

Frowning, Margaret said, "I don't remember saying anything out of the ordinary."

"You didn't have to. I can read between the lines." She shifted her plump frame in the chair. "Your letter was also short. Five lines, I think? Usually they're two pages long."

Margaret sighed. She tucked her lavender dress under her legs, which were curled up in her seat, and wondered how much she should tell Nina about her struggles. The two of them had become unexpectedly close through their letters over the past year, in spite of how they first met. She remembered how Nina had admitted that the first time she saw Margaret, which was when Ira had brought her along on one of Nina and Ira's Saturday fishing trips, she'd thought Margaret and Ira were romantically interested in each other, not knowing that they were cousins. Margaret found that amusing, because anyone could see that Ira liked Nina for more than a friend and that she felt the same. They were the ones who were clueless about each other's feelings. Late last year she was invited to their wedding but had to miss it because she had come down with the flu the day before she was supposed to leave. Ever since, she and Nina had written each other often, deepening their friendship.

But despite their closeness, she had never admitted her past to Nina, and although Nina knew that Margaret had worn makeup during her *rumspringa*, she thankfully hadn't brought up the subject again. *If only that was all I'd done.* She wasn't ready to disclose the details of that regretful time to anyone, but she could explain to her closest friend one of the reasons for her visit. "I'm here because of the mail-order bride advertisement."

Nina's thick, pretty brows lifted up. She leaned toward Margaret, a spark of interest in her eyes. "You are?"

"Now wait a minute, let me finish." She didn't need Nina thinking she was serious about finding a husband. "*Mamm* has been bugging me to get married ever since I joined the church, so I let her think that I'm looking for a husband during *mei* visit here."

"You lied to her?"

"Not exactly." She didn't like the guilt that was now nagging at her conscience. "I didn't correct her assumption, that's all."

"Then you lied by omission." Nina shook her head, clucking her tongue.

Margaret scowled, wishing she'd kept her mouth shut. "You sound like a judgmental old *frau*." The guilt bloomed like a violet in springtime. She shouldn't have deceived *Mamm* and her father, if *Mamm* had even bothered to tell him about the bride advertisement. But none of that was Nina's fault. "I'm sorry. I didn't mean to snap at you."

"It's okay." Nina gave her a sympathetic smile. "I understand why you let her believe you were looking for a husband. There's *nix* worse than someone else sticking their nose in your social life."

Buoyed by Nina's response, Margaret continued to explain how things were strained at home. "I'm trying to be more like *mei schwesters*," she said, struggling not to show her irritation that being boring and humorless was an ideal she had to strive for. "But *Mamm* is still disappointed in me. The only way I'll make her happy is if I get married."

"That's a terrible idea," Nina said. "You should only get married when you meet the right man. And even then, you should wait until you're both ready and sure that you want to marry each other."

"I agree with you. Don't worry, I'm only here to visit family and friends, not to *geh* on a husband hunt. I'm not going to get married anytime soon."

"*Gut.* Not that I don't want you to get married, but if you're not doing it for the right reasons, it's better to stay single." The sensor light above the back door had turned on, casting low light over the patio and extending a few inches into the backyard. Margaret could now see Nina's face and the annoyance in her eyes. "I remember how *Grossmutter* was always pressuring me and Levi to marry. More than once we had to tell her to mind her own business."

"I could never tell *Mamm* to do that. She wouldn't talk to me for a week if I did."

"Really?"

"Really." The one time Margaret had sassed her mother, she was twelve and *Mamm* had just finished lecturing her about how she talked too much and needed to learn to be quiet and follow her sisters' examples. She'd been tired and moody and popped off a few choice words. She wasn't sure what she'd even said, but she would never forget how her mother's face turned the color of an eggplant, and then she'd given Margaret the silent treatment for the next twelve days. Out of the blue, she started talking to her again as if nothing had happened, but Margaret had learned her lesson.

"The thing is," Nina said, "even though she drove us *ab im kopp* with her meddling, we always knew *Grossmutter* wanted the best for us."

Although Margaret had only met Delilah a few times, Nina had told her enough about her grandmother through her letters that Margaret felt like she knew her well. Delilah had raised Nina and her older brother Levi since they were young children, after their mother died. She was a strong-willed woman who didn't hesitate to give her opinion or meddle in her family's lives if she thought they needed it, a characteristic that had caused some friction over the years. According to Nina, her grandmother had learned her lesson and fortunately hadn't interfered in her and Levi's marriages. At least not yet.

"I'm sure that's what your *mutter* wants for you too," Nina added.

"I find that hard to believe."

"Have you ever talked to her about it?"

After a pause, Margaret shook her head. There were a number of reasons why she couldn't talk to her mother about not being ready to get married, the biggest one being that she was tired of feeling like a disappointment to her family. Her mother would no doubt bring up her failings yet again, reminding her that good Amish women didn't sneak out of the house and go to parties with "those wild English fools." Whenever that subject was brought up, Margaret quickly switched the topic, usually saying she agreed with her mother that she was stupid and wrong and made a bad choice, just so *Mamm* wouldn't ask her questions she wasn't prepared to answer—at least not honestly.

"She wouldn't understand," Margaret finally said, then sat up and shifted in her seat until her toes touched the deck floor. As she did so many times with *Mamm*, she decided to change the focus of the conversation. "Enough about me. What's new in your life since your last letter?"

"Well . . ." Nina glanced down at her lap, then back at Margaret. "There is some brand-new news." After a pause, she added, "I'm expecting."

Margaret clapped her hands. "That's wonderful! I'm thrilled for you."

"Shh. *Nee* one knows. I haven't even told Ira yet."

"Why not?"

"He's been busy with the harvest. I didn't want to bother him."

But she wasn't looking at Margaret when she was talking. Now who's lying by omission? She moved her chair closer to Nina so she could lower her voice. "I'm sure he wouldn't consider this news a bother. And Delilah is going to be thrilled."

Nina bobbed her head but didn't say anything.

Alarmed by her friend's odd behavior, she asked, "Do you feel all right?"

Pressing her lips together, Nina nodded again. "But I felt the same way last time."

Margaret's heart dropped to her stomach. "Nina, why didn't you tell me?"

"I didn't tell anyone. Only Ira. I didn't expect to get pregnant so soon after . . ." She wiped her eyes with the heel of her hand.

"What if something happens to this *boppli*?" she whispered, her voice so quiet and thin Margaret almost didn't hear her.

Taking Nina's hand, Margaret said, "That's why you're not telling Ira."

"I'm scared." She squeezed Margaret's hand. "I don't want to disappoint him again."

"Oh, Nina." Margaret's heart went out to her friend. Nina was terrified and for some reason felt like she had to carry that fear alone. "Don't you think he'd be upset if you didn't tell him?" she said gently.

"I suppose he would."

"And isn't a part of marriage being able to share each other's burdens? I'm sure you didn't disappoint him. We both know that God is in control of these things."

"You're right. And I am six weeks along. Further than I was before." She glanced at her stomach, which had been slightly rounded ever since Margaret had known her. "I haven't had any morning sickness, thank goodness. But that could change, and I don't think I could hide that from him."

"Not if you end up with the morning sickness *mei schwesters* had. June was sick more than the other two." Or so she said. Margaret hadn't been around her sisters too much when they were pregnant. She'd been too busy having fun—or what she had thought was fun—at the time. Now she knew she had been immature. "I know *mei* cousin, Nina. He loves you more than anything else in this world. You need to tell him."

As if on cue, the back door opened and Ira stepped out. He came over to Nina and put his beefy hand on her shoulder. "We should be heading home," he said, stifling a yawn. "We've got to harvest the corn tomorrow. That's going to take the whole day." He turned to Margaret. "You have *nee* idea how excited *Mamm* was when she told us you were coming for a visit."

Margaret smirked as she stood, determined to lighten the mood for Nina. "And how about you, cousin? Are you glad to see me?"

He shrugged. "I guess." When she pinched his arm he said, "Ow! That hurt. I didn't think a little thing like you could squeeze so hard." But he was laughing as he rubbed his shoulder.

"Let's *geh*, weakling." Nina stood next to him, then slipped her hand into his. "You're right. We need to get home. I have something important to talk to you about." She gave Margaret a sweet smile, and any hint that she had been upset moments ago was gone. Ignoring Ira's puzzled look, she led him back into the house to say goodbye to his parents.

Margaret stayed behind and sat back down on the chair, still filled with joy about Nina's pregnancy, although that joy was tempered by knowing about her friend's miscarriage. She was glad Nina had decided to tell Ira about the baby. She said a quick prayer for all three of them, asking God to keep the baby healthy and strong and to give Nina and Ira peace about this pregnancy.

When she finished, her thoughts shifted to her own future. Seeing her cousins and aunt and uncle happily married hadn't changed her mind about waiting on marriage, but she couldn't help wondering if children were in her future when—or if—she did marry. She hadn't allowed herself to think about babies, but like getting married, having children would be expected too.

The idea seemed so distant to her. She couldn't imagine herself as a mother, at least not a good one. That reminded her that she needed to visit *Aenti* Carolyn soon. The snickerdoodles had been so delicious and addicting that she ate way too many of them. She needed to start watching how much she was eating. Her mother would notice if she put on any weight and wouldn't hesitate to comment on it, and she'd point out how her sisters managed to keep thin even after having babies. *Ugh*. She needed to stop thinking about her family, or they were going to ruin her trip.

The back door opened again, and Mary poked out her head. "Seth and Martha left. They told me to tell you *gute nacht*. Ivy and Karen had to leave too. Ivy asked you to stop at the store when you get a chance."

Margaret started to stand. "I didn't realize I'd been outside so long."

Mary held up her hand. "That's fine. Stay out here as long as you like. It's such a lovely evening. Freemont and I are going to bed, but make yourself at home." She smiled, opening the door a little wider. "Did I tell you I'm glad you're here?"

Chuckling, Margaret replied, "Once or twice."

After Mary shut the door, Margaret settled back in the chair. Mary was right. This evening was made to be enjoyed. The air was cool but not too crisp, and what few clouds had dotted the sky earlier had cleared. When she looked up, she could see thousands of twinkling stars. As soon as she could, she would visit the antique store Ivy and Noah ran together, and she would also make sure to visit Karen and Adam, who lived near the Chupps and owned a farm with that family.

A feeling of contentment came over her, and the last bit of tension in her shoulders finally released. Just like her last visit to Birch Creek, she felt welcome and comfortable. It was nice to be wanted by family for a change.

Chapter 4

Three days into his forced vacation, Owen was at his wits' end. Saturday had been tough, knowing his father and brothers were working hard outside and his mother, along with Phoebe and her sister-in-law, Leanna, were in the kitchen cooking and canning jars of vegetable soup. He decided to spend the day in Barton, walking around the hardware store and Walmart, then getting lunch at a Mexican restaurant that he'd heard through the grapevine had decent food. Meandering through a day without doing farmwork or accomplishing a single work-related task unsettled him. If he couldn't get through one day without going nuts, how was he going to manage the rest of the week?

But if he thought Saturday had been bad, Sunday was worse. Church service had been held last week, so he was at loose ends having an entire day to do nothing but rest and read. Normally he didn't mind that too much since he usually engaged in a lot of physical work on Saturdays. That hadn't been the case the day before. After taking two brief naps, one before lunch and one after, he grew restless and went outside for a short while. But that didn't last either. He couldn't bear to look at the farm, knowing he couldn't do even a single evening chore. He went back inside and took a third nap, then went to bed early out of sheer boredom.

By Monday he realized he had to make a change. After the rest of the family finished breakfast and went outside to work, he grabbed a book about foraging off his dresser, along with a small pocket compass, and left the house. As he walked along the asphalt road, the strain of the past two days started to ease somewhat. Being outside never failed to calm him, other than yesterday when he had gone in the backyard, and that had to do more with him wanting to work than not enjoying the outdoors.

A buggy approached, and when it was close enough that he could recognize the driver, he realized it was Martha Yoder, Seth's wife. He waved at her as she drove her buggy past him, and she returned his greeting. He imagined she was headed to her mother-in-law Mary's house, probably to cook and can like his mother, sister, and Leanna were doing.

He didn't have an end destination in mind, and he figured he had walked a little more than a mile when he saw a grove of trees to his right. A walk through the woods was a luxury he hadn't indulged in for a long time. Now that he thought about it, he couldn't remember the last time he'd taken a nature walk just for fun. He had brought the pocket compass for just this reason, in case he decided to detour from the road. Good thing he did because these woods were unfamiliar to him.

As he walked farther into the woods, he searched for a stump or log where he could sit and read for a spell, figuring he might as well learn about something while he was on vacation. Being surrounded by a variety of trees that were already starting to change color was much better than staring at the four walls in his bedroom.

Owen kept walking, not bothering to keep track of how long he'd been strolling through the woods, when he saw a small building in the distance. He squinted and sped up until he was facing what appeared to be a garden shed but was somewhat larger than the usual size shed. Strange. Why would someone build a shed in the middle of the woods? He walked around the wooden structure, looking for some sign of ownership, but didn't find anything. When he rounded back to the front again, he noticed the door was slightly ajar.

His curiosity getting the best of him, he lightly knocked, not surprised he didn't get an answer. Unable to stop himself, he opened the door and stuck his head inside. Empty. That wasn't a surprise either. *I've come this far. Might as well go all the way in.*

Stepping inside, he surveyed the single room. Once his eyes adjusted to the dim interior, he was able to see that the dusty, paned window on the far-left side of the building provided a halfway decent amount of light. He saw a long table attached to the back wall, and above the table hung an empty pegboard. Sawdust scattered the table surface, and when he turned around, he spied a tall, empty metal shelving unit on the adjacent wall. There wasn't any indication that this shed was used for gardening or storing firewood. The large amount of sawdust made him think this was, or had been, a workshop of some kind.

He walked over to the window and ran his index finger down the thick layer of dust on the glass pane, then looked at the dirt covering his finger. He wiped it off on his broadfall pants, then he glanced around the shed again. Obviously no one had been here for a long while. Confident the place was completely abandoned, he sat down on the plywood-covered floor and leaned against the wall under the window. It wasn't hot outside, but he was enjoying the coolness inside the shed, and the sunbeam of light streaming through the window was enough for him to clearly see the cover of his book, *God's Garden*. This place beat an old stump any day.

Owen opened the book to an entry about fiddleheads, a type of ostrich fern. Good, he was learning something new right off the bat. He didn't know anything about fiddleheads, but by the time he finished reading, he'd gleaned some useful information. The author thought the plants tasted like a cross between asparagus and young spinach, with a hint of mushroom. Interesting. The green, unfurled fronds were edible, and the book included details about where to find and harvest them, with an additional section on how to cook the plants. He paid attention to an important warning—undercooked fiddleheads could make one sick, so it was crucial to cook the plant thoroughly. Duly noted.

As he continued to read, his mind turned to business again. Who said the farm had to be his single source of income? Once he became proficient at foraging, he could teach his younger brothers the skill, and they could sell what they foraged at the farmers market along with their produce and baked goods. The more he thought about it, the more he warmed to the idea of making some money off of something that took little effort and would actually be enjoyable, as long as they made sure to put a warning label on the fiddlehead fronds so no one got a bad case of food poisoning. That would ruin business for sure.

Stop. He set the book down on his lap and gave his head a hard shake. There was one thing his parents didn't want him to do—think about work and business—and all he could think about was work and business. Somehow, he had to separate his newfound interest in foraging from his inclination to think of everything as a business opportunity. "Just relax and read," he said, picking up the book again. "Relax and read." This time he made sure he was simply absorbing the information, not trying to apply it to anything. A difficult task, but he kept at it. Eventually he was able to concentrate solely on the book, and before long he became engrossed in the world of foraging, ignoring everything else around him. *Relax and read . . .*

Margaret kept a sharp eye on the ground as she wound her way through the woods, making sure she didn't accidentally crush a hidden wildflower or miss seeing a pretty or interesting new plant she wasn't familiar with. She had discovered this wooded area yesterday when she left her aunt and uncle to take a leisurely Sunday afternoon walk. This morning when she'd finished helping *Aenti* Mary clean up the kitchen after breakfast, she asked her aunt if she needed help with anything. When *Aenti* Mary said no, Margaret decided to return to these woods and do a little more exploring.

Nature walks and hikes had always saved her sanity back in Salt Creek. She loved going through the wooded areas back home to find flowers to place between the pages of the three old encyclopedias she used for pressing the blooms, and now that she was interested in medicinal herbs, she had even more enthusiasm to seek out interesting flora. If she found anything, she planned to pick only a few of the plants, not wanting to waste anything. She didn't yet know enough about using herbs but wanted to make sure she had enough to study.

Today she was on the hunt for one particular herb—burdock. She wasn't sure if the plant grew in these woods, but she had read in her book that it was native to Ohio, so the search was justified. As she continued to walk, she inspected the ground, searching through old leaves, short plants, and the mosses and lichen that covered the bottoms of some of the trees. She also made sure to watch her step. She didn't want to trip and fall over any large tree branches, logs, or roots—something she'd done more than once back home. Avoiding those things was a job in itself. The forest floor was covered with detritus.

After what seemed like a long time of searching, she hadn't found anything, unfortunately, not even a decent flower to take back to the Yoders. How disappointing. The tree cover was too dense in this part of the woods for the sun to fully break through. Figuring she'd probably have better luck if she moved to a thinner area of trees, she decided to find her way back out of the woods. She'd always had a good sense of direction, so she wasn't worried about getting lost.

A few minutes later, she stepped over a large log. When she glanced up, she saw something she never expected to see—a shed in the middle of the woods. How odd. The small structure was made with weathered wooden slats, but they didn't look all that old, and the brown roof sloped to the back. She tried to imagine who would have built the structure. Was it a hunting cabin? She crossed that guess off her list. The shed was too small for a cabin, although it did look like one or two people could fit inside it. Her curiosity piqued, she slowly moved toward the shed, then saw that not only wasn't the door locked, but it was also slightly open.

She paused and looked around. Surely this shed belonged to someone. The place didn't look like it had been abandoned for years, but it didn't appear to be in great shape either. She tapped her finger against her bottom lip. She should just walk away and continue looking for the burdock. To do anything else would be trespassing.

But who would know if she just took a peek inside? Ignoring her conscience, she slowly opened the door, ready to jump back if a chipmunk or squirrel or other woodland animal had decided to use the shed for shelter or a home. Then she peered inside. To her surprise there was a window on the left side, and faint sunlight streamed through the glass pane. Her gaze followed the beam to a large lump on the floor. That was strange. She walked farther inside, and when she got close enough to the lump, she flinched. The lump was a body. A deathly still male body.

Panic shot through her and she didn't think, only reacted. She ran to him and knelt down, quickly putting her ear against his chest. Oh, thank God, she heard a heartbeat—

"Hey!"

The man jolted to life, flinging Margaret off his chest and onto the floor beside him. When she looked up, she realized she was face to face with Owen Bontrager. "Owen!" she cried as she scrambled away from him. She slapped her hand over her heart. "You about scared me to death!"

"I scared *you*?" He sat up and scowled at her. "Imagine waking up from a nice nap to find a woman with her ear on your chest." He frowned and rose from the floor. "On second thought, don't imagine that. What are you doing here?"

Embarrassment replaced panic and she jumped to her feet. This was what she got for being nosy—first shock and then embarrassment. "I'm sorry," she began to babble, taking several steps back. "I was taking a walk and I saw your, uh, cabin . . . shed . . . whatever this place is." Oh boy, now she was insulting his little building. "I shouldn't have come inside uninvited."

A shamed expression crossed his face, and he jabbed the heel of his work boot—a shoe that had seen better days—against the plywood floor. "Um, this isn't *mei* cabin. It's not actually a cabin either, as you can see. Nobody but a hermit could live here for more than a couple of days." He straightened his crooked straw hat. "I just found it myself. I hadn't intended to stay long—just to read a chapter or two. Guess I fell asleep." He bent down and grabbed his book off the floor.

"Then you're trespassing too?" She didn't know him very well, but she wouldn't have pegged him for a rule breaker. He seemed too self-contained and serious for that.

The hazy sunlight shone from a window that needed a good cleaning and lit up his red cheeks. "Ah, seems like I am. I hadn't thought of it that way, but I should have." He closed his eyes for a moment.

Had he gone to sleep again? Could someone even sleep standing up? She doubted that, but it was weird he was just standing there with his eyes closed. "Are you okay?"

He opened his eyes. "I'm fine. Just asking for forgiveness. We should *geh* now."

They left the shed and Owen shut the door behind him. When

it didn't latch properly, he tried again. He let go of the knob, but the door cracked open again, looking the same as it had when Margaret had arrived. She stared at it and frowned. "I'm confused," she said, more to herself than to him.

"About what? The door not latching? I think it needs some oiling."

The broken latch wasn't her concern. She faced him, wondering if she should explain herself. "I should know this," she mumbled.

"Know what?" He adjusted his hat again, pushing it farther back off his forehead.

"Do we have to confess our trespassing in front of the church next Sunday?" She hoped not. She'd promised her mother she wouldn't get into trouble, and she hadn't even been in Birch Creek for a week and had already broken the law. Or at least a rule. If she and Owen had to get up in front of the congregation and tell everyone, her mother would surely find out. Not to mention she would shame *Aenti* Mary and *Onkel* Freemont. Actually, that would be double shame since he was the bishop. *Why didn't I turn around and leave when I was supposed to?*

"Margaret."

Her gaze shot up when she heard his calm voice.

"I think it will be okay if this stays between us. We didn't mean any harm. We just weren't thinking."

"Oh, thank goodness. I can't *geh* through—" She caught herself before she admitted that she couldn't go through another public confession again, especially in front of a bunch of strangers. She cleared her throat. "I'm surprised to see you here," she said. "Aren't you supposed to be working right now?"

"I'm supposed to be," he muttered. "But *mei* parents had other ideas." He glanced at the book in her hand. "Still reading about herbal medicine?"

She nodded, then pointed to the book he was holding. "Still reading about farming?"

"Nope. Foraging." He held up the book so she could see the cover. "This was one of *mei grossvatter*'s books. I inherited several of them when he passed away, including the one I was reading the other day. It's old, but it has a lot of *gut* information."

"I'm sure it's special to you too."

"All his books are, although I'll admit I haven't had much time to read them. I guess that's changed now." She had no idea what he was talking about, but before she could question him, he asked, "Have you found what you're looking for?"

"*Nee.*" She cast a glance around the woods. "I was trying to find some burdock, but I think there needs to be more sunlight in order for it to grow. I didn't find any wildflowers either, probably for the same reason. The trees are really dense around here."

"That they are." He brushed at a gnat flying nearby. "What do you use burdock for?"

She moved closer to him and opened her herbal medicine book. "According to this," she said, pointing to the earmarked page, "it's supposed to help with diabetes, stomach issues, and wrinkles."

"Wrinkles?" He half grinned, enough to show his overlapping front teeth. "You don't have to worry about those for a long time. How old are you? Twenty, twenty-one?"

"Twenty. What about you?"

"Twenty-three." Behind him a few oak tree branches rustled

against each other. Several brown leaves broke free and floated to the ground.

"And you're still single?" She cringed. Why had she said that? He didn't have a beard, so obviously he wasn't married, but that didn't mean he didn't have a fiancé or girlfriend. "It's just that back home in our little district, a lot of people your age are already married."

Now he was smirking. "*Ya*, I'm still single." Then his expression turned impassive, and he started to look around again.

She closed her book and rocked on her heels. Then she inspected the ground. A small spider scurried in front of the toe of her shoes.

After several moments of silence, he finally said, "Guess I better get back to my walk." He still wasn't looking at her.

"And I should get back to looking for the burdock. Just not around here."

"Okay. See you, then." He started to walk off.

"Bye."

Margaret turned and walked in the opposite direction from the shed. Well, that was awkward. Not as awkward as their ride back from the bus station the other day, but close. Despite herself, she sized him up in her mind. Even if she hadn't decided not to be interested in anyone in Birch Creek, Owen wouldn't be in the running. There wasn't a single iota of connection between them. As he had in the car the other day, the only thing he wanted to talk about were plants. While she liked plants, a person couldn't exactly base a relationship on them.

"Do you want some help?"

His voice yanked her out of her thoughts. She spun around,

surprised not only to see him standing there, but more so by his offer. When she met his gaze, she noticed his eyes again, particularly those exceptionally long lashes. They didn't look the least bit feminine on him, highlighting instead his unique blue-gray irises. They're just eyes . . . just eyelashes. But they were the most remarkable eyes and eyelashes she'd ever seen.

"If you don't, I understand." His grandfather's book was tucked under his arm, but he was digging at the dirt with his boot heel again. "Just thought I'd offer. In case you needed some. Help, that is."

His gawkiness was kind of cute, she had to admit. Especially the way he shyly lifted his gaze to hers for a second, then looked back down to the ground. And it would be nice to have some company while she searched for the burdock—

Hold up. What was she doing thinking Owen was sort of cute? *Even though it's true.* His offer was nice, but she couldn't accept. She knew better than anyone what happened when a man and a woman were alone. A few minutes ago, she decided there was no spark between them, and she hadn't changed her mind. She didn't expect anything untoward to happen, but why take the chance? "Ah, actually, I don't think that's a *gut* idea."

He frowned. "Why not?"

"Because . . ." Oh boy, how could she explain herself to him without sounding dumb? Then again, it was better to be straightforward than coy. In the past she had played mind games, mimicking the behavior of the English girls she hung out with. No more of that nonsense. She squared her shoulders. "I don't think it's a *gut* idea because I'm not in the market for a husband, and it's inappropriate for us to be alone together." There. The truth was out. If she'd only took that advice back in her *rumspringa* days, she wouldn't have so many regrets.

"Huh." Amusement entered his eyes. "I gotta say, I wasn't expecting you to say that." Rubbing his chin, he added, "Let me put your mind at ease, Margaret Yoder. I'm not looking for a *frau*. Or even a date. I didn't offer to help you look for burdock because I was interested in you—I just need a way to kill some time before I *geh* home. Don't worry, I won't treat you any different than I would treat my *schwester*. The thought never crossed *mei* mind."

She stilled. Not interested? Killing time? *His sister?* She should be happy he was being as candid as she was, but instead she was insulted. For the first time, a man was telling her he wasn't interested or attracted to her, and she couldn't believe what she was hearing. Even Timothy, the boy whose sole focus had been baseball when they were both in their early teens, had asked her out right after she had turned sixteen and before she had ditched the Amish boys in her community for the English ones she found more exciting. She had refused to go out with him of course, her mind and heart determined to experience freedom—or what she thought would be freedom—for the first time. She didn't need a baseball-loving Amish boy dragging her down.

The thought never crossed mei *mind.* She pinched her lips together. "Why would you say that?" she snapped, seeing his eyes widening. "Is there something wrong with me?"

Owen stumbled back, knocked off-kilter by her question and the spark of fire that suddenly appeared in her eyes. Clearly, he had said the wrong thing, but he had also said several things, so he had no idea what specifically set her off. Whatever it was, she was hopping mad and it was his fault. Attempting to smooth things over, he said, "There's *nix* wrong with you. At least from what I can tell."

Her pretty face scrunched into an impressive and quite sulky scowl. Guess that was the wrong thing to say too.

Her small chin lifted, and she marched toward him until only a few inches separated them. The top of her head reached his upper chest, but that didn't keep her from staring him down. "I'll have you know that I'm a perfectly fine woman. Make that a perfectly fine *Amish* woman."

"Uh, I'm sure you are." He thought it was weird that she had emphasized she was Amish since it would be obvious to anyone that she was. He began to back away but succeeded in hitting a tree instead. He'd have to jump aside to get away from her, and he wasn't sure she wouldn't chase after him in her agitated state.

"I would make any man a *gut frau*," she continued, pointing her finger at him.

"I have *nee* doubt about that." He could feel the rough tree bark scratching through the back of his shirt, but the discomfort was nothing compared to how the little dynamo in front of him was making him feel. He needed to calm her down, but he had no idea how. He did have to make one thing clear, though. "I'm sure you'll make some man happy in the future, Margaret. But I'm not that man."

She blinked several times. Then her small hands flew to her cheeks. "Oh *nee*," she said, moving away from him. Then she covered her face with her hands. "This is so embarrassing."

It sure was, for both of them. And if he was smart, he would turn around and walk away. No, make that run away, because he couldn't make heads or tails of what had just happened during the last couple of minutes. He had to wonder if she was just a little *ab im kopp*.

But his common sense must have taken a vacation because he couldn't leave her like this, alone in the woods, thinking she had humiliated herself in front of him. He still wasn't sure how it had happened, but he had somehow flipped a switch inside her, and he needed to fix whatever it was that needed fixing. This was one reason why he stayed away from women. They were too complicated.

Taking a deep breath, he said, "Hey." When she didn't respond, he took one tentative step toward her, then another. "I'm sorry."

Margaret's hands fell from her face and she looked at him, her cheeks as red as fresh-picked apples off the tree. "This isn't your fault. It's mine." She walked over to a nearby stump and plopped down, her small shoulders drooping. "I made such a fool out of myself in front of you."

She looked so forlorn he couldn't stop himself from going to her. He hunkered down until they were at eye level. "It's okay," he said, trying to measure his words so he wouldn't set her off again. "If I had a dollar for every time I made a fool of myself, I'd be a wealthy man."

"*Ya* right. You're just trying to make me feel better." She tugged at a leaf on a nearby bush, but not hard enough to break it off the twig. "I can't imagine you making a fool out of yourself."

"Well, my folks think I'm a fool for working too hard. Does that count?"

She shook her head, but a hint of a smile appeared on her face. A sardonic smile, but he would take it. "That sounds more like a strength instead of a flaw," she said.

"Not to *mei* parents." He sat down, then bent his knees and rested his forearms on them. He loosely clasped his hands before continuing. "Earlier you mentioned that I should be at work. The reason I'm not is because *mei mamm* and *daed* made me take a vacation."

She let go of the leaf and the twig snapped back, barely missing her elbow. "They made you?"

"Yep. For one week I can't do any work. I can't even wipe off the table after supper."

"Wow. That would never happen to me. I love to *geh* on vacation, but *mei familye* doesn't. *Daed* doesn't like to travel and *Mamm* is happy at home. Same thing with *mei schwesters*. They're all homebodies."

"*Mei familye* are fine with staying home, but we've always gone somewhere for two weeks in the early spring, right before plowing time. Last year they went to Ephrata for vacation, and the year before that it was Colorado."

"And you didn't *geh*?"

He hadn't intended on bringing up his enforced time off, but he was glad to see she was calm and they were able to have a normal conversation, although he wasn't sure it was normal to admit he was a workaholic to a woman he barely knew. "I haven't been on the last three trips with them. You would think with so many people in our family they would be glad to be minus a person. But they weren't."

"Why didn't you *geh*?"

"Somebody needed to watch the farm while the *familye* was gone."

"That's reasonable." She leaned forward and rested her elbow on her knee.

The strands of her white *kapp* were tied together and trailing down the back of her sage-green-colored dress. He noticed that she looked pretty in that color, although she had been pretty in the light-purple dress she had on the other day. He figured she'd look nice wearing a grass seed sack. But that was just stating a fact. "Well, we're the only ones who are reasonable then."

"If there isn't anyone that's able to take care of the farm while the family is gone, then why would they complain when you said you would?" she asked.

"We have other *familye* who can keep an eye on the place and our animals."

Margaret sat back, the space between her eyebrows wrinkling. "Then why didn't you *geh* on those vacations?"

"Because they're a waste of time." He'd never admitted that thought out loud before, but that was the reason. Even if he had, his parents would have a counterargument. But that didn't mean he didn't think he was right. "There's never enough time to finish all the work on the farm. There's always something that has to be done or planned for or taken care of. Taking off for a couple of weeks to do nothing isn't productive."

"But the work will always be there, *ya?*" she said softly.

He leveled his gaze at her. "I can see you're agreeing with *mei* parents on this." He almost laughed. His father and mother had wanted him to get to know some of the single women in their community, and he was at least talking to one. Little did they know they had an ally in the great vacation debate.

She smiled, and this time any trace of bitterness was gone. "They sound like wise people."

"They are," he grumbled. "I love *mei* parents, even though I don't agree with them about this issue. But that's neither here nor there. The bottom line is I have a week off."

"And you're spending it in the woods reading about foraging."

"I'm expanding *mei* knowledge," he said, moving his arms from his knees and straightening his shoulders. "I also find foraging interesting. I've never had the time to read *grossvatter*'s books before. I figured I would plow through as many as I can now that I have the time to spend."

"Or the time to kill." She sniffed.

Ah, there it was—what he had said that upset her. He should have realized it too. No wonder she was bent out of shape. Using her as an excuse to kill time sounded bad, even if he didn't mean it that way. He should have said he wanted to help her because he was interested in the burdock. That would be the partial truth. The other part was that he was finding that he enjoyed her company, especially since they had a common interest. There was nothing amiss about that. "Sorry. That comment came out wrong."

"It's okay. I overreacted." A dreamy look filled her eyes. "If I had a week to do anything I wanted to, I would definitely *geh* somewhere part of the time. Maybe spend a few days in a cabin on Lake Erie. At the very least I'd *geh* to a different town."

"Like you're doing now?"

Her placid expression shifted. "I am not on vacation."

"You're not? Are you working for the Yoders then?"

"*Nee.*"

He rubbed his chin. "Are you working somewhere else?"

"I'm not working anywhere. But I'm not on vacation either." She sat back up and sighed. "You probably think I'm completely nuts now."

"I don't think that."

Tilting her head, she smirked. "Even after *mei* tirade?"

"Little tirade." He held his thumb and forefinger together for emphasis. Then her smirk transformed into a smile, and he couldn't help but smile back. "Then why are you in Birch Creek if you're not working or on vacation?"

He thought he heard her sigh, but when she spoke, her eyes were resolute. "I'm here to find a husband."

Chapter 5

Margaret squirmed. She could have told Owen anything instead of the truth, like she was looking for a job or she was here helping her aunt with the canning or her uncle and cousins with the harvest. But she couldn't bring herself to be anything but honest with him, even though her honesty contradicted what she'd told him earlier. Now he had to think she was off her rocker. Even she was starting to wonder if she was getting a little *ab im kopp*.

He leaned back and nodded slowly as if he were trying to absorb what she just said. "But I thought you told me—"

"That I wasn't looking for a husband. But *mei familye* thinks I am."

"That makes . . ." He paused for a moment before saying, "Actually, that doesn't make sense at all."

"I know. But *Mamm* wants me to get married, and she won't stop bugging me about it." She wasn't about to tell him that her mother thought she needed a man to set her straight, and she absolutely wasn't going to reveal anything about her *rumspringa* to him. "All *mei schwesters* were married at twenty. That's some kind of magic number to *Mamm*."

He nodded. "Weird how our parents are so concerned about their kids getting married. Do you know about the mail-order advertisement?"

"*Ya. Mamm* showed it to me."

Owen sat cross-legged, not seeming to care that he was sitting on dirt, old leaves, and pebbles. "*Daed* told me the other day he thought *Mamm* had put it in there since she'd been concerned about her *sohns* being able to find spouses due to the lack of single women in our community."

"Did she?"

"She told *Daed* she didn't, and he believed her. I believe her too. That doesn't change the fact that she's been praying for all her *buwe* to find *fraus*, though. At one time that was a tall order, but now there are plenty of single women to choose from."

"And you're not interested in any of them?"

He shook his head. "Nope. I'm not ready for marriage, despite my old age."

She flinched. "Sorry. I didn't mean to insult you."

"You didn't. I'm just teasing you." He smiled.

He has a great smile. Margaret paused, stunned by the thought that had popped into her head. Moments ago she was sure he thought she was crazy. He had a right to think so, considering how she had flown off the handle. Now they were having a nice conversation, and the awkwardness was disappearing between them. He had such a calm demeanor that made her feel comfortable around him. What a welcome change from what she was used to. She also appreciated that he had called her meltdown small, which it definitely wasn't. She wasn't sure how he'd managed it, but he had made a humiliating situation lighthearted, and that was impressive.

And then he smiled at her, and suddenly she didn't notice his crooked teeth or his sharp jaw. She just saw Owen.

"Marriage is a big step," he continued. "It's not like the English world, where people get divorces at the drop of a hat. I know not all English couples do, but it seems like divorce is always an option for them. It's not for us."

"Exactly. What if we make a mistake? When we get married, we get married for life." She had made so many mistakes over the years that when it came to the biggest decision of her life—other than joining the church—she questioned her own judgment.

"Bingo. I don't want to be stuck with someone I don't get along with. Or worse, end up resenting *mei frau*. That wouldn't be fair to either of us."

She liked his logical perspective. "*Nee*, it wouldn't. You'd think our parents would know this."

"My folks have a terrific marriage. They're always a united front, even during the rough times."

"That's *gut*. *Mei* parents are . . ." She realized she had never thought much about her mother and father's relationship. They did seem distant with each other, and she had never seen them exchange any affection in front of her. She couldn't imagine having a marriage like that. She might not be ready to get married, but she was positive she didn't want a cold relationship like her parents had. "They get along all right," was all she could say.

"That might be the reason why our parents are so eager to push marriage, because they have *gut* ones," Owen said. "Or they're too old to remember what life was like when they were single."

"I'm sure mine don't."

He rubbed his chin again, as if he were settling something in his mind. Then he dropped his hand and said, "Regardless of their reasons, it's not right for them to put pressure on us to get married. I'm not ruling it out, but it's going to be a long time before I tie the knot."

"Me too. A very long time."

He grinned. "There, I'm glad that's settled."

"Agreed." Finally, she'd found someone who felt the same way about the marriage issue. He'd also unexpectedly helped her figure out the real reason she didn't want to jump into a relationship, much less get married. She didn't exactly have the best track record in the romance department, and lately, making mistakes was her specialty. Marriage was for life, and there was no need to rush into it, despite her mother's opinion. There was also no reason to discuss the topic with him again since they both felt the same way.

But there was still one more thing she had to clear up with him. If she was smart, she wouldn't bring it up. Yet for some reason she couldn't go back to the Yoders without explaining the real reason she'd lost her cool with him. Oh, this was so embarrassing. *Just let it drop.*

However, she had never been one to listen to her own common sense. He started to stand up when she said, "I still haven't told you why I was so upset earlier. I, uh . . . I'm not used to being told I'm not pretty."

He sat back down, and his affable expression vanished. "When did I say that?"

"When you said I didn't have to worry about the two of us being alone."

His brow furrowed. "We just discussed why I said that, and it doesn't have anything to do with how you look."

She crossed her arms. Why was he being so dense? *I guess I have to spell it out for him.* "You compared me to *yer schwester.*"

"And you think Phoebe's ugly?"

Margaret paused. She hadn't seen Phoebe since she'd come back to Birch Creek, but she had met her on her last visit. Phoebe was attractive. Definitely not ugly. "Um, *nee.* She's pretty."

Owen leveled his gaze at her. "You realize you're not making much sense again, right? I wasn't insulting you. I was trying to reassure you that I didn't have any ulterior motives."

Uh-oh. Apparently, she had misunderstood him. Which she wouldn't have, if she hadn't let her ego get in the way. She and Owen were getting along just fine until she had to open her mouth. No, they were doing more than fine. She hadn't felt this relaxed in a long time, or at least she hadn't until a few moments ago, and then she had to go and ruin everything. "Well, I'm not used to that," she said in a small voice, too embarrassed to look at him.

"To being reassured?"

"*Nee.* Not by a *mann* anyway." Wow, she was making a real mess of things now. She leapt from the stump. "I've got to *geh,*" she said, her face heating up again. If he hadn't thought she was odd before, he surely did now. She didn't seem to be able to relate to a man unless she was flirting with him and he wanted a date . . . or something more. How pathetic.

Then again, why did she care if Owen thought she was strange? His opinion shouldn't matter to her. But for some reason it did.

Owen scrambled to his feet and blocked her path so she couldn't get away, although he was keeping a respectable distance. "Margaret, let's clear this up right now. You're definitely pretty."

Now she was even more mortified. She hated how her pride kept getting the best of her. "You don't have to say that."

"I wouldn't have said it if it wasn't true."

She looked up at him, and she felt a tiny flutter in her stomach. Not attraction, of course, since she knew without a doubt that she wasn't attracted to him. But if she ever did meet a man who made her heart sing, he would surely be as nice and understanding as Owen Bontrager. "I'm sorry I made things awkward . . . again. And I want you to know that I don't *geh* around fishing for compliments." What was it about this man that she felt like she could reveal so much of herself to him? "I have a problem with pride, and I'm trying to work on it."

"I don't know about that," Owen said. "I mean, all of us need to work on our pride. But I'm not seeing a prideful woman in front of me."

Her brow lifted, surprised by his statement. "You're not?"

"*Nee.* You're dealing with a lot of pressure from your family. Pressure can make people do—and say—strange things. I'm a little familiar with pressure, too, you know. Some of it's self-inflicted. Or so I'm told." He chuckled, then turned serious again. "*Mei daed* suggested I use *mei* free time to pursue a hobby or learn something new. I decided to read those books *mei grossvatter* gave me."

"Do you feel any better?"

"*Ya.* I guess I do. I'm learning about foraging, which is interesting and might be something I'll pursue more seriously in the future. I'm also catching up on *mei* sleep. Not because the books are boring, but I'm discovering that I'm more tired than I thought. I'm not saying that you don't enjoy spending time with your family, but is there anything that you wanted to learn or do that you haven't had a chance to? Within the boundaries of Birch Creek, of course."

She had to smile at that because he was right—if she had a choice, she would go somewhere she'd never been before. But since she was confined to Birch Creek, which she didn't mind one bit, she considered his question. "I like walking through the woods and meadows. I love picking wildflowers and pressing them in books. I recently started making pictures with them. I'm enjoying learning about medicinal herbs."

He nodded, as if he were focused on every word she was saying. Such a change from the dismissive way her family treated her and from the English guys she had gone out with. He made her feel like what she was saying was important to him, even though she was just talking about flowers and herbs.

"I thought about searching for some fiddleheads tomorrow," he said. "The weather is supposed to be nice for the rest of the week. If you'd like, you could join me, since we, uh . . ."

"Got all the awkwardness out of the way," she supplied.

"That's a *gut* way to put it. Maybe we'll find some wildflowers for your collection or that burdock you were looking for. If both of us are looking, we have a better chance of finding what we're searching for."

Again, she liked how he was so practical. "That's a great idea."

"Do you want to meet back here in the morning? Around eight?"

"Sure. Oh, wait." She pursed her lips to the side. "I'm supposed to help *Aenti* can green peas tomorrow. We should be done by lunchtime, though. How about we meet at one instead?"

"Fine by me." He glanced around the woods. "I'm guessing it's near suppertime, so I should get back home. I don't want to be late and put *Mamm* out."

She looked up at the sky and saw that the dappled sunlight had moved to the west. She had no idea how much time had passed, but Owen was probably right. "I need to get home, too, and help Mary with supper," she said.

"Do you need any help finding your way out of here?"

"*Nee.* I remember the path I took."

He gestured with his thumb. "We're going in opposite directions, so I'll see you tomorrow."

"See you then." She gave him a little wave before she walked away and headed for her aunt's house. Making her way through the woods, she felt lighter than she had in a long time. She hadn't told Owen everything that had been bothering her, but he knew more than she had revealed to anyone else, including Nina. He could have written her off as daffy, but instead he encouraged her. And she couldn't wait to search for fiddleheads, something she hadn't done before.

When she exited the woods, she walked back to the Yoders'. Along the way she glanced down at the grass and weeds growing on the side of the road and spotted a few stems of Grass Pink orchids. She picked the pretty flowers and grinned. She couldn't wait for tomorrow afternoon.

Rhoda breathed in the mild evening air as she stood on the front step of Cevilla and Richard Thompson's small house. She glanced at her shaky hands and tried to control them. Cevilla had surprised her by inviting her over for supper, something she hadn't done in a long time. Then again, how many times had she been invited over to the Yoders, Beilers, Millers, and other families over the years, and had refused? She was fine meeting with her women friends alone, but she avoided any invitations that involved being around families. The only exception were Sol's and Aden's families, and even then she wasn't completely at ease. That saddened her. She shouldn't feel like an outsider in her family or community, but she did. Thanks to Emmanuel.

Not wanting to be rude, she had accepted Cevilla's invitation. Cevilla, who was in her eighties and had been a part of the Birch Creek community almost from the beginning, spent most of her life as a single woman. Her marriage to Richard, a friend from her childhood, had been a welcome surprise to everyone. If there was one woman in the district who truly understood what it was like to be alone, it was Cevilla. The difference was that Cevilla had seemed content with her single life. Rhoda couldn't say the same.

But there was also another side of Cevilla, one that had trouble minding her own business. During Emmanuel's stint as bishop, Cevilla had been more reserved, but since Freemont had taken over leadership, she was more like the woman who had moved to Birch Creek over twenty-five years ago—opinionated, outgoing, and a little nosy but good intentioned. Emmanuel had oppressed everyone in the community, not just his family.

Rhoda shook her head, pushing Emmanuel out of her mind, resenting that he still held her thoughts captive. She couldn't stand outside musing about the past while Cevilla and her husband were waiting for her. She knocked on the door. A few moments later, Cevilla opened it, her face beaming. "Hello, Rhoda," she said, opening the door wider and motioning with her cane for her to come inside. "*Danki* for coming."

"*Danki* for having me." She stepped into the foyer and looked around the small living room. A cozy fire was already burning in the tiny woodstove in the corner of the room, blanketing the area with warmth. A little too much warmth for Rhoda's comfort, but she didn't say anything. Cevilla was known to wear a sweater in the summer, explaining that age thins the blood. Rhoda held up the basket she was carrying. "I brought some apple turnovers."

"Wonderful. Do you mind putting them in the kitchen? Supper's almost ready." Cevilla shut the door, then walked toward the kitchen, her cane thumping on the wood floor. "It's just the two of us right now. Richard went to visit with Asa, and who knows when he'll be back. Those two men love to talk about numbers. Did you know Richard was an accountant before he was a businessman?"

"*Nee*, I didn't." She followed Cevilla into the kitchen, now feeling a little guilty for not bringing over more than just turnovers. She had noticed the older woman's movements were slowing down over the past year, something she didn't like to think about. She couldn't imagine Birch Creek without Cevilla Schlabach Thompson. When Rhoda saw the meatloaf, fresh bread, green bean casserole, whipped potatoes and gravy, and a plate of sliced fresh apples on the table, her guilt increased. It must have taken her all day to prepare this food.

"I hope you don't mind, but Naomi made supper tonight. She

insisted when I told her you were coming over." Cevilla sat down at the head of the table and balanced her cane to a standing position. Rhoda noticed she had four-pronged rubber attachments at the bottom of her cane. "Richard and I are used to smaller meals."

Rhoda sat down across from Cevilla. Of course she didn't mind if Naomi made supper. Knowing that she did eased her conscience about not bringing supper instead of counting on an eighty-plus-year-old woman to feed her. "It looks and smells *appeditlich*."

"Doesn't it? She set the table, too, bless her." Cevilla smiled, the wrinkles at the corners of her mouth deepening. "Shall we pray?"

Nodding, Rhoda bowed her head, the tightness across her shoulders loosening. She said a silent prayer of thanks for the abundance of food, then lifted her head.

"Don't be shy, Rhoda." Cevilla pointed to the meatloaf. "Eat all you want. There's enough here for ten people. Naomi always overcooks." She laughed. "Then again, don't all the Amish women in this community do the same? In this case I'm glad. Richard and I are happy to have the leftovers."

"Can I fix your plate?" Rhoda asked.

Cevilla nodded. "That would be lovely, thank you. One extra spoonful of potatoes, please."

Rhoda smiled and prepared Cevilla's plate and then her own. They both started eating, and as she suspected, the food was wonderful. Cevilla asked her about her grandchildren, and how Aden's honey business was going, and was Sol still making those pretty birdhouses and selling them at Schrock's. Rhoda filled her in about her family between bites of food, while Cevilla nodded and listened with rapt attention as she ate small bites of her supper.

"Now that we have all the pleasantries out of the way"—Cevilla put down her fork, although most of her supper remained uneaten. "Let's talk about you and Emmanuel."

Rhoda's fork, filled with green beans, nearly flipped out of her hand. "What?"

Cevilla dabbed her mouth with her napkin as if she had just asked Rhoda to pass the gravy instead of dropping a bombshell. "To tell the truth, I sent Richard over to Asa's knowing he wouldn't come home in time for supper so we could be alone. I think it's high time you and I had this conversation. Eight years have passed since that man turned a coward tail and ran away from his family and his sin."

"Cevilla, I . . ." Rhoda looked down at her plate. The pat of butter she placed on her potatoes had melted into a yellow stream running down the side of the mound. She was tempted to dash out the door to avoid discussing her wayward husband, even with a woman who knew everything that had happened. Not everything. Not the most shameful parts. But she wouldn't be any better than Emmanuel if she did. Still, she had to be honest. "I'm not sure I'm ready to talk about this."

"I know, honey." She reached across the small table, took Rhoda's hand, and gave it a gentle squeeze. "But don't you think you've been putting your life on hold long enough?"

Tears welled in her eyes as she lifted her gaze to Cevilla's. "What else am I supposed to do? He's *mei* husband. How can I give up on him?"

"He didn't have any compunction about giving up on you.

Or your *sohns*. Or this community." She scowled. "I've kept *mei* peace about him. *Nee* gossip, *nee* slander. But I've known you for a long time, Rhoda. You are unhappy, and you have been for a very long time. That needs to change."

She nodded, wiping the tears from her cheeks. "I'm lonely," she admitted. She was lonely before Emmanuel left, but she couldn't tell that to Cevilla. The woman was wound up enough. "But I believe it's God's will I stay that way."

"How do you know?"

Because it's what I deserve. She couldn't bring herself to say the words out loud, not even to Cevilla, who she knew wouldn't judge her. "If I wasn't, I would know what happened to him by now."

Cevilla released her hand. "What if you could find out?"

"I don't know how I would. Not unless he came back, or . . ."

"Have you thought about hiring someone to find out what happened to him?"

Rhoda stilled. The idea had never crossed her mind. Then she shook her head. "I'm not sure I want to know."

Cevilla peered at her over her silver-rimmed glasses. "You don't need closure?"

Rhoda rubbed the center of her forehead. The tension in her upper back returned. "I don't know that either. For years I prayed for him to return. I'd forgiven him for what he'd done to me and the community." But she hadn't forgiven him because she wanted to. Her faith required her to, and to not forgive him would be against her beliefs. That didn't mean it hadn't been difficult or that she didn't have to renew that forgiveness almost every single day. Perhaps that was part of her sin, too, that she couldn't fully forgive him. Or even wanted to. She turned away from Cevilla.

"He did some unspeakable things," she whispered, her voice thick with pain.

"*Ya*, he did." When Rhoda jerked around and looked at her, she added, "I don't know all the specifics of course, and I'm not here to ask you about that. I also don't want you to think people have been discussing him behind your back. In fact, no one does anymore. Emmanuel Troyer and his sins are in the past. We're free of him, and honey, I want that freedom for you."

"Did *mei sohns* put you up to this?" They were the only ones she knew who had said anything close to what Cevilla was telling her now. They had wanted her to give up on Emmanuel's return for years. His legacy of pain and shame was far-reaching and had affected everyone. After he disappeared, the community had split, and several families moved away. But now it was more tightly knit than it ever could have been under her husband's iron boot, and many new families had moved in, enough that the community was bursting with people.

"*Nee*, they didn't. This is all *mei* doing. Richard doesn't even know." Cevilla lifted her chin. "And he won't know because I'm not saying a peep about it. This is between you and me, Rhoda. That's the truth." She sighed, the first hint of doubt appearing in her expression. "I don't want to upset you. But I didn't want to wait to talk to you about this. I'm not getting any younger, you know."

Rhoda's heart clenched. "You're not ill, are you?"

"Of course not. I'm still kicking, and as long as the Lord wills, I'll continue to. However, I also know that there's *nee* need to keep putting off this discussion."

Knowing how difficult this had to be even for a confident

woman like Cevilla, Rhoda was touched. "I appreciate that you care enough to talk to me about him."

"And I appreciate you listening. I know how painful this subject is for you."

Nodding, Rhoda said, "It is. And I'm not sure I'm ready to find out about Emmanuel just yet."

Cevilla didn't say anything for a long moment. "I understand. And that's your decision to make. But if you ever change your mind, Richard has the number of a private detective he knows in Los Angeles. I don't think it would be against the *Ordnung* to call him."

She didn't know if that was true or not. Was it wrong to hire someone to search for Emmanuel? How would she pay for a detective? He would be expensive for sure, and she didn't have much money. The house she and Emmanuel had lived in was paid for in cash when he and a few other men in the brand-new community built it, so she had very few bills. And although Sol and Aden took care of her every financial need, she had refused to move in with either of her sons, telling them that she needed to be there when their father returned. If he ever returned.

Cevilla picked up her fork and cut a small bite of meatloaf from the slice on her plate. "Whenever you're ready to go down that path, just say the word and I'll be right beside you." She gestured to Rhoda's plate. "Let's finish eating before the food gets cold. Naomi will be disappointed if we have too many leftovers."

They resumed the casual conversation they'd engaged in before Cevilla brought up Emmanuel. Rhoda was only half-interested in what Cevilla was saying, though, and in addition to her back aching, her stomach had flared up again. But she choked down her food, including half of the apple turnover she'd split with Cevilla, although she had refused the woman's offer of coffee. Her stomach couldn't take that abuse right now.

"How about some tea?" Cevilla said. "I prefer that anyway. I have some delicious peppermint if you'd like that."

Normally she would have accepted, but all she wanted to do was go home. She was suddenly worn out, which was strange because she only had a meal and some dessert. And a talk about Emmanuel. "I should be getting home."

"All right." Cevilla's smile was kind, but her eyes were filled with sympathy.

Rhoda fought the urge to frown. She didn't want anyone, including Cevilla, pitying her. Then again, perhaps the entire community did pity an old woman whose husband deserted her without a word.

The outside kitchen door opened, and Richard walked inside. "Hi, Rhoda," he said, eyeing the spread that was still on the table. "I'm sorry I'm so late. Asa and I got to talking and I lost track of time."

"That's all right, dear." Cevilla winked at Rhoda.

"Ooh, meatloaf. One of my favorites. Who brought it over this time?"

"Naomi."

As Richard washed his hands in the kitchen sink, Rhoda said, "I'm sorry to eat and run, but I should be going."

Richard turned off the tap and reached for the white dish towel hanging near the sink. "Next time I'll make sure to check the clock on the wall when I visit someone. I'm still used to wearing a wristwatch or having a phone in my pocket to check the time."

Rhoda stood. "*Nee* need to apologize." When Cevilla started to stand, she held up her hand. "I'll see myself out. Enjoy the food, Richard. Naomi's outdone herself again."

Cevilla met Rhoda's gaze and nodded. "Drive safe, *mei* friend."

Rhoda quickly left the Thompsons' and climbed into her buggy. As she headed home, her mind swirled with Cevilla's words. But there was something else she also thought about, and she gripped the horse's reins. Why should she continue to wait for Emmanuel to return? It was obvious he wasn't going to. She shouldn't be surprised either. During the first four years of their marriage, he had been trustworthy, or so she thought. But looking back, she saw that there were signs during that time that she had ignored—the way he wanted to know where she was whenever they weren't together, and how he insisted that she be seen and not heard when it came to his disciplining their sons and being in charge of the community. He controlled everything in her life, and she'd been powerless to stop him.

How could I ever have loved him? He obviously doesn't love me or Sol or Aden.

As Rhoda continued home, the anger brewed inside her. Eight years. Eight long, lonely years. And it wasn't just the loneliness that upset her. She didn't want anyone feeling sorry for her anymore. She wasn't ready to hire a detective, and she didn't think she ever would be. But she could move on with her life. She didn't have to be unhappy and disappointed all the time. She had her sons. Her grandchildren. Good friends, like Cevilla, Mary, and Naomi. She could also have more friends, too, if she would open herself up to new people.

If she didn't constantly wear the shame of her husband as a shroud.

That ends now. From this point on she would live without Emmanuel Troyer. She didn't care where he was or what happened to him. And she would never look back on their life together ever again.

Chapter 6

*H*ow's your vacation going?"

Owen glanced at his father and then poured a ladleful of white peppery gravy over his mashed potatoes. He and his family had just started filling their plates after saying grace before supper. "Boring," he said. Then he paused, realizing that wasn't a completely truthful description. His compelled vacation had been on the dull side for the most part, but reading about foraging had been interesting. So had meeting Margaret earlier today. But he didn't correct himself. His parents didn't need to know he was enjoying any part of the break they'd foisted on him. If they did, they might make it an annual event.

"What have you been doing with your time?" *Mamm* passed a large platter filled with fried pork chops to Elam, who plopped the biggest chop on his plate. She turned to her youngest son. "Your eyes are bigger than your face. Put that back and choose a smaller one."

Elam scowled, but did as he was instructed.

Owen hoped the distraction would make *Mamm* forget her question, but Jesse, who was always up for annoying his brothers, was the picture of innocence when he said, "*Ya*, Owen. What are you doing tomorrow while the rest of us are mucking out the pigpen?"

He opened his mouth to tell Jesse to mind his own business but stopped himself. *Mamm* had asked the question and he didn't want to insult her. As Nelson passed the pork chop platter to him, he speared one with his fork and shrugged. "Not much. Just meeting Margaret Yoder in the woods tomorrow. We're going to search for fiddleheads."

A resounding clatter made him flinch as eating utensils hit dinner plates. Owen looked up to see every single family member gaping at him in shock.

"You're seeing Margaret Yoder?" Nelson lifted an eyebrow.

"She's pretty," Mahlon said. Moses nodded in agreement.

"Very pretty." Ezra nodded approvingly.

"I'm surprised he actually talked to a real-life *maedel*. Didn't know he had it in him." Jesse took a huge bite of corn on the cob, then looked up. Now all eyes were on him. "What?" he said, the words almost unintelligible through all the corn in his mouth.

"Don't speak with your mouth full," *Mamm* said sternly. "And don't say anything if you can't say something nice." Then she looked at Owen, her face beaming with delight. "I'm glad you're making the most of your vacation, dear."

Everyone, including *Daed*, snickered.

But *Mamm* ignored them, used to dealing with boys and men of all ages—and maturity levels. "What time are you meeting her tomorrow?"

Owen was sorry he said anything. He slunk back in his chair. "One o'clock."

"If you and Margaret need any help, I can *geh* along," Jesse volunteered.

"*Nee!*" *Mamm*, *Daed*, and Owen all said at the same time.

Jesse lifted his shoulders. "I'm just trying to be nice." He smirked at Owen, then chomped on the corn cob again.

Great. Just great. Now he probably wouldn't hear the end of his brothers' teasing. But he could deal with it. This wasn't the first time he'd been ribbed by his siblings, and he'd been known to give back as good as he got on occasion. But despite his mental reassurances, he didn't like being teased about Margaret. That didn't seem fair to her, especially in light of what she told him today. He was surprised she'd been so open with him about what was bothering her, and because she had, he wanted to reassure her. He also thought she was fun to be around, her unexpected outburst notwithstanding. He noticed the spark in her eyes when he invited her to look for fiddleheads with him, and he was looking forward to foraging with her tomorrow.

But none of that meant he was interested in her, beyond her being someone to forage with.

But there was something else he'd been thinking about on his way home from the woods, and he couldn't get it out of his mind. He didn't have much experience with women. Zero to be exact. But he wasn't clueless either. Clearly, whatever had happened to her in the past when it came to her dealings with men, she was bothered by it. Very bothered.

He stared at the uneaten pork chop on his plate. Margaret's past was her own, and he didn't need to be speculating about something that had nothing to do with him. And his family's teasing was pointless. Just because she agreed to help him find fiddleheads didn't mean there was anything going on other than the obvious—two people spending an afternoon together pursuing a common goal. End of story. There were no misunderstandings between him and Margaret, and that's what mattered.

"Why fiddleheads?"

His father's question pulled him out of his thoughts. "What?" he asked, turning to him.

"Why are you looking for fiddleheads? I haven't done that since I was a *kinn*." His expression grew wistful. "I remember foraging for those with your *grossvatter*."

Owen went on to explain how he'd gotten the idea, reminding *Daed* about the books he'd received from his grandfather. "I'm hoping to read through several of them before the week is out."

"You won't get through one with Margaret distracting you."

"Jesse!" Both parents exclaimed as every one of his brothers giggled like silly schoolgirls.

Owen scowled. Jesse in particular could be a pain in the backside.

"You've said enough tonight." *Daed* pointed his fork at him.

Jesse shrank back, as if he realized he'd finally crossed the line. "Sorry. I'll keep *mei* lips zipped from now on."

Several conversations ensued during the rest of the meal, thankfully none of them about him and Margaret, and Owen was glad he could start eating his pork chop and potatoes in peace. He didn't care for lima beans so he took double portions of the Bodacious corn. But he was so distracted he didn't fully enjoy the delicious meal *Mamm* prepared, and he made sure to stay quiet for the remainder of supper, not wanting to add fuel to his brothers' childish behavior.

After polishing off a small serving of apple crisp with home-made vanilla ice cream, he went upstairs for the rest of the night to read. The next chapter in *God's Garden* was about finding butternuts, but he read only half the page before he started nodding off. One thing was for sure, he didn't have any problem sleeping on his vacation. He had to give his parents a little bit of credit. Obviously he was overtired, something he had refused to admit even to himself until he mentioned it to Margaret earlier.

Margaret. He closed his eyes, still seeing her pretty face. Then he chuckled, remembering how put out she'd been when she thought he had compared her looks to his sister, and how dumb he'd been to make such a comment. When she had explained why she was so upset, he understood, and he'd told her the truth when he said he didn't think she was prideful. Admitting that she had a problem with pride was a humble thing to say, although he doubted she knew that.

Wide-awake now, he stared at the page again, but all he could see was Margaret's pretty face again. When he realized he was smiling, he snapped the book shut. Turning on his side, he shut off the battery-operated lamp on his bedside table, punched his pillow, and then closed his eyes. Once he fell asleep he would be able to get her out of his mind.

Nope, there she was again, giving him a cute little wave—the same way she had when they parted company in the woods.

His eyes flew open and he flopped over onto his back. Thank

God he and Margaret had gotten all that romantic stuff straight between them and were both in agreement that neither one of them wanted a relationship—with anyone. But there was a tiny part of him that knew that when he was ready to get married, he wanted a woman as fun and forthright as Margaret Yoder.

Margaret placed the Grass Pink orchids between the pages of a large sewing book that *Aenti* Mary had let her use for pressing flowers. Using the pair of tweezers she'd brought with her for just this purpose, she arranged the delicate petals in a natural way so when they dried and flattened, they would still look as close to their original state as possible. Satisfied, she closed the book at the exact moment *Aenti* Mary entered the kitchen.

"You certainly enjoy working with your pressed flowers." Her aunt smiled as she opened the gas-powered cooler and pulled out a carton of milk. "Do you want some? I usually find a glass of milk before bed helps me sleep."

"That would be nice."

Aenti Mary filled two glasses half full, put the carton away, then brought the drinks to the table and placed one in front of Margaret. "*Danki*," Margaret said as *Aenti* Mary sat down at the kitchen table across from her.

Nodding, she took a sip of the milk. "Did you enjoy your walk today?"

Margaret stared at the milk in her glass and smiled, thinking about Owen and the time they spent together in the woods. "*Ya.* I had a *gut* time."

"I didn't realize you enjoyed being out in nature so much. You seem happier today than you were yesterday."

She looked at her aunt. "Did I seem unhappy yesterday?"

"Not exactly. But I could see that you weren't as relaxed as you usually are."

Margaret frowned. Could everyone read her emotions that easily? Then she realized that couldn't be the case because her family didn't seem to understand her feelings at all.

"Where did you *geh* on your walk?" her aunt asked.

She explained about her walk in the woods, leaving out the part about finding the shed. She didn't want to give any hint that she and Owen had been trespassing. "I didn't find the burdock I was looking for, though."

"I saw that you were reading about herbal medicine yesterday," *Aenti* Mary said. "How long have you been interested in the topic?"

"Not very long. I never knew there was so much to learn about medicinal herbs."

Her aunt nodded. "When I was growing up in Iowa there was a *frau* in our community who knew every plant and what it was used for. She could cure anything that ailed you. I have some of her recipes, along with a few from *mei mamm*. When I met Freemont and moved to Ohio, I brought them with me. But when we moved to Birch Creek, no one was allowed to use any of their own home remedies. Only the ones that were bishop-approved."

Margaret was stunned to hear that. "Why?"

Sighing, *Aenti* Mary touched the side of the glass. "Bishop Troyer was a difficult man, and he wasn't a *gut* leader. When Freemont decided to move here to build his own farm, we had no idea that was the case. But we didn't have a choice. Your *onkel* knew he wouldn't be able to make it as a farmer in Salt Creek. There were too many farms in the area to be successful."

Margaret wasn't surprised to hear that. Her father had complained more than once in the past that it was getting harder to make a living being a farmer. Still, that didn't make him want to change his occupation or move to a place where there was more land and less competition. Her family not only didn't like change, but they also were content with the status quo, at least for the most part.

Aenti Mary continued. "Over the years, it became apparent that something was wrong with how Emmanuel was shepherding the community." She looked at Margaret and shook her head. "That's all I'm going to mention about him. To say anything more would be gossip. Besides, it was God's will for him to be bishop during that time, just like it's his will for Freemont to be bishop now. Who are any of us to question the Lord's plans?"

Normally Margaret would have been curious to hear more and might have even prodded her aunt to continue talking about this mysterious bishop. But the pain on her aunt's face brought her up short. This was a topic not to be discussed.

"Freemont relaxed the *Ordnung* when he was ordained bishop, and each family is free to do pretty much what they want to, within reason, of course. As long as they aren't violating what God says in the Bible, or the *Ordnung* as it is now, he doesn't step in. Fortunately, he hasn't had to discipline anyone since he became the bishop."

Margaret stiffened. She hadn't realized how close she and

Owen had gotten to being the first people disciplined in Birch Creek. That was a distinction she didn't want any part of.

"You know, Rhoda Troyer has an interest in herbal medicine," *Aenti* Mary said. "Her remedies were the only ones Emmanuel approved. I'm sure she wouldn't mind sharing her knowledge with you." A shadow of sadness appeared in her eyes. "She's Emmanuel's wife. I know she would like the company. I'm going to visit her tomorrow afternoon, if you'd like to come along. I usually go over to her *haus* once a week."

"*Danki*, but I have plans. I'm meeting Owen Bontrager tomorrow."

"Oh?" An interested expression immediately crossed her aunt's face.

Oops. She hadn't realized how casually she'd mentioned Owen until the words were out of her mouth. Before *Aenti* Mary got any ideas about her and Owen being a couple, she needed to make things clear. "I'm not interested in him," she said quickly. "And he's not interested in me. He simply invited me to forage for fiddleheads with him. That sounded like fun, so I said I'd *geh*."

Aenti Mary slowly took another drink of her milk, as if she were deep in thought. When she set the glass down on the table, she said, "It's not every day a *yung mann* asks a *yung maedel* to forage for fiddleheads." Her lips twitched. "How do you know he's not interested in you?"

"Because we talked about it." Margaret squared her shoulders.

"On the ride home from the bus station?"

"*Nee*. I saw him in the woods today. He was, uh, reading a book." That was close. She'd almost told her aunt about the shed.

"I see." Now *Aenti* Mary was almost fully smiling. "Then you made plans to meet yesterday."

"*Nee*, we didn't. We just ran into each other in the woods, that's all."

"How serendipitous."

Margaret wasn't sure what that meant, but it didn't matter. She could tell that Mary was coming to the wrong conclusion and she had to steer her back to reality. "Yesterday when I was walking in the woods, I saw Owen. He was reading a book and then we got to talking. He likes plants. I like plants. Then he asked me to forage for fiddleheads with him and I said I would." Hopefully the condensed version of the afternoon would make things clear enough.

Her aunt frowned a little. "But neither of you like each other."

"Oh, I like him." She couldn't help but smile again. Her aunt had no idea how wonderful it was to like a man and not think of him in a romantic way or worry that he was only after her for one thing. "He's nice." *And kind of cute.* "But it isn't a date or anything."

Aenti Mary didn't respond right away. Finally, she said, "I hope you two find lots of fiddleheads."

Margaret grinned, pleased her aunt understood. "I hope we do too. Maybe I can meet Rhoda another day."

"I'm sure that can be arranged. I'll mention it to her tomorrow, and you two can get together and make plans."

"*Danki, Aenti* Mary." She continued to smile. Not only was she going foraging with Owen tomorrow, but she would also get a chance to meet with Rhoda at some point during her visit and learn more about herbal medicine. She also needed to visit her *Aenti* Carolyn, and of course see Nina again, both of which she looked forward to. She hadn't been this relaxed or happy in a long time. Coming to Birch Creek was the right decision.

Aenti Mary finished drinking the rest of her milk, then rose from her chair. "If you want to meet Owen earlier tomorrow that's fine with me. I don't have as many peas to can this year, so it won't be a problem to do them myself."

"I'll help you," she said, unwilling to going back on her word. "I told him I'd be canning in the morning."

"I appreciate that. Any kind of work is always much easier to do with an extra pair of hands, and we should zip through those peas in a jiffy." *Aenti* Mary walked to the sink and rinsed out her glass. She set it on the counter to be washed in the morning. "I'll see you at breakfast," she said. "*Gute nacht.*"

"*Gute nacht, Aenti.*"

After she finished her milk, Margaret also rinsed out her glass, then decided to wash both hers and her aunt's before turning in for the night. After she finished, she picked up the book with the orchids inside, then shut off the gas-fired lamp in the kitchen, plunging the house into darkness. She knew her way around the Yoders' home as accurately as she did her own, and she had no problem navigating the dark as she went upstairs to the guest bedroom that used to be the room Seth and Ira had shared.

When she walked inside the room, she closed the door but didn't bother to turn on the light. She set the book down on the dresser, undressed, and got ready for bed. A few minutes later, she knelt at the edge of the mattress and said her nighttime prayers. *Oh, and if you can keep me from making a fool of myself in front of Owen tomorrow, I would appreciate it. Being foolish once is enough.*

Margaret climbed into bed and snuggled under the cool sheets and then brought the white-and-blue checked quilt that covered the twin bed over her body. As she lay in the dark, the quilt tucked under her chin, she thought about her conversation with Owen again. She'd never had to worry about being foolish in front of a man before. Actually, they were the ones who were usually tongue-tied. Except for Dylan. He'd always been smooth, always in control, always sure of what he wanted and how he would get it. She'd been drawn to his confidence, not to mention being with him fed her rebellion.

She cringed, the shame that always seemed to be hovering over her shoulder, ready to pounce, appearing again. She squeezed her eyes shut, saying another prayer, thanking God that he had saved her from making more mistakes than she already had.

Desperate for a distraction, she shifted her thoughts to Owen again, still marveling at his insight and kind, steady presence. No one could call him exciting, that was for sure. But she'd had enough excitement to last a lifetime. All she wanted now was to find some fiddleheads and be with someone who didn't judge her or entice her.

She sighed, smiling again. Who cared about romance? She and Owen had companionship. That was all she needed.

Lester stood at the edge of the road and aimed his flashlight at the thick woods in front of him. Midnight had come and gone several hours ago. Unable to sleep, he'd driven over here, leaving his car two blocks down the road and walking up to this point. His heart hammered in his chest. Years had passed since he'd been here, and he still wasn't sure he should be. It was one thing to work at Stoll's Inn as a handyman. The Stolls were still fairly new to Birch Creek and unaware of the community's past, except for whatever information the long-term district members had decided to reveal. From what he could tell, no one had revealed much of anything. Thank God.

Although he'd been in Birch Creek for over a year, making sure to stay as unassuming as possible at his job and returning home to a small house he'd purchased on the outskirts of the community, the time had come for him to face the past he'd been fleeing from. Even so, he still fought his cowardice. It had taken him this long to build the courage he needed to come here tonight, the place where everything had started almost thirty years ago . . . and had all come crashing down eight years ago. If he ran away this time, he would never come back.

He'd lost track how many times during those twenty years he wound his way through these woods, in both daylight and darkness, until he reached his destination—the remnants of a shanty he built and only he had known about. The isolated building was his refuge, his hiding place, and eventually his downfall. *Do it, you lily-livered chicken. Take that step forward.*

Sweat broke out on his forehead, and he entered the woods.

He walked a familiar path, the cacophonic sounds of insects and the creak of moving tree branches adding to his fear. The woodsy dankness of the plants and trees filling his nostrils. He resisted the urge to turn around and run away. He could continue ignoring his past and no one would be the wiser. What was one more failure on top of countless others?

But he would know. And that was enough to spur him on.

Refortified, he continued walking until the beam of his flashlight landed on a wooden structure. He froze. The last time he'd been here, a storm had torn his shed to pieces, but now he was looking at what seemed to be a brand-new building. Surely there wasn't another destroyed shed hidden in this same area. Someone had rebuilt his private edifice, staking their claim on his section of the woods. How dare they.

He shook off his indignation. He was the one who had abandoned everything and everyone. He shouldn't be surprised that some enterprising person had decided to piece the shed back together. Perhaps they found the purpose they needed, just as he had before . . .

Lester gripped his flashlight, shoving aside his thoughts, and kept his gaze glued on the closed door. The door was new and different from the one he had chosen when he built the shed. As he reached for the doorknob, a strong wind kicked up. He yanked his hand back, closing his fingers into a fist. He had no claim here anymore, just like he didn't have a claim to Birch Creek. Maybe that was why God had brought him here tonight, planting the idea in his head until he couldn't think about anything else until he had gotten in the car and had driven over. The Lord had a point to prove. Everyone had moved on. Had she moved on too?

He spun around and darted out of the woods, nearly tripping over a tree root in the process. A long branch scraped his cheek and he winced with pain. Once he reached the road again, he stopped, his chest heaving. He hadn't run that fast since he was a young man, and his rampant pulse let him know his heart wasn't happy with him. He touched the skin above his full mustache and beard, then shined his flashlight on his finger. Blood. Not a lot, but enough that he needed a bandage. He'd take care of the scrape when he got home, but right now he had to leave before anyone saw him, even though the street was deserted and every house in the vicinity was dark. He couldn't risk being found out. Not now. Possibly not ever.

But he was fooling himself. The day would come when people would know who he was. The day of reckoning always did, and he would eventually have to face his. And when he did, there would be a steep price to pay . . . one he should have paid a long time ago.

Chapter 7

Margaret arrived at the shed at one o'clock sharp. The door was ajar of course, due to it being broken, but that didn't mean Owen was inside. However, when she walked into the shed, he was in the same place she'd found him yesterday, reading a book under the window. He must not have heard her since he didn't look up from his book. His straw hat lay next to him on the dirt floor, and hazy sunlight shone across the top of his thick black hair. She started to take a step forward when she saw him close his eyes and lean the back of his head against the wood-planked wall.

Was he praying or sleeping? She wasn't sure, so she waited a few seconds. He didn't stir, confirming that he had fallen asleep. Now what should she do? Wake him up? That wouldn't be right. He wasn't exactly in a comfortable napping position, and she remembered he'd mentioned yesterday that he was more tired than he thought. If he could fall asleep sitting up, he definitely needed to slumber.

There was also another reason she didn't want to wake him

up. She crept over to him, then quietly crouched beside him. Not too close. She didn't want to wake him. But something compelled her to study him. His long eyelashes touched his cheeks, and his lips parted slightly as his breathing became steady and shallow. The more she was around Owen, the more she was starting to change her mind about his looks. Despite his slightly imperfect teeth and thin, wiry body, she was starting to think he was somewhat handsome, in an ordinary kind of way—

"Are you going to sit there and watch me all afternoon?"

Margaret toppled over as Owen's eyes flew open. Casually he lolled his head toward her, the biggest grin she'd ever seen plastered on his face.

"Ooh," she hissed, her heartbeat pounding in her ears. "You scared me again."

"Don't blame me." He closed his book and jumped to his feet, still grinning. "You're the one who was spying on me."

He had her there. She stood and brushed off the dirt from her dress. "How long did you know I was here?"

"From the moment you walked in the door." He chuckled. "Thanks for the laugh."

"I don't think it's funny." She lifted her chin and glared at him. "I don't like being scared."

His mirth disappeared and he walked toward her. "I'm sorry. I was just kidding you."

He seemed so sincere she couldn't be mad at him. "Just because I didn't like it doesn't mean I don't deserve it. I shouldn't have been watching you." Her cheeks flamed as she searched for an explanation. "I, uh, thought you might have been, ah, having a problem and I didn't want to . . . um . . ."

Owen laughed. "Margaret, it's okay. I know I'm irresistible."

She knew he was still teasing, but something stirred inside her. Then again, she was still recovering from her heart leaping to her throat when he scared her, so whatever she was feeling right now had to be due to that and not his claim that he was hard to resist.

"I gotta say," he continued, "I've never been around a *maedel* as unique as you." He brushed past her and headed for the door, leaving her standing alone in the middle of the shed.

What was that supposed to mean? Was she unique in a good way or bad? Unique meant peculiar in her family, and that wasn't a desirable trait. But when Owen said the word, she didn't feel inadequate or that she was being made fun of. Just the opposite. Unique also meant special. *I like that definition better.*

He poked his head into the shed. "Are you coming or not?"

"*Ya.*" She hurried to him, a thought occurring to her. "Aren't we trespassing again?"

"I don't think so. I asked *Daed* about this place and he said that as far as he knows, no one owns this parcel of land."

"And he's sure about that?"

He gave her a confident nod. "He knows every landowner in Birch Creek, even the English. Your *onkel* Freemont has introduced him to almost everybody over the years."

"Did he think it was strange that there was a shed in the middle of the woods?"

"I decided not to mention it to him. Since we're on common land and the shed seems to be abandoned, it's obvious someone built it a while back and forgot about it. I'm sure we don't have to worry about getting in trouble for being here."

"Thank goodness. I don't want to break any more rules."

He tilted his head. "More rules?"

She almost gasped. How could she have admitted her fear to him? She was feeling too comfortable around him. That had to be the reason. She had to be careful about what she said to him in the future. "I meant any rules," she said, laughing and batting her eyelashes, her go-to method when she wanted to distract a man.

Instead he frowned. "Is there something in your eye?"

"*Nee*, why?"

"You keep blinking."

Her eyelids froze. The thing about her go-to method of blinking and laughing insipidly is that she felt stupid doing it. She was glad Owen wasn't affected, but she still had to cover for what she'd said. She blinked like a normal human being this time and said in a crisp tone, "I thought you wanted to find fiddleheads."

"I do but—"

"Then you *geh* that way and I'll *geh* this way." Before he could answer her, she headed in the opposite direction of the shed. A few minutes later she glanced over her shoulder. When she didn't see him, she let out a long breath. She certainly was living up to being unique.

She spent the next hour searching for fiddleheads and not seeing a single one. They regrouped at the shed and found out Owen hadn't come across any either. "I don't think there are any fiddleheads in these woods," he said.

"Is there any other place we can look?"

He rubbed his chin. "There's a field with a few trees not too far from the edge of the woods. Maybe we'll have more luck there."

Margaret followed him to the field, and they began to search. There didn't seem to be any fiddleheads among the grasses and weeds either, but she was finding some lovely wildflowers. She picked a few and continued her search. She wasn't sure how long she'd been on the hunt when Owen came up alongside her.

"This is a waste of time," he muttered, shoving his hands in his pockets. "We haven't found anything."

"Speak for yourself." Margaret beamed as she held up more Grass Pink orchids, along with three New England asters and a stem of Butterfly Weeds.

"As nice as those are," he said, arching a brow, "I've seen exactly zero fiddleheads. I suspect that's your tally too."

"Foraging takes patience." She now realized that her searches for wildflowers were a type of foraging, and she had learned early on it took time and perseverance to find what she wanted. "We haven't been looking for very long."

"Three hours isn't long?" At her surprised glance he pointed at the sky. "The sun will be setting in about an hour or so."

"Oh." He was right, the sun was hovering above the horizon. She'd been so engrossed in looking for fiddleheads and flowers she hadn't noticed how fast the afternoon had gone. "*Aenti*'s probably started supper by now." When she heard his stomach growl, she grinned. "Sounds like *yer* a little hungry."

He looked around the field. "Acres of land and not a bite to eat." He looked at her with his usual half-grin. "Although we could probably find something edible if we had to."

"True." While she should probably head back to her aunt and uncle's house, she discovered she wasn't in a hurry to leave yet. Not because she dreaded cooking or doing any other chores. She had never minded housework or yard work, and more often than not she enjoyed those tasks.

She was hesitant to leave because the fall afternoon had been perfect, despite the dearth of fiddleheads. The nearly cloudless sky, warm sunshine, and fresh air added to the happiness she felt just by being in Birch Creek. Facing the fading sun, she said with a sigh, "There's nothing more amazing than a sunset."

"Or a sunrise." He moved to stand beside her as they watched the sunset in the distance. "*Nix* better than getting up before daylight and seeing the sky grow lighter and brighter while letting the cattle out into the pasture."

"You're not supposed to be thinking about work," she reminded him with a nudge of her elbow.

"Oops. Sorry."

She smiled, taking in one last look at the lavender and peach streaks slashing the vibrant blue of the sky. She sighed. "I should head home now. I don't want to keep my *aenti* and *onkel* waiting."

He nodded, tucking his foraging book under his arm. "*Mei haus* is on the way, so I'll walk with you."

They left the field and walked along the side of the road. "How long have you lived in Birch Creek?" she asked.

"Let's see. Phoebe married Jalon six years ago. We moved here several months before the wedding."

"It's a nice community," she said.

"Agreed. I can't imagine living anywhere else. I thought all *mei bruders* felt the same, but Devon ended up moving back to Fredericktown after he married Nettie Miller last year." He shook his head. "We've had two weddings and three marriages in a year in our family."

"Two weddings?"

"Zeke and Zeb had a double wedding. Have you met their *fraus*? Darla and Amanda?"

"*Nee*, but I'm sure I will at church."

"You can't miss them. You can't tell them apart either."

Margaret giggled. Somehow, they had gotten on the marriage subject again, but the conversation wasn't awkward this time. She liked learning about his family. They were so much different from her own.

"How's your study of herbal medicine going?" he asked after a few minutes of silence.

She told him about making plans to visit Rhoda Troyer. "*Aenti* said she might be willing to share some of her herbal recipes with me."

Owen nodded. "I can see her doing that."

"Do you know her very well?"

"*Nee*, but *Mamm* goes and visits her once a week."

"So does Mary." Margaret paused. "She says Rhoda is lonely."

"I suspect she is, living by herself for so many years. I don't know much about what happened when her husband was bishop here. That's the one topic no one in this community will talk about."

"Do you think it's strange that they don't?"

"I'm sure it's out of respect for her. Besides, there's *nee* need. Your *onkel* is an excellent bishop."

"I think so. Then again, I'm biased."

"In this case your bias is spot-on."

As they continued to walk, several cars passed by, along with two buggies. Inside one was a blond-haired, stocky man who waved at Owen. "That's Andrew Beiler," he explained. "He owns a farrier business." Hezekiah Detweiler was in the other one with his wife, Amanda, and they also waved. Their niece Martha was married to Margaret's cousin, Seth. If Owen was worried about anyone in the district getting the wrong idea about them walking together, he didn't show it. She wasn't going to worry about it either.

A short while later, Owen slowed down in front of a huge house. The two-story home was instantly recognizable as Amish, with its white siding, shutter-free windows, and fresh-washed laundry on the line. The flower bed lining the base of a long front porch still looked lush even this late in the season. She could only imagine how pretty it was in full bloom.

"I knew it," Owen said, coming to a halt in front of the driveway. He put his hands on his slim hips. "The twins promised me that one of them would mow the lawn today, and of course they haven't."

She was surprised by his annoyed tone. He'd been frustrated about not finding fiddleheads, but he sounded downright irritated with his brothers. "The lawn looks nice," she said, speaking the truth. In her opinion it didn't need to be mowed.

"It's too long. Tomorrow it will be harder to mow, and the longer it's put off, the more difficult it will be to cut it right. Then there's all the grass that has to be raked up afterward. I doubt they'll get all that cleaned up either."

"You sound like you've had a lot of mowing experience."

"I'm usually the one who does it." He studied the yard again, then shook his head, turning to her so his back faced the house. "I'll talk to *Daed* about it. Maybe he'll agree four days of vacation is enough and I can mow our lawn properly."

Margaret's eyes widened. "You're going to forgo the rest of your free time so you can mow a lawn?"

"*Ya*. It's important." He didn't budge from her direct look.

"It's just grass, Owen."

"Just grass?" He leaned forward so he could meet her gaze. "Just grass?"

He seemed so serious she couldn't keep from laughing. "*Ya*," she said, moving closer to him. "Who cares about a little grass?"

"I do, that's who." But a smile was playing on his lips.

"Next you're going tell me that you bring out a ruler to make sure all the blades are even."

"That's not a bad idea." He straightened, chuckling. "All right, I get your point. I can be a little obsessive about the farm. And the grass."

"I wouldn't say obsessive. But obviously you like things done right."

"Shouldn't everyone? When work is done on time and correctly it saves a lot of time and money."

She couldn't argue about that. "Spoken like a *gut* businessman."

He smiled, her comment seeming to please him.

"But that doesn't mean you can quit your vacation."

He groaned, his smile disappearing. "Fine. Since I'm still on vacation, what are we going to do tomorrow?"

The question was out of his mouth before Owen could stop it. Doing something with her tomorrow had been the furthest thing from his mind. Well, maybe he had thought about it a little when he'd taken a few breaks looking for those annoyingly hidden fiddleheads. Who knew they would be so hard to find? He had paused and watched her gather wildflowers. She was so excited to see the orange ones, which she said were called Butterfly Weed. He had to admit the flower was on the pretty side for a weed, and she had looked so pleased when she added it to the other flowers in her small wildflower bouquet. But seeing her enjoy herself didn't mean he wanted to spend another day with her. Yet here he was, asking her to do just that. Even more baffling, he was hoping she would say yes.

She crossed her petite arms over her chest and leveled her gaze, giving him a penetrating stare. "Are you using me to kill time again, Owen Bontrager?"

"Uh . . ." He wasn't sure about how to answer her question because he didn't know why he had asked her in the first place. It was definitely true that time went faster when he was with her. Not just faster, but it was also more enjoyable. "I'm determined to find those fiddleheads," he said, focusing on the task instead of his motivation. That was something he didn't want to dwell on too much. "I figured we could try searching another field. You're not ready to give up, are you?"

Her lips twitched. "I don't back down from a challenge. But I can't *geh* with you tomorrow. I need to visit *mei aenti* Carolyn. I haven't seen her since I've been in town."

"Oh." That was disappointing. But he understood her reason. Family comes first.

"How about Thursday? I can help you look for them then. Or are you in a hurry for a fiddlehead salad?"

"I think I can wait a day." He'd have to figure out what to do with his time tomorrow, but he was glad she was agreeing to get together with him the day after. "What time do you want to meet?"

"The same time we met today. At the shed. But only on one condition."

Wary, he asked, "What's that?"

"You have to promise to stay away from the lawn mower for the rest of your vacation."

What a taskmaster. He tried to hold back a smile but failed. "I promise."

"Then I will happily accept your invitation." She returned his smile with a bright one of her own.

Without warning, his breath hitched in his chest. This wasn't the first time he'd seen her smile today, but for some reason the way she was smiling at him now hit him hard. He gave himself a mental shake. Smiling made everyone look more attractive, not that Margaret needed any help in that department.

"I'll see you on Thursday then." She lifted her small hand and waved before turning around and walking away.

Instead of going inside his house, he watched her leave. There was something about Margaret Yoder that made him happy. She was turning what had promised to be a difficult week into a fun time. He didn't realize until that moment that he was missing fun in his life. He had satisfaction from work, stability through his faith and family, and a secure future in front of him. But when was the last time he'd had any fun before he met Margaret? He couldn't remember. He also couldn't keep his eyes off her as she headed to the Yoders'.

"Some gentleman you are."

Owen groaned and turned to see Jesse. And of course, he wouldn't be fortunate enough to have only Jesse spying on him. Moses and Mahlon were nearby, snickering behind their hands covering their mouths. He glowered at them. "How long have you guys been watching me?"

"Not long," Moses said.

"A few minutes," Mahlon added.

"Why aren't you walking her home?" Jesse asked.

He peered at his pesky brother, who at fourteen years old had shot up five inches over the summer and stood nearly up to Owen's chin. Owen gave him a glare he couldn't miss. "I don't have to walk her home. She knows her way back to the Yoders'."

Jesse scoffed. "Men are supposed to walk women home. That's what *Mamm* always said."

"When did she say that?" Owen asked, befuddled. "She never told me."

"She probably thought you'd never be close enough to a *maedel* to find out."

Moses and Mahlon snickered again, and Owen had enough. He was about to set Jesse straight about respecting his elders when his conscience took hold of him. Should he have offered to walk her home? Did she think he was a heel because he didn't? He looked over his shoulder and saw her tiny figure in the distance. If he left now, he could jog at a brisk pace and catch up to her. Thanks a lot, Jesse. "*Geh* mow the lawn," he told the three of them as he started after Margaret. At this point he didn't care who mowed it, as long as someone did.

"*Daed* said it could wait until tomorrow," the twins said in unison.

He rolled his eyes and started after her. "Margaret!" he called out as he closed in on her. He didn't want to scare her again. He couldn't resist surprising her back in the shed when she was watching him. But he didn't want to do that to her now.

She stopped walking and turned around, looking surprised. "Did you forget to tell me something?"

"*Nee.*" He pulled up short but didn't say anything. He couldn't tell her that Jesse had made him feel guilty for not walking her home. No one liked being shown up by a younger brother. But he had to give her an explanation. "I, uh—"

"Owen! Look!" She breezed past him and knelt down in the tall grass on the side of the road. "Fiddleheads!"

He crouched down next to her. Sure enough, there was a patch of fiddleheads in front of them. He also realized they were still on his family's property, but just a few feet from the property line. Pastureland spread out in front of them, and he couldn't remember the last time he'd been this far back on their land. It had never dawned on him to look for fiddleheads by his house.

Margaret pinched off two of the unfurled fronds from one of the plants, and Owen followed suit until they both had a single handful, enough for a snack.

"Quest complete." She sniffed the fronds in one hand, hanging on to the wildflowers in the other.

"Make sure you cook those thoroughly. You don't want to get sick."

"*Danki* for the warning." Then she lifted her head and smiled.

This time it wasn't just a hitched breath that set him off-kilter. More like a jolt of lightning went right through him. Although he doubted a lightning strike would make him feel this good. When he knelt next to her a few minutes ago, he hadn't realized how close they were to each other. But now he was keenly aware that there was very little space between them. When he breathed in, he could smell a pleasant, flowery scent. Naturally she would smell like flowers. *Better than flowers.*

Her smile faded. "I guess we don't need to meet on Thursday. We know where the fiddleheads are now."

He tried to nod, but he couldn't. Suddenly this wasn't just him offhandedly offering to do something with her to make time go faster. And forget the fiddleheads—they were just an excuse. They were becoming friends—at least he thought so. And friends liked to spend time together. He wracked his brain trying to come up with another reason to see her again.

She stood up. "Well, I guess I'll see you around."

Was that disappointment he saw in her eyes? He wasn't sure, but a part of him hoped it was so he wasn't the only one feeling let down. After the longest minute of his life, she turned around to leave.

Finally, an idea kicked in. "Butternuts!" he called out.

She faced him. "What?"

"I was reading about butternuts last night. We could search for those. There's another area of woods nearby that I've never been to. Did you know butternuts are a *gut* source of pantothenic acid?" He had no idea what pantothenic acid was, and he said a quick prayer that she wouldn't ask him about it.

"*Nee*, I didn't know that." She regarded him for a minute, and he couldn't tell if she thought he was serious. "Sounds important, though."

"Very. We all need our, uh, pantothenic acid." It took every ounce of restraint not to face palm himself for that statement.

Margaret nodded. "Okay. Foraging for butternuts sounds fun. And nutritious. See you Thursday." She turned and started walking away.

Once again, he stared at her as she left. Then he really did slap his hand on his forehead. He was supposed to walk her home. He spun around and looked behind him, then let out a long breath when he didn't see his brothers lurking around. No one was mowing the lawn either, but for once he was glad they'd disregarded his orders. He turned again and looked at Margaret. He couldn't chase after her a second time. She would definitely think he'd lost his mind.

He was starting to suspect he might have.

Chapter 8

Rhoda slid a heaping serving of brownie à la mode in each of her sons' dessert bowls, then took them over to the table. Solomon, her oldest, was sitting in Emmanuel's vacant chair. Appropriate, since Sol had taken over as head of the family after her husband's disappearance, although he never did anything without consulting his brother, Aden, first. It was a testament to God's healing that her sons, who were pitted against each other as children, had grown into men who had repaired their relationship, and had even become friends in the process.

Aden's eyes lit up at the sight of one of his favorite desserts. "This looks *appeditlich*." Aden picked up his spoon and dug right in.

Sol was more deliberate, taking his time as he spooned equal amounts of vanilla ice cream and warm brownie into his mouth. "*Gut* as usual," he said with a faint smile above his red beard that reached almost to the middle of his chest.

Rhoda sat down at the table and picked up her coffee cup, watching her sons as they ate their dessert and talked about their workday. At least once a week they came over for dessert and coffee, leaving their wives and children at home. Although she enjoyed spending time with her daughters-in-law, it was nice to have this time alone with her boys.

Sol managed his own carpentry business and had taken on Atlee Shetler as a partner a little over three years ago. Business had increased so much that Atlee had hired Peter Kauffman a year later to help them keep up with demand. Aden experienced his own success, having taken over Schrock's Grocery, Birch Creek's only grocery and tool store, when he married Sadie Schrock. He had a beekeeping business on the side and produced the best honey in the area, not only according to her but also according to his many satisfied customers. He had even taken Malachi Chupp under his wing and was teaching him how to manage hives and harvest honey.

She smiled. If only Emmanuel could see them now. Then her smile dimmed at the thought. He had always been impossible to please, and although their sons had a strong bond with each other and took excellent care of their wives and children, he would find something to criticize and possibly outright sabotage. She gripped the cup handle so tight her knuckles hurt. Emmanuel's disgrace and disappearance had brought her sons together. That was one good thing about what had happened, and she suddenly realized she was glad he wasn't here to undermine what they had worked so hard for.

Sol stopped talking and looked at Rhoda, his intense green eyes filling with concern. "Is everything all right, *Mamm?*"

She set down the coffee cup and put her hands in her lap. "*Ya,* everything is fine," she said as she rubbed her aching knuckles.

But Aden eyed her dubiously. He had the same dark-red hair and green eyes as his brother, but that was where the similarities ended. Aden had always been the softhearted of the two, taking more after her than Emmanuel. Her husband had seen that as weakness, and had used Sol to toughen him up, damaging both sons in the process. *I was also at fault.*

Sol set down his spoon. "There's something going on," he said.

"We can tell," Aden added.

She paused. She couldn't reveal what she was thinking. Dredging up that part of the past was off-limits, and she rarely thought about it herself. But ever since her talk with Cevilla last night, memories she had been unaware of kept coming to the surface, and she grew angrier with each one. She waved her hand, trying to dismiss their concern as she picked up her coffee again. Decaf with cream, a treat since her stomach hadn't bothered her all day. "You're imagining things."

Both Sol and Aden looked at her, then picked up their spoons and began eating again. She sighed inwardly, glad they believed her, or at least pretended to.

"I noticed the woodpile is full," Sol said, scraping the side of his spoon against the dish to scoop up the last few brownie crumbs.

"I did too." Aden grabbed the napkin off the table. "You didn't hire anyone to do the firewood, did you?"

She shook her head. "Loren Stoll dropped off a split cord this morning. He said their handyman, Lester, had chopped too much."

"For the inn?" Aden said. "I wouldn't think there could be enough firewood for that place, especially with winter coming up.

They're always full, especially since Birch Creek is now known as the bachelor capital of Amish country."

Sol nodded but didn't join in his brother's chuckling. Rhoda paused. She hadn't thought about what Aden pointed out. She'd been surprised when Loren arrived shortly after ten, pulling a wagon of firewood behind his buggy. The wagon wasn't full by any means and had been easy for the horse to manage, but there was enough wood to last her a good long while. "I figured you could use it," Loren had said before he started unloading it. "This will take some of the work off your *sohns* too."

"Has Loren been by before that?"

She turned to Sol, not liking the hardness she saw in his eyes. They reminded her too much of his father, even though he had more compassion and mercy than Emmanuel ever possessed. "He's only visited once before. Delilah had made some extra food, and he dropped off a basket of the leftovers."

"Seems like they have a lot of extra stuff at the inn."

"They're just being kind, Sol. You know the Stolls. They're very hospitable people. That's why their inn is so successful. Besides, Delilah had a cold. If she hadn't been ill, she would have brought over the food herself."

When Sol didn't reply, Aden stepped in. "We'll tell Loren we appreciate his generosity when we see him on Sunday. Won't we, Sol?"

"*Ya.*" Sol's expression tempered. "That was nice of him and Delilah. But if you ever need anything, *Mamm,* you know you can ask us. Doesn't matter what it is or what time of day you need it—we're here for you."

His words nearly brought tears to her eyes, but she choked

them back. They were so good to her. "I know." And then something inside her broke. Her sons had never pressured her to accept that Emmanuel was gone for good, but until right now she'd never thought about how it affected them that she still clung to the miniscule chance he would return. Now that she no longer believed he would, she needed to let them know. "I wasn't truthful a minute ago when I told you everything was all right," she said. "It isn't. I've been thinking about your father."

Both men froze. If they were surprised about Loren stopping by with firewood, they were floored by her most recent words.

"Have you heard from him?" Aden asked, his expression nearly as hard as his brother's.

She shook her head, setting down the mug on the table again. "I haven't heard anything from him, or about him, since he left."

In unison, Sol and Aden sat back in their chairs. "Didn't think so," Sol muttered.

"Don't start," Aden whispered, but Rhoda still heard him.

Of her two boys, Sol had borne the brunt of Emmanuel's wrath, although Aden had also been abused. She wasn't surprised that her oldest was still bitter, and she wasn't helping things by denying reality. Her sons had tiptoed around this subject long enough. If she didn't tell them now, she might not ever, and she had to say the words out loud in order to move on. "It's clear your *daed* isn't coming back."

Sol's eyes widened. "What?"

"It's taken me a long time to accept this, but if Emmanuel was intending to return, he would have done so by now."

Neither of her sons said anything for a long time. Then Aden spoke. "We believe that too."

"It's better that he doesn't come back." Sol pushed his plate away, staring at the table.

Rhoda tensed and looked down at her folded hands on the table. Old hands, with aching fingers and wrists. But that pain didn't compare to the heavy guilt that broke through any moment of happiness, as if she didn't deserve to experience anything but shame, remorse, and regret. Still, she wasn't going to change her mind. Emmanuel was gone, and she had finally accepted that fact.

"What if he's . . ." Aden rubbed his eyebrow.

"Dead?" Sol didn't hesitate to say the word. "If he is, he's getting his just reward."

"Sol," Aden warned, glancing at Rhoda.

"It's okay, Aden. He might very well be. We probably won't ever know." That she could say those words and mean them encouraged her.

"Then what about you?" Sol asked. "Are you supposed to live alone forever because he's a coward?"

Rhoda thought Sol had forgiven Emmanuel, but by his flared temper she could tell there was still more forgiveness needed. That was something between her son and God, though. "If I don't know that he's passed away, then *ya*. That's what I will do."

"You don't have to be alone, *Mamm*," Aden said. "You can move in with us."

"Or us." Sol looked at his brother. "Either one," he said as Aden nodded. "You can choose."

"*Danki*," she said. "But I'm fine staying here. I know after your *daed* left you wanted me to leave this house. But I want to stay. This is *mei* home." She also didn't want to be a burden to either of her sons. They wouldn't see her that way, but she did. One step at a time.

"Are you sure?" Sol looked at her from across the table.

She smiled at him, then at Aden. "I'm sure. I'll be fine here."

Sol shook his head. "I don't understand, but I'll respect your decision."

"Me too." Aden paused, then added, "I'm glad you realize he left for *gut*. There's *nee* use hoping for something that will never happen."

"I see that now." A lump formed in her throat, but she had to finish speaking. "I'm sorry for what he did to you. For the part I played—" She couldn't stop the tears from falling down her face, and she was kicking herself for being so weak. She didn't want to upset her sons. She just needed to ask for forgiveness from them again.

"*Mamm*," Sol said softly. "You don't have to apologize."

"We know how he is . . . was." Aden touched her hand. "You did the best you could."

"I should have done better." She lifted her gaze to both of them. "I should have been stronger." She grabbed her napkin and wiped her cheeks, then lifted her chin. "From this moment on, I will be."

Sol and Aden stayed for the next half hour, and they would have been there longer if she hadn't made them leave. "I'm fine," she said when they lingered in the doorway. And it was true. She was more than fine. The weight she had been carrying for so long was a little lighter, and she was looking forward to living without wondering when or if Emmanuel was going to show up.

"Now *geh* on home before Irene and Sadie start worrying about you because you're late."

Sol leaned over and kissed her cheek, then walked out the door. Aden hugged her. "Love you, *Mamm*."

"I love you too."

After her sons left, Rhoda set to washing the bowls and cups from dessert and coffee. As she dipped the dishes into the hot soapy water, Sol's question came back to her mind. *Are you supposed to live alone forever?* No one lived forever, but she knew what he meant. Loren suddenly came to mind. Although there was nothing between them, and unless God willed it, there never would be, she allowed herself another thought. *What if we were both free?*

Her cheeks grew red and she smiled, imagining a future she knew she wouldn't have. She hadn't allowed herself to think or feel like this for a long time. And while the emotions were temporary and she would soon have to lock them away forever, she allowed herself to wish for the impossible a little while longer before finishing up the dishes. She turned off the gas lamp in the kitchen, then went to her bedroom and turned on the small lamp on the nightstand.

She stared at the bed she had shared with Emmanuel for so many years, longer than she'd slept alone. The quilt had belonged to his mother, he'd bought the furniture before they were married, and even the dresses in her closet, which were showing a little wear and tear, were the colors he approved. Everything in this room, in this house, had his stamp on it, and she suddenly realized that although she told Sol and Aden that the house was her home, it really wasn't. It was still Emmanuel's.

Rhoda tore the quilt off the bed and tossed it on the rocking chair in the corner of the room. Then she went to her closet and looked at her dresses—dark blue only. No light colors, like lavender or pale green. She loved pale green. She grabbed all the dresses except one and stacked them on the chair. Tomorrow she would fold the quilt and set it aside to donate later. After breakfast she would call for a taxi, go to the fabric shop in Barton, and buy all the light-colored fabric she wanted for new dresses, then sew them up.

She undressed and climbed into bed. Even though she only had a sheet covering her, she felt warm. She'd pick up some quilting material at the fabric shop, too, and make herself a new coverlet in the colors she liked. She would even throw a little pink into the pattern, a color Emmanuel disliked but she had always thought was pretty.

Rhoda smiled. This house might not feel like hers now . . . but it would soon enough. Then she could really call it her own.

"Here, have another pumpkin cupcake, Margaret."

Margaret took the cupcake from her *aenti* Carolyn that was piled high with fluffy cream cheese frosting and took a big bite. Oh, this was heaven. She had skipped breakfast this morning knowing her aunt would have a treat or two available, and she'd been correct. In addition to the moist cupcakes, *Aenti* Carolyn also had apple coffee cake and lemon pie on the table, a serving utensil stuck in both pans. "*Gut* as always, *Aenti.*"

Carolyn smiled, wrinkles creasing the corners of her eyes.

"Sorry there's so much food here, but I was trying a new lemon pie recipe last night, and Atlee's on a dessert strike. He says his spare tire is getting too round. I think he looks just fine. Nothing wrong with a little extra weight in *mei* opinion, but he disagrees. Make sure to take the leftovers with you, or else he's not going to be happy with me."

"I will." She'd already tasted the pie, which was divine, but had to refuse the coffee cake. Fortunately, there was black coffee to cut the sweetness of the desserts. She took a sip, then asked, "Does Junior normally take naps in the morning?" She had arrived at *Aenti* Carolyn's half an hour ago, and had expected to see her young cousin, but he was still in bed.

"*Nee*, but he was up most of the night. He was a colicky baby, and sometimes he still has tummy aches. I fed him breakfast around five thirty, and when he almost fell asleep in his oatmeal, I knew he needed to *geh* back to bed." She pressed the side of her fork into the coffee cake. "I'm glad he's napping. That gives us some uninterrupted time together."

For the next twenty minutes, the two of them talked about their families, *Aenti* Carolyn saying more than Margaret. She could tell how happy her aunt was, even though she did look a little tired. Considering she was up most of the night, that made sense. Otherwise, her aunt was lively and entertaining as usual, and Margaret could hardly believe that she and her father were brother and sister. *Daed* never revealed much about his childhood, at least not to Margaret. It was beginning to dawn on her that just like she was so different from her siblings, her father was also dissimilar from his.

The sound of a buggy pulling into her aunt's driveway came

through the open kitchen window. "I'm not sure who that could be," she said. "I'm not expecting anyone this morning. Then again, sometimes friends just drop right in. *Gut* thing I have plenty of dessert." Her aunt laughed and got up from the table. "I'll be right back."

Margaret polished off the rest of the cupcake while her aunt answered the front door. She picked up her napkin and wiped the extra frosting off her chin. There wasn't a neat way to eat an overly frosted cupcake—not that she was complaining.

Aenti Carolyn dashed into the kitchen. "I'm so sorry! I totally forgot I was supposed to *geh* with Mattie to Schrock's this morning. I'm going to have to cut our visit short."

"That's all right." She had plenty of things to do, one of them being to find out if there was an herbal recipe for colic in her book. She didn't remember seeing one. Then again, she would have glossed over it if there was since she didn't know any colicky babies. "I'll be here for another two and a half weeks."

"Wonderful, that's plenty of time to get together. If you're not too busy, that is."

"For you, I'm never too busy."

Her aunt grinned. "That's because I feed your sweet tooth."

A muffled cry came from the back of the house. "Oh *gut*, Junior's up," *Aenti* Carolyn said. "I wasn't eager to wake him and have a cranky toddler on *mei* hands while I'm shopping. Mattie is dropping off a bakery delivery for *mei* English neighbor, Tina. That will give me enough time to get him ready to *geh*."

Margaret paused. Her aunt looked frazzled enough, and it couldn't be easy dealing with a busy toddler in a grocery store. Then again, if *Aenti* Carolyn was willing to take him, he couldn't be that much of a handful, despite *Aenti* Mary's warnings. "I can watch Junior," she said, a bit surprised at herself for offering.

Her aunt paused. "Are you sure? He's a busy *boppli*."

At two years old he wasn't exactly a baby, but Margaret had noticed that mothers called their children babies even when they were past the baby stage. "If it will help you, I don't mind at all."

"That would be great." *Aenti* Carolyn beamed. "Mattie and I can get our shopping done a lot faster then. Come, I'll introduce you and show you where everything is."

Margaret followed her back to Junior's bedroom, which was at the opposite end of the house but still on the same floor. Although she'd spent little time with children, she had seen how her sisters took care of their kids when everyone was together for a family supper or holiday. Their children were always well behaved, just like their mothers. Despite her lack of babysitting experience, Margaret was confident she could handle Junior. How hard could it be to keep an eye on a two-year-old for a couple of hours?

Owen pulled a small wagon filled with ears of corn, jars of spaghetti sauce, and a few jars of green beans and green peas behind him as he headed for Carolyn Shetler's house. His mother had mentioned at the breakfast table that she was planning to drop off the produce later that morning, and Owen found himself volunteering for the job. Even when she insisted she could do it herself, he stood his ground.

"It's not that far of a walk and it won't take me long to drop the stuff off," he said as she cleared the breakfast dishes.

Mamm eyed him for a moment before finally relenting. "All right, but only because I want to get the laundry out in time to dry this afternoon."

"I'm glad to do it." But he didn't reveal why. One reason was because he needed something to do other than read and nap. He'd even thought about going to Akron for the day. He'd been to the large city once before years ago with his father and older brothers. They attended a garden show at the convocation center, then had lunch at a restaurant nearby. Owen didn't care for crowds or big cities, but he thought he might give Akron another chance. At least that had been the plan last night. This morning he had changed his mind. Going to Akron alone wasn't his idea of a fun time.

Not that dragging produce a half mile away was a blast either, but at least he had a chance to catch a glimpse of Margaret again. Just to see if she was enjoying her visit with her aunt. He cringed at that lame excuse as he turned into Carolyn's driveway. Of course she would enjoy her time with Carolyn. *Just admit you want to see her again.* But he couldn't quite acknowledge that either.

When he was a few feet from the front door, he heard a yelp coming through the open screened-in window. A female yelp. He dropped the wagon handle and ran up the front porch and knocked on the door. "Carolyn?" he called. Another yelp, and this time he recognized the voice. "Margaret?" When she didn't answer, he turned the knob, which wasn't locked, and opened the door. He was stunned by what he saw. Toys were scattered all over the floor and the couch pillows were on the coffee table, a corner of one pillow hanging over the edge as if someone had tossed it there. That mess wasn't bad, but the trail of cloth diapers on the floor leading to the kitchen was a surprise. Thank God they were all clean.

Yelp!

He almost stepped on a diaper as he hurried to the kitchen, grabbing it off the floor on the way. When he walked inside, his jaw dropped. Flour covered the floor, and he saw an open bag near the pantry. What a disaster. But where was Margaret? And Carolyn and her son were nowhere in sight.

Then he heard a child giggle, and he walked over to the other side of the table. There were Margaret and Junior, sitting on the flour-covered floor playing peekaboo.

Margaret's hands were covering her face. "One, two, three!" She opened them and squealed. There was the explanation for the yelping he'd heard. "Peekaboo!"

Junior dissolved into a fit of giggles. What was it about peekaboo that kids found so funny? Elam loved the game when he was a *boppli*.

"Now it's Junior's turn." She took his pudgy hands and put them over his face. Flour covered every inch of his body. "One, two, three!" She opened his hands and squealed again. "Peekaboo!"

"Peeka!" Junior put his hands over his face, then opened them. "Peeka!"

Owen was charmed by the scene. He leaned against the doorjamb and watched them complete two more rounds. When they were finished, Margaret said, "Now it's time for a bath."

"*Nee.*" Junior scrambled to his feet and started to run off. "No baff."

But Margaret grabbed him around the waist and pulled him into her lap. "*Ya*, bath."

He squirmed and tried to get away, but she held fast, and somehow got to her feet as she held on to him. Junior Atlee was large for a toddler, but that didn't affect Margaret. She turned and—

"Ahh!"

Owen jumped and dropped the diaper. "What!" he yelled.

"You scared me again!"

"You scared me too!"

Junior started to wail. "Oh *nee*. We both scared him." Margaret held him close, running her hand over his flour-covered back. "We were doing just fine before Owen got here, weren't we?" she cooed.

He snatched the diaper off the floor and shook it. "If you call being coated in flour just fine," he muttered as fine white flakes fell to the floor.

"I was going to clean that up." She placed her hand against Junior's head, which was now resting on her shoulder. Thankfully, he had stopped crying.

"I'm sure you were." He walked over to Margaret. "I'm sorry I scared you. I didn't mean to this time."

"I know. And I'm sorry I scared you." She frowned. "What are you doing here?"

He explained about bringing the vegetables to Carolyn. They were still outside in the wagon, but they would be fine there for a little while. The corn was still in the husk and the beans and peas were sealed in glass jars. "I heard you yelping so I came inside. I'm glad *nix* is wrong."

She glanced around the kitchen and sighed. "That's not

exactly true, but I'm getting things under control. At least I was."

Why was he the one feeling guilty when all he did was check on her? Then again, he should have told her he was there, instead of watching her.

"I've got to give Junior a bath," she said, her frown deepening. "Then I have to clean up the kitchen, obviously. And the front room. *Aenti* Carolyn's been gone for an hour and I don't want her to come back and see this mess. She'll never let me near Junior again if she does."

"I can bathe him," Owen said.

Her brow lifted. "What do you know about bathing *kinner*?"

"You forget I have seven younger siblings. I'm fourteen years older than the youngest one. I've given plenty of baths. While Junior's in the tub you can clean up . . . this." He gestured to the flour.

"*Gut* idea. I haven't bathed a *kinn* but I do know how to clean up a kitchen."

"What happened here?"

She sighed as she handed Junior over to him. "I took *mei* eye off him for a few seconds while I put away the books he'd pulled off the bookshelf in the living room. I didn't realize he could reach the two bottom rows. Why don't *Aenti* Carolyn and Atlee put those books higher?"

"Probably because he knows not to touch them when his parents are around." Wow, Junior was a chunk. He looked into the child's hazel eyes and discovered Junior was also investigating him. The kid touched the brim of his hat.

"By the time I was finished, he had disappeared. I found him in the pantry, and by that time he'd gotten into the flour. I ended up chasing him around the kitchen table, and this is the result." She held out her arms.

He was tempted to laugh, but he knew better. He also knew better than to tell Junior he was getting a bath, so he said, "Let's *geh* see some of your toys." When Junior's eyes lit up, Owen knew he had him. Hopefully, there were toys in the bathtub. "I'll be back," he said, then left the kitchen, toddler in tow. *This kid's getting a bath whether he likes it or not.*

Margaret swept up the last bit of the flour off the floor. The last person she'd expected to see in her aunt's kitchen was Owen, and although he had scared her for a third time, she was grateful he had shown up. She wouldn't have been able clean up Junior and get the kitchen and living room back in order before her aunt got home. Now she had a fighting chance.

She dumped the contents of the dustpan into the trash can, blinking at the puff of flour she created when it hit the rest of the trash. Then she wiped the table a second time. Fortunately, *Aenti* Carolyn had wrapped up the desserts and put them on the counter before she left with Mattie, or else they would been covered in a light dusting. Margaret rinsed off the cloth and wiped off the counters for good measure, then surveyed the entire room. *Aenti* Carolyn would never know what happened.

Satisfied she had covered her tracks, she went to the living room, picking up diapers as she walked. Junior had dragged the diapers out of his room while she was waving goodbye to her aunt. Now she knew she couldn't let the little booger out of her sight.

She was fluffing the couch cushions when Owen appeared—without Junior. She hurried to him. "Where is he? You didn't leave him alone, did you? Not-so-*gut* things happen when he's unsupervised."

"Relax, he's taking a nap. Nothing like a nice warm bath to make you sleepy."

She was so relieved she nearly fell against him. "Did he give you any trouble?"

"He protested a little, then settled down. He's a typical *bu*."

Margaret had no idea what a typical boy was, but if they were like Junior Atlee they sure did need close supervision. "I got everything cleaned up."

"Even yourself, I see." He gave her that half-smile of his.

"*Ya.* I didn't realize how much flour I had on me. But it brushed off easily." She heard Mattie's buggy pull in the driveway. "Just in time too. Carolyn's home."

"I'll bring in the vegetables." He started to open the front door.

"Owen?"

He turned around. "*Ya?*"

"*Danki* for helping me. I don't know what I would have done if you hadn't shown up."

"You would have done just fine." He smiled, this time a full one.

And her heart skipped a beat. Actually, two. *What in the world?*

She blinked, then finally hurried to the kitchen to meet Carolyn and help put Owen's vegetables away. When her aunt walked into the kitchen, Margaret plopped down on one of the chairs as if she'd been sitting there for a while. "Hi," she said, trying not to smile too brightly. "How was your trip?"

"Successful, thanks to you." Carolyn set three canvas shopping bags on the counter to her right.

"How was Junior? He didn't give you any problems, did he?"

Margaret paused. Junior's misdeeds weren't all his fault. If she'd been more experienced with small children, she would have watched him more closely. "Not too much. He's taking a nap right now. I do owe you a bag of flour, though."

Aenti Carolyn gave her an odd look, and Margaret was just about to explain when Owen walked through the door. "Where do you want the corn, Carolyn?"

"You can lay it on the counter." She gestured to the counter on the left side of the sink. "Miriam's so thoughtful to send those vegetables. Everyone knows I have a black thumb. I did manage to get a few tomatoes this year, though."

He nodded, not looking at Margaret. "I'll be right back with the jars."

"I'm going to take a peek at Junior," her aunt said. "I'm so glad he was *gut* for you while I was gone."

Once Carolyn was gone, Margaret leaned back in her chair. She'd explain everything to her aunt later, but right now she was glad to have a few moments to catch her breath.

A couple of minutes passed, and she looked through the window on the kitchen door to see Owen standing there, his arms full of glass jars. "Can I help you with those?" she said as she opened the door for him.

"Nah. I'll set them here." He went to the table and carefully put the jars down. Then he turned to her. "Everything's unloaded."

"Carolyn's checking on Junior."

"I guess you tuckered him out." He smirked.

"More like the other way around." She looked at him, oddly at a loss for words.

"Well," he said, shoving one of his hands in his pockets. "I better get the wagon back to *Mamm*. I'm sure she's got plans for delivering more vegetables around the community."

"That's very generous of her."

Owen's expression turned grim. "There was a time when we were on the receiving end of other people's kindness. She's never forgotten that. None of us have." Before Margaret could say anything, he added, "See you tomorrow." Then he left.

Margaret's heart pinched. She had never seen him look so somber. Whatever happened to his family in the past must have been serious.

"He's conked out," Carolyn said as she walked into the kitchen. "How about I fix us some lunch and you can tell me how everything went. I'm sure it was an interesting morning."

She looked at the kitchen door again. It definitely was.

Chapter 9

The next morning, after getting a good night's sleep and then eating a hearty breakfast, Margaret helped Mary bake bread for the week. She liked that her aunt didn't just make plain old white bread, but also cinnamon raisin and a small loaf of wheat for Freemont. Back home her mother only baked white bread. Maybe when she went back home, she'd ask her mother to try *Aenti* Mary's cinnamon bread recipe.

That thought brought her up short. She knew exactly how that conversation would go. "We've always had white bread," *Mamm* would say. "There's *nee* reason to change that now."

But that wasn't the only thing that gave her pause. Even though she'd only been in Birch Creek a week, she didn't feel a drop of homesickness. She would have to return in two more weeks since she had promised her mother she would. Then again, maybe she could tell her she needed more time to find a husband.

No, that wouldn't work. That would be outright lying, and she refused to do that.

"Ira stopped by before heading out to the field this morning,"

Mary said, adding a handful of raisins to the cinnamon-flavored dough on the kneading board. "Nina's been asking after you. He wanted to know if you could *geh* visit her this afternoon and then stay for supper."

Margaret froze, her hands dusted with flour and hovering over a ball of yeasty bread dough she was about to roll out. Uh-oh. She did want to see Nina again, especially to find out how her talk with Ira went. She'd seen Ira briefly yesterday morning before she went to Carolyn's, and he didn't seem any different from how he usually was. Then again, she knew about the miscarriage, and like Nina, he probably didn't want to share the news just yet.

But she also wanted to spend the afternoon with Owen again, even though she'd just seen him yesterday. She needed to thank him again for helping her out. Fortunately, *Aenti* Carolyn found the situation amusing and wasn't upset that Junior had made a mess. "It's not the first time and it won't be the last," she said, laughing. Even Margaret could see the humor in it, but she was certain she wouldn't think her babysitting disaster wasn't so bad if Owen hadn't given her an assist.

She also had to admit he was cute when he brought up the butternuts the other day. She wondered if he knew how red the tops of his ears were as he was talking about panta-whatever acid, something she was fairly sure he'd made up just to get her attention. He'd gotten it, and she was excited to look for butternuts. They had them back home in Salt Creek, and she enjoyed eating them when they were ripe. She had searched for the acid Owen mentioned in her book last night, to see if it had any healing properties. Although there was a chapter on butternuts, the acid wasn't mentioned. She didn't have any luck finding a recipe for colic either, but maybe Rhoda had one, or she could go to the Barton library and check their resources—

"Margaret? Did you hear what I said?"

Oh, right. Her aunt had asked a question. She looked at her and nodded, unsure how to answer. How was she going to tell *Aenti* Mary that she would rather go forage for butternuts with Owen than visit with Nina? And would Nina be upset about being ignored? Surely her friend would understand. Owen only had a few days left of vacation and then he would go back to work. There would be plenty of time for her to see Nina after today. She wanted to find butternuts, and of course the burdock, too, and she would find those faster with his help.

"It won't take long to finish this bread. We'll be done before lunch, and I can put the loaves in the oven later after they rise. *Geh* on to Nina's and enjoy yourself."

Margaret couldn't believe her luck. All she had to do was tell her aunt that she would be at Nina's for the afternoon, and she wouldn't even have to mention Owen. Then when she returned, she could say that she had a headache or wasn't hungry or come up with some other excuse so that if her aunt asked Ira about it, he could say she wasn't there. Perfect.

Her shoulders relaxed and she reached for the bread dough . . . then stopped. How could she possibly be considering lying to *Aenti* Mary? That was not only wrong, but it was also insulting to her aunt and uncle who were treating her so kindly and letting her stay in their house for almost a month. Sure, she was family, but she knew better than anyone that not all family was regarded the same.

She couldn't believe she had almost lied to her aunt so she

wouldn't have to admit that she wanted to be with Owen. Which was dumb. She'd already explained her nonrelationship with him to her aunt. Why did it matter if she knew she was going to spend another afternoon with him?

"Margaret? Is everything okay?" her aunt asked, a concerned look on her face. "You seem preoccupied this morning."

Margaret picked up the dough and tried to be nonchalant as she formed it into Parker rolls. "I can't *geh* to Nina's today," she said. "I have, um, plans. With Owen. To find butternuts." She looked down at her hand. The shape looked more like a pancake than a roll.

"That's nice." Her aunt tucked the cinnamon loaf into a metal baking pan, unfazed by Margaret's announcement. "I'm sure Nina will understand that you're busy today with Owen."

"Um, I was kind of hoping she didn't have to know." It wouldn't be just Nina who would find out who she was spending the day with, but Ira would too. She didn't want either of them jumping to the wrong conclusion. She'd rather explain the situation to Nina herself. Then she could tell Ira if she wanted to.

Aenti Mary paused, tilted her head, then finally nodded. "I'll let Ira know you can come another day, but I won't tell him why."

Relieved, Margaret relaxed. "*Danki,*" she said, thankful her aunt was so understanding. Her mother wouldn't have been. *Mamm* would have wanted to know her detailed plans, questioning her mercilessly about Owen, even though it was common among young Amish men and women to keep dating private.

Dating? Why had that popped into her mind? *We're not dating.* Good grief, she needed to stop thinking about her mother. Even from two hours away the woman was driving her crazy.

It's not her fault. Margaret had to admit she wasn't being fair, blaming her mother for her confusion. She wasn't used to having a male friend, and she was having a hard time shifting her thoughts from her normal interactions with men, which always led to a date or a very superficial relationship, to the enjoyable, no-strings-attached friendship she had with Owen. If she could keep that straight in her mind, she wouldn't be confused at all.

Like her aunt predicted, they finished with the baking right before lunch, and while *Aenti* Mary cleaned up the kitchen table, Margaret prepared roast beef and cheddar cheese sandwiches with tomato, lettuce, and pickles, potato salad, sliced apples, and oranges for her uncle and cousins. Then she filled a basket of cranberry muffins she'd baked early this morning before starting on the bread. The pumpkin cupcakes she'd brought home from *Aenti* Carolyn's had disappeared last night. She'd even had one more before she went to bed, promising herself that today she would try to burn off the extra calories while she foraged in the woods.

Freemont, Seth, Ira, and Judah came into the house and washed up for lunch. Margaret was pouring lemonade into Judah's glass when she glanced up at the clock. Oh no, it was almost twelve. If she stopped to eat lunch, she would be late meeting Owen. As everyone sat down at the table, she grabbed a cranberry muffin, paused, then grabbed two before trying to slip out of the kitchen unnoticed.

"Hey, Margaret," Ira said, grabbing two sandwiches off the plate. "Nina wants you to come over today."

Margaret froze and looked at her aunt before shifting her gaze to Ira. "I'm, um—"

"She's going on an errand for me this afternoon." *Aenti* Mary sprinkled salt on her potato salad. "Tell Nina they can get together another time."

Ira nodded, picking up a pickle off his plate. "Sure," he said. Then he took a crunchy bite. "I'll let her know. What about tomorrow?" He leveled a look at Margaret. "Can you make it then? She's really eager to see you."

Not missing Ira's meaning, she nodded, now positive that he not only knew about the pregnancy, but also that Margaret was aware of the miscarriage. Thankfully, he didn't seem upset, just eager for her to visit his wife. "I'll be over tomorrow morning. She and I can spend the day together."

Her cousin grinned. "She'll like that."

Now that Ira was placated, she looked at her aunt, who gave her a quick nod, her blank expression never changing. She owed *Aenti* Mary a favor in the future. A big one. She was also relieved that her aunt wasn't suspicious of her short conversation with Ira.

She ran upstairs and picked up a basket that *Aenti* Carolyn had let her borrow last night to bring home the cupcakes. She laid the muffins inside on the two pale-yellow napkins lining the basket and then added a thermos of cold water she had filled right before lunch. She closed the basket lid, went downstairs, and dashed out of the house before anyone stopped her again.

Despite the cloud-covered sky, Margaret grinned as she headed for the woods. Ah, freedom. She couldn't wait to see Owen. Oh, and to search for butternuts.

⌐◡⌐

As he had the last time he met Margaret, Owen arrived at the shed earlier than he needed to. Two hours early, to be precise. But unlike the last time he was here, he couldn't relax. He sat down under the window and stretched out his legs and then opened his book. Today he brought a novel about early pioneers and tried to lose himself in the story. The sky was overcast and gray, which limited the light coming through the window, but he could still see the words. What he couldn't do was focus on what they meant.

He set the book aside and closed his eyes, trying to pray, hoping concentrating on the Lord would keep his brain on track. But all he saw was Margaret covered in flour and comforting Junior in her arms. The memory still touched him. It also baffled him. Why was he so affected by her holding a toddler? She wasn't the first woman he'd ever seen comforting a small child, and it was such a common sight in his community that he paid no heed to it. Why was he thinking about it now?

He had to admit Junior was a pistol. He was also cute, and with all his chunky rolls, he was pretty cuddly. He hadn't minded giving him a bath yesterday. In fact, he kind of enjoyed it.

Groaning, Owen opened his eyes. Sitting here was pointless. He jumped to his feet and started to pace, trying to figure out why he was thinking about babies and Margaret at the same time. Then he grew annoyed. He wouldn't have this problem if he wasn't on vacation. Right now, he should be out with his brothers digging up more root vegetables. The turnip crop still needed to be harvested and he noticed last night that the potato patch needed more work. The entire farm was going to pot because he wasn't there to make sure everything was done the right way.

He halted and shook his head. What was he even thinking?

Number one, the farm was fine, and number two, he was being prideful. He wasn't in charge of the farm. His father was. And his brothers were doing what they usually did. He just wasn't there to go back over everything with a fine-tooth comb. The farm wasn't imploding because he wasn't there. Maybe that's what was sticking in his craw right now. Obviously he was expendable, or at least he wasn't as crucial to the daily running of the place as he thought.

Sure, it bothered him some that everyone seemed to be perfectly fine without him there working, but not enough to knock him off-kilter like this. His current turmoil was totally due to Margaret, and it wasn't even her fault. Earlier this week they had come to an agreement about keeping their relationship friendly, and he had genuinely thought that the subject was closed. But for some crazy reason he kept trying to pry it open, at least in his mind. It wasn't just that she was pretty. She was also funny, spunky, adventurous, and smart. She was humble and didn't have a problem admitting when she was wrong. How could he not be intrigued by a woman like Margaret?

Then he remembered what she'd said the day she got mad at him, about men not reassuring her, whatever that meant, and also about her family troubles. Instead of reminding himself that her problems weren't his business, he was wondering if he could help her. He didn't like the idea of her having to fight something by herself, and he hoped she was leaning on God in the process. *I wish she could lean on me too.*

Feeling like a sap, he went to the window, pushed back his hat, then peered outside. Rats, it looked like rain. Hopefully any showers would hold off until they were done foraging. He should have checked the weather forecast before he left. Normally he checked it every day, even obsessing over it after spring planting and then later in the season when frost threatened. But he hadn't given the weather a thought recently. There was no room in his mind when he was always thinking of Margaret.

Owen yanked off his hat and slapped it against his leg a few times. He shouldn't have come here early. He had way too much time to stew in his own absurd thoughts. She had made herself crystal clear—she didn't have any romantic intentions toward anyone, specifically him. He had said the same about her, and he needed to stick to what he told her. What he still believed. *I'm not interested in Margaret Yoder.*

As he plopped his hat back on his head, he heard a rustling sound outside the shed. He paused, waiting for a few moments for Margaret to come through the door, and ignoring how his hands suddenly became damp. He ran his palms over his broadfall pants and stared at the unlocked door.

When she didn't appear, he frowned. Had he imagined the noise? One of the things he liked about coming to the shed was how quiet everything was this deep into the woods. He was so used to the constant cacophony of his family and farm animals that only ceased when he slept, and he hadn't realized how much he appreciated peace and quiet until he had experienced both when he was here. That was another thing he liked about Margaret. When they were foraging, she was totally focused and rarely said anything.

When he opened the door and looked outside, Margaret was nowhere in sight. He left the shed and explored the perimeter, which only took him little more than a minute. There wasn't a sign that anyone had been there, so he stopped to listen, but he only heard the usual soft hum of birds tweeting, insects clicking and whistling, and an owl hooting in the distance. Immediately he relaxed. He was too jittery, and he needed to settle himself down. He closed his eyes and drew in a deep, long breath of fresh forest air.

"Hi, Owen."

His eyes flew open at the sound of Margaret's light and airy voice. He was startled a bit, but not nearly as much as he had been yesterday when she had yelled at him at Carolyn's. He almost laughed. Somehow, they always managed to catch each other off guard. "Hi, Margaret."

"Why were your eyes closed?"

Owen made the mistake of not keeping his gaze on her face, and his palms became clammy again. She was wearing a dark-green dress today, appropriate for being inconspicuous in the woods, save for her white prayer *kapp*. She really did look pretty in everything she wore.

"I expected you to be inside napping again," she added with a little smirk. "Don't tell me you can sleep standing up."

"I, uh, was just enjoying the fresh air. I also just got here, by the way." He cringed inwardly at the fib, but he couldn't admit that he couldn't get comfortable enough to sleep because he couldn't stop thinking of her. She'd flee like a scared bunny if he did. "Is that basket for the butternuts?" he asked quickly, attempting to turn her attention to something else.

"*Ya*, but it also has something in it." She opened the lid and pulled out a muffin. "I grabbed two on the way out. I figured we could have a snack before we started. I hope you like cranberry."

That was thoughtful. "I do." He took the muffin and jerked his head toward the shed. "Want to eat in there or out here?"

"Probably in the shed. It's more comfortable to sit on the floor than on the rough ground out here."

A few moments later they were seated next to each other underneath the window. Owen made sure there was a good amount of room between them as they ate the muffins and shared the thermos of water she brought. Smart thinking. It hadn't crossed his mind to bring anything, including a container to carry the butternuts, which should have been the first thing on his mind before he left the house. Fortunately, she didn't say anything about him being empty-handed.

"Have you ever eaten butternuts before?" Margaret asked.

"I remember having some when I was little, but it's been a long time." He ate the last half of the muffin in one bite. When he finished chewing, he added, "I don't recall what they taste like, though."

"They have their own flavor." Unlike him, she had nibbled on her muffin, and almost three-quarters of it was left. She picked up the thermos and unscrewed the top, then poured a cup of water and handed it to him. "I enjoy them, but I can't eat too many. They're a little rich for me. Now, I do love peanuts and anything with peanut butter. That's *mei* downfall."

"Chocolate is mine. I can eat half a cake by myself."

Her gaze traveled over him as he took a drink. "Where do you put it?"

He lifted his chin in mock indignation. "Are you saying I'm too skinny?"

She looked horrified. "I'm sorry. I didn't mean to insult you."

163

"It's okay." He laughed and then shrugged. "You're not the first person to ask me that question. I've always been thin. *Daed* used to say it was because I worked twice as hard as anyone else, but I just think that's how God made me."

"Like me being so short." She looked at her muffin.

"Does it bother you to be short?"

"It used to when I was younger. For a long time, people who didn't know me thought I was still a child, even when I was a teenager."

"That had to be annoying."

"*Ya*, it sure was." She pinched off another bite of the muffin. "Being this short has other drawbacks too. I don't like asking for help to reach things. I have trouble getting clothes out of the wringer washer if I don't have a stool, and putting them out on the line takes me longer than it took *mei schwesters*. Stuff like that."

He tried not to look at her too much, because now that she was talking about her petite stature, he thought about how easy it would be to pick her up. *And hold her in my arms.* He instantly derailed that train of thought, knowing he would regret where it would end up if he didn't. Staring at the other side of the room he said, "I can see where that would be a problem."

"I manage." She turned to him, holding out the muffin. "I don't think I can finish this."

"You don't like it?"

"Oh, I do. I'm just not that hungry. I ate too many of *mei aenti*'s pumpkin cupcakes yesterday. Do you want the rest?"

"I never turn down food." He took the muffin and finished it off along with the rest of the water in the thermos while she fiddled with the basket. He handed her the thermos lid, then stood and said, "Ready to butternut hunt?"

"*Ya*." She started to stand, but she slipped on some of the sawdust on the floor and her legs shot out from underneath her.

He lurched, ready to help her up, then held back. Despite all of his inner chastising, he couldn't be sure he could let her go if he touched her. Great, now his forehead broke out in a sweat even though it was cool in the shed. He had to get out of there. Pretending he didn't see her slip, he hurried out the door, not only feeling like a fool but also a jerk at the same time for letting her fall—all because he couldn't trust himself to do the right thing. He'd always been so sure of himself and who he was. Or so he thought. Now he didn't know what to think anymore.

Margaret rolled her eyes, irritated with herself for landing on her backside while trying to do something as simple as standing up. She frowned and looked at the door Owen left open. He seemed to be in an awful hurry to go foraging, considering how he'd dashed out of the shed like his pants were on fire. Then again, getting back on the foraging track was a good thing. She had enjoyed talking to him too much as they shared the muffins, and she could have lingered in the shed with him the whole afternoon, chatting and getting to know him better. In fact, she'd been thinking about that very thing when she started to stand, focusing more on him and not paying attention to what she was doing.

But the fall had brought her back to reality. They weren't here to socialize. They were here to find butternuts. Sighing, she got up from the ground, brushed the dust off her dress, and picked up the basket. He was probably far ahead of her by now. The other day she'd noticed and appreciated how tenacious he was in his quest to find the fiddleheads, so much so that they had said few words to each other while they foraged. She didn't mind, preferring to put her energy into searching rather than talking.

But when they were sitting next to each other on the floor of the shed, things were different. More companionable. There was something freeing about being able to sit and talk and share cranberry muffins together, without the pressure of attraction or romance. During their conversation she'd only been unsettled once, when she had pointed out how skinny he was. As usual when she was with Owen, she spoke without thinking. Maybe it was because she didn't have to be on her guard with him or turn on her flirty charm and bask in his attention. Fortunately, he hadn't been offended. Although it wasn't fair that he could eat half a chocolate cake if he wanted to without any consequences.

When she had taken a good look at him, she realized he wasn't as slender as she thought he was. She noticed the outline of his biceps under his light-blue long-sleeved shirt, which was rolled up to his elbows and revealed well-defined forearms. He wasn't as muscular as a bigger built guy, her preferred type. And yet his wiry body had suddenly become attractive to her. And that was worrisome. She had to remind herself that she was drawn to his personality, not his looks. Finding him physically attractive changed everything, and not in a good way. She had to set that aside permanently. She wasn't about to ruin her time with him because she couldn't keep her eyes to herself.

Tamping her muddled thoughts down deep, she hurried

outside and saw Owen searching the base of a large tree a few yards from the shed. No surprise, he was already focused on their objective. Time for her to focus too. She joined him, and neither of them said anything as they searched for the nuts.

"I thought this was a butternut tree, but it's not," he said, looking at the tree in front of him. "I guess I'm not sure what they look like."

"I'm not either. I've never looked for them before. I've just eaten them."

He turned to her, putting his hands on his slender waist. She tried not to notice. "That doesn't mean we shouldn't keep looking. There might be some here. We should probably split up like we did the other day."

"I think you're right." It hadn't dawned on her to pay attention to what the tree looked like when she was reading about the butternuts. Then again, her thoughts weren't completely on the butternuts last night when she was reading either. "I'll *geh* that way," she said, pointing to the east.

"Then I'll *geh* this way." He gestured with his hand to the west.

They split up, Margaret still carrying the basket, determined to keep her mind on the butternuts and not on Owen's . . . physique. Soon she was immersed in her search, spying several pretty green plants at the base of a birch tree. She walked over to them and crouched down. She wasn't sure what they were, but she was drawn to the rich green color of their feather-like leaves and thought how pretty they would look in a frame. She picked a few and carefully placed them in the basket.

The sound of thunder rumbled in the distance. She lifted her head and peered at the sky through the dense branches of leaves for the first time since she and Owen had separated. She hadn't noticed how dark the atmosphere had become. Instead of a blanket of gray, there were now charcoal-colored thunderheads above them. When she stood, she felt a drop of rain hit her arm. Then another, and then a downpour of rain whooshed from the clouds.

"Bother!" She put her hand over her head as if the token act would prevent her from getting wet and ran toward the shed. A thunderclap snapped above her, and right after, a large bolt of lightning flashed a short distance away, lighting up Owen as he ran in her direction.

"Big storm's coming!" he called out. A huge gust of wind rocked the tree branches back and forth.

"I think it's already here!" she yelled back.

"We need to get to the shed!"

She nodded, concentrating on not tripping over anything as she ran as fast as she could. Every bit of sunlight had disappeared, leaving behind near darkness while the rain continued to pound her body and obscure her vision. She arrived at the shed at the same time Owen did. He thrust open the door and shoved her inside, slamming the door behind them.

Margaret set the basket down and shook out her hands. "I'm soaked to the skin!"

"So am I."

Another flash of lightning illuminated the interior of the dark shed, enough that she could see he was right. His shirt and pants clung to him and water dripped off the brim of his hat. Bother again. "Now what do we do?" she muttered, averting her gaze even though it was too dark to clearly see him. She knew herself well enough that if she looked at him again and another lightning strike hit, she wouldn't be able to pull her gaze from the rest of him, something he would definitely notice. If that happened, it would put all her other embarrassing moments to shame. Turning around, she squeezed out the water from the hem of her dress.

"We wait out the storm."

His logical tone calmed her. But she wasn't irritated by the storm. Well, a little. God decided to put a crimp in their plans, and she was really hoping to eat a few butternuts today. She was more annoyed with herself. She shouldn't be paying attention to how physically attractive he was. That wasn't a friendly thing to do. But here she was, afraid to look at him again, and now that her eyes had adjusted to the dim light in the shed, he wasn't just a figure in shadow. Maybe the storm would pass by quickly and they could go back to foraging. *Dear Lord, I hope it does.*

Chapter 10

*L*ester finished raking up the last of the leaves that had been scattered over the parking lot in front of Stoll's Inn. He put them in a wheelbarrow and wheeled it out to the compost pile located past the inn and the barn that his boss, Loren Stoll, owned. By the time he reached the pile, his shirt was soaked with sweat, and he was breathing hard, despite the cloud-filled gray sky. He was in his late fifties, and hard work didn't come as easy to him as it had when he was younger.

But hard work was also good for the soul, so he wasn't going to give up working. He dumped the leaves into the pile and stirred them into the compost pile that had grown at least a foot over the summer. Then he put a tarp over the pile and secured it with small stakes he poked through premade holes in the blue covering before taking a mallet and tamping them down. By next spring, this pile would turn into some of the best fertilizer around, and he would use that in the flower beds and Delilah's garden in the back of the Stolls' small house. *If I'm still around by that time.*

He took off his overly large hat and wiped his forehead with the red handkerchief he always kept in his shirt pocket and tried not to think about his cowardice the other night. At one time he thought he was a strong man, stronger than any man he knew—or so he thought. But that high opinion had been brought low over the years. God had a way of doing that, bringing the prideful down from their pedestal. Lester had fashioned his pedestal himself, and that made the fall longer and harder. Even now he was still falling.

He was placing his hat on his head when Katharine, the young woman who was living with Loren and Delilah, approached. He gave her a curt nod, but his aloof manner belied his thoughts. There was a time when he would look at this girl and judge the extra pounds she carried and the spots on her face that should have cleared up when she stopped being a teenager, along with her habit of looking down at her feet when she talked. Instead he felt sympathy for her. *At least I've changed that much.*

She arrived several weeks ago, along with four other young women who were now taking up residence in the inn—they'd all come to Birch Creek due to that foolish bachelor advertisement. But it was clear from the start that she was separate from those girls, so much that when Delilah asked one of them to stay with her so they could free up two of the rooms for other guests, Katharine hadn't hesitated. Although he didn't pay much attention to other folks' social lives, he'd seen how happy and giggly the other women were, and he figured they were being courted by someone in Birch Creek, or at least having fun with the prospect. Not Katharine. If she wasn't looking for a husband, then why was she here? But he stuck to his policy of minding his own business and never asked her about it.

"Hi, Lester."

She smiled and he had to admit that was her best feature. Too bad she didn't do it often. "Hi, Katharine."

Her gaze shifted to his cheek. "What happened to your face?"

He resisted touching the long scratch above his beard. He'd bandaged the cut after he returned from the woods the other night, and it stopped bleeding by the morning. Now his skin was forming a noticeable scab. "Went fishing after work the other day," he mumbled. "Branch scratched my cheek."

"I hope it didn't hurt too bad."

"Do you need something, Katharine?"

"*Nix*." She stared at her feet again. "I just wondered if you needed any help with anything."

He paused, recalling another young woman, Amanda King, now Amanda Bontrager, who had stayed with the Stolls and had offered to help him. She also seemed lost and troubled like Katharine. Difference was, Amanda was conventionally attractive, along with being a nice girl. He hadn't been surprised to hear that both her and her twin sister, Darla, had gotten married.

But Katharine . . . he had to keep from shaking his head. Poor girl had the odds stacked against her. "I'm sure I can come up with something," he said. "The weather's getting cooler, and I need to stockpile the firewood soon."

"I can split it for you." She glanced up. "I do it at home."

That surprised him. He didn't know a single woman who split firewood. That was a man's job, and he wasn't going to turn it over to a woman, even though she looked big and broad enough to handle it. "How about you work on trimming the bushes in front of the inn? They're getting a little out of control."

Her face lit up and she nodded. "Thanks, Lester," she said. "I'll be happy to do that."

"The clippers are in the shed behind the barn."

Grinning, she nodded, then headed toward the barn, her walk lighter than he'd ever seen it. She wasn't his daughter, although she was old enough to be . . .

He banged the mallet on one more spike, even though it was already secure, then tossed the mallet in the wheelbarrow. He'd put both of them away later. Before he could work on the woodpile, he remembered that he'd promised Delilah he would replace the doorknob on the inn's back door. He went inside the inn to the combination mudroom and storage room and opened the cabinet where he kept odds and ends. There was the doorknob on top of a package of nails he'd purchased last week. After fishing out his small knife from his pants pocket, he was prying off the package's plastic casing when he heard Delilah's and Loren's voices through the interior door that led to the inn's common area.

"I just thought I'd stop over at Rhoda's after work today." Loren's annoyed tone carried through the wooden door. "I don't know why you're making such a fuss."

"I'm not fussing," Delilah said, sounding defensive. "I'm concerned."

"You're always concerned," Loren mumbled.

"What did you say, *sohn*?"

"*Nix*. Don't worry, I'll be back before supper tonight."

"You were just there the other day working on her firewood pile. And then the time before, you insisted on taking over a basket of food that I was planning to give her the next day."

Loren cleared his throat. "I was saving you a trip."

"Now why don't I believe you?" She paused. "Loren, what are you doing?" Delilah asked.

Lester couldn't help himself. He cracked open the door so he could hear their conversation better. Delilah had her hands on her hips, staring Loren down. For his part Loren looked irritated, something he was from time to time when dealing with his busybody mother.

Loren sighed. "I just said I'm—"

"I know what you said." Delilah shook her head. "I want to know what your intentions are."

"To do *mei* Christian duty, *Mutter*. That's all. I saw a nice planter box that was on clearance at the hardware store yesterday. She has a lot of flowers and plants in containers on her front porch."

"You noticed that, huh?"

"I notice a lot of things."

Another pause. "Tell me the truth, Loren. Are you interested in her?"

Lester squeezed the plastic doorknob packaging, a sharp corner cutting into his skin.

"She's . . . nice." At Delilah's huff he added, "*Mamm*, she's a decent sort. There, are you satisfied?"

"*Nee*, I'm not. Far be it from me to stick *mei* nose into your business—"

"Why stop now?" he muttered.

"But you realize Rhoda isn't a free woman. She may not ever be."

"You think I want to court her?" He shook his head. "She lost her spouse, *Mutter*. I don't know the reasons why and I'm not going to ask. But I do know what it's like to be married one day . . . and to be alone the next. We may not have lost our spouses the same way, but the pain is there. Did you ever think that maybe she'd like to talk to someone who knows that kind of grief?"

"Oh." Delilah's expression softened. "*Nee*. I didn't think about it that way. But, *sohn*, you have to be careful. Talking about such a thing might lead to something neither of you anticipate."

"I know." He took her hand and squeezed it. "And I won't bring up the subject unless it comes up naturally. But if she ever wants to talk, I'll be there for her."

"Even if she can't be there for you?"

He nodded. "Even then."

Lester closed the door, his heart galloping in his chest. He looked down at the doorknob poking out of the plastic. Right. He was supposed to fix this. He tore off the packaging and shoved it in the cabinet. Then he rushed outside and tried to start working on the door. The knob fell out of his hand. He picked it back up, only to drop it again. By the time he snatched it off the ground a second time, Loren and Delilah were coming outside.

"Oh hey, Lester," Loren said. "Thanks for taking care of that doorknob."

"No problem," Lester said gruffly, not looking up.

Delilah bustled over to Lester. Like Katharine, she carried more than a few extra pounds, but that never got in the way of her energy. Sometimes Lester was worn out just watching her work. "When you're finished with that, would you mind looking at the sink in Room 4? One of the girls was complaining that the faucet wouldn't stop dripping."

"Next on my list, ma'am."

With a nod, Delilah turned and followed her son, who was nearly to their house. "Loren, we're not finished talking," she said, only to have Loren let the screen door slam on her. "Oh, for goodness' sake," she said, then opened the door and flounced inside.

Normally Lester chuckled at their interactions, which usually consisted of Delilah demanding something and Loren wearily acquiescing. But he wasn't laughing now. He leveled his gaze at the house and glared. If things were different, he wouldn't be standing there fiddling with the doorknob. He would be in that house, setting Loren Stoll straight.

Instead he finished replacing the doorknob, noticing a small cut on his hand that wasn't there before. Probably from the sharp edge of the plastic packaging. A boom of thunder sounded in the air. He looked up. A huge storm gathered in the distance. Quickly he ignored his latest cut and turned the screwdriver one more time, securing the knob to the door.

But he couldn't ignore the jealousy churning inside him . . . or his anger that he couldn't do anything about it.

All we have to do is ride out the storm. How hard could that be?

It turned out that staying in the shed together while the rain hammered the roof and the wind shook the small structure was harder than Owen thought. Not because he was worried about the shed crashing on top of their heads. At least not too worried. The small building appeared to be solidly built. His bigger concern was being alone with Margaret again, this time in the dark and with both of them soaking wet.

"I'm surprised it's so dark in here," she said, crossing her arms over her small body.

It wasn't that dark. There just wasn't as much light as there usually was. Which was fine by him. He didn't need to be looking at her when her dress was clinging to her every curve. But if she was bothered by the dark, they could stand near the window, and he would just have to keep his eyes on something else. The last thing he needed was for her to catch him looking at her, because he knew she would be highly offended if she did. He had promised her she wouldn't have to worry about him making her feel uncomfortable, and that was a promise he would definitely keep.

"Do you want to move closer to the window?" he asked, untucking his shirt out of his pants so the cotton fabric would dry faster. "There's a little more light over there."

"Uh, sure."

She didn't sound so sure, but she walked to the window anyway. He kept his head down as he pulled his wet shirt away from his torso. Out of the corner of his eye he saw her shiver. "Are you cold?"

Margaret shook her head, then paused. "Maybe a little," she said. "But I'll be all right."

He moved as close to her as he dared, noticing for the first time that the window was almost too high for her. The sill was parallel with her chin. "Too bad there's not a blanket in here. I'd give you *mei* shirt but it's still wet—"

"I said I'm fine." The words shot out of her mouth and she moved farther away from him.

Owen took a step back. What had her all up in a spin? Then again, they were both wet and she was cold, so she had a right to be irritated. He looked out the window. The wind was so strong the trees' limbs were all leaning in one direction, and the rain was blowing sideways. "I had *nee* idea we were going to have a storm today."

"Me neither." Another boom of thunder followed by a bright flash of lightning made her jump. "Goodness," she said, sounding a little breathless. "This is a serious storm."

"*Ya*. It is." But he wasn't paying attention to the weather. He could see her profile in the faint light coming through the window as she stared straight ahead. Even the howling wind seemed to disappear as he looked at her. She was perfectly featured—her eyes, eyebrows, and nose symmetrical, her hair, even when wet, a warm shade of dark brown, and her mouth . . .

He looked away, pretending to be enthralled by the storm and not the woman standing next to him. Lord, he was in trouble. Lots of trouble.

"Are you okay?"

He couldn't resist her soft voice, and although he knew he shouldn't, he turned to her. "*Ya*," he said, his gaze meeting her eyes. "I'm okay." Far from it, but he wasn't going to let her know that.

"*Gut*," she said, her eyes locking with his. "It's a bad storm out there—wait, I already said that, didn't I?"

Unable to keep from smiling, he nodded. "You're right, it's bad." When he saw her shiver again, he said, "I'm going to check this place out more thoroughly. It's a long shot, but maybe there's something you can wrap around your shoulders." Plus, it was an opportunity to put some distance between them.

Without waiting for her to respond, he started searching around the shed, looking underneath the worktable first and then rifling through the cabinets on the other side of the room. This was the first time he'd done such a detailed search of the place, not wanting to disturb anything during his previous visits here since this wasn't his shed. But he wasn't concerned about that now. There wasn't much hope he would find anything other than dirt and sawdust, but he would pore over every square inch just to make sure. He didn't like the idea of her being cold. Even he was starting to get a little chilly.

Suddenly the door crashed open and a strong gust of wind blew into the shed. He ran and threw his weight against the door. The wind must have shifted direction. When he stepped back, the door started to bang against the frame. That would be torturous to listen to if they were stuck here for much longer. He went to the shelving unit and pushed on it. Good, it wasn't attached to the wall. He shoved it over in front of the door at the same time another gust kicked up. The door moved but the shelving unit kept it from batting back and forth against the frame.

Owen turned to Margaret and halted, not liking what he saw. She wasn't just shivering now, she was shaking. He slipped off his shirt and set it to the side, then went over and put his arms around her.

"Owen? What are you doing?"

What am I doing? If someone from his community walked in here and saw the two of them together like this, he would have some explaining to do, not that anyone would believe anything he said anyway. Being locked in an embrace with Margaret was the very definition of a compromising position. But that didn't matter right now. She did. "I'm warming you up," he said, tentatively putting his arms around her. "I had to take off my shirt because it's wet and cold. If that's not okay, I'll put it back on—"

"*Nee,*" she said quickly. A pause. Then she added, "It's okay."

He tightened his embrace around her until she rested her head against him, the top of her head touching the middle of his chest. He absorbed the cold of her dress and skin until she stopped shaking. "Are you warmer now?" he asked, thunder and wind whipping outside the window behind him.

"*Ya*," she said, nodding her head at the same time. "Very warm."

"Do you want me to let you *geh*?" He held his breath as he waited for her to answer him.

Margaret couldn't move, and she didn't want to. She'd never been so thoroughly held before. Not by her parents, and definitely not by Dylan or any of the other guys she'd gone out with. A minute ago, she had been shaking from the blast of cold wind that shot through the shed. Now she was toasty in Owen's arms, despite her wet clothing.

"Margaret? Did you hear me?"

His voice rumbled in his chest, and she smiled. She could stay here for the duration of the storm locked in Owen's arms—his strong arms—listening to his steady heartbeat as the wind and rain raged around them. She was tempted to close her eyes and pretend he hadn't said anything and continue to enjoy his warmth. But that wouldn't be right. First off, he was probably freezing, and secondly, she would be taking advantage of him. It was bad enough that she had paid attention to him when he untucked his shirt a little while ago, and thankfully, he didn't notice.

"*Ya*," she said, wriggling in his arms. But just because she was doing the right thing didn't mean she wanted to. "Please let me *geh*."

His arms fell to his sides, and then he turned and picked up his shirt. She stared out the window again, standing on her tiptoes. So much for the storm easing up quickly. Instead it seemed to gather more force. At least she wasn't cold anymore, thanks to Owen. But she was already missing his embrace. "*Danki* for warming me up."

He nodded, still keeping a respectable distance between them. "I didn't do much."

She squared her small shoulders and looked at him. "Just accept the thanks, all right?"

"Yes ma'am," he said.

Margaret faced the window again. There wasn't much else to do but wait, and she was never good at waiting. "How long do you think the storm will last?"

"No idea. Probably a cold front coming through. Spring and fall are when we have our strongest storms."

Spoken like a true farmer. Out of the corner of her eye she could see him buttoning his shirt. Thank goodness. She crossed her arms again. "I remember going fishing in a storm once," she said.

He moved closer to her until they were both standing in front of the window. "You? Fishing?"

"Yeah, me. I used to love to fish when I was a *kinn*."

"I didn't care for it as much as some of my *bruders*," he said. "Except for Zeke. He was afraid of the water."

"Are you?"

"Nah. I just like climbing trees and playing in the dirt more."

"And reading books."

He smiled. "And reading books." Another lightning strike, but she was used to it by now. "That went to the wayside as I got more involved with the farm," he added.

"I wasn't allowed to play in the dirt. *Mamm* didn't like us getting soiled."

"But she didn't mind you fishing?"

"As long as I stayed clean, she was okay with it. Until I was twelve or so, and I got stuck in a storm when I was fishing by myself. I came home covered in mud, and that was the last time I went fishing." *That* Mamm *knew of.* She'd fished a couple more times before giving up on it completely.

She looked out the window again. Whoever had the idea of placing the window so high wasn't all that smart. Or he was tall and didn't think about it, which was a more likely answer.

"Forgive me for saying so, but your *mamm* sounds hard to get along with."

Inexplicably, Owen's statement made her feel a little protective. "She likes to have things a certain way," Margaret said.

"Which is different from your way." He wiped a strip of dirt and sawdust off the white windowsill with his finger, then rubbed it on his pants, which were still wet, but at least water wasn't dripping from the dark-blue fabric anymore. "I guess the challenge is figuring out how you can both compromise."

She shook her head, any remnants of protectiveness disappearing. "There's *nee* compromising. I don't know how to talk to her," she said. "She doesn't understand me, and I've never understood her."

They didn't say anything for a few minutes, just watched the storm continue to surge.

"I'm sorry," Owen finally said. "I shouldn't have told you what you and your *mamm* need to do. It's not like I'm an expert on relationships."

He sure seemed to be, despite his self-doubt. "It's okay," she said, turning to him. "You're right, though. We need to figure out how to get along or else we never will." She let out a bitter laugh. "Finding a husband would do the trick." Uh-oh. There she went again, speaking the first thought that came to mind. Time to yank that idea right back into her head. She stared out the window again, annoyed that she kept putting her foot in her mouth. "I, uh, mean—"

Crack!

"Margaret, look out!"

Before she could take another breath, she saw a tree falling toward her. Owen grabbed her and put his body over hers. The tree crashed through the window.

Margaret's cheek slammed against the shed floor as Owen fell on top of her. Glass flew all around them.

"Margaret!" His mouth was near her ear. "Are you—"

The tree shifted and a limb slammed him in the head. He slumped on top of her.

"Owen!" With all her strength she heaved him onto his back. His eyes were closed, and blood trickled from the side of his temple. *Oh no, oh no, oh no.*

His eyes fluttered open. "Margaret?" he murmured.

Thank God he wasn't passed out and he still knew who she was. She pushed back a thin limb from her shoulder.

"Hey. You're bleeding." His eyes closed again.

She cupped his face in her hands. "Don't you fall asleep on

me, Owen Bontrager." When he didn't respond, she said, "Where am I bleeding?"

His eyes opened halfway. "Here." He touched her cheek, the one she had scraped against the plywood floor.

"Well, you're bleeding too. Can you sit up?" She had no idea if he should be sitting up or not, but it was better than lying on the floor with so much glass around.

"I think so."

She let go of his face and helped him to a seated position.

"The storm's stopped."

Margaret looked outside the window, at least what she could see around the tree that was lying next to them. Indeed, the rain and wind had stopped, as if the tree falling down had flipped a nature switch. At least they had that going for them. Now they could walk home and get their wounds looked at. She turned to Owen. His eyes were closed again. "Do you think you can stand?"

He shook his head, then fell against her.

"Owen? Owen!"

He didn't move.

Panic filled her. He was truly passed out now. She looked at him, and this close up she could see the glass and bark from the tree embedded in the cut in his scalp. There was also a large lump forming around it and blood continued to run down the side of his head and face. She had to stop the bleeding. She looked at her dress, but with him leaning against her, she didn't have both hands free to rip the fabric.

Then she thought about her *kapp*. That would have to do. With one hand she pulled out the clips holding her *kapp* to her hair and tossed them to the ground, then pulled off her head covering.

Somehow, she managed to place the *kapp* on his wound and wind the strings around his head as tightly as she dared. She waited to see if blood seeped through the makeshift bandage and was relieved when it didn't.

He moaned and shifted against her.

"Owen?" When he didn't answer, she turned on her chatterbox. She didn't know for sure, but if she talked enough, maybe he would wake up. "I'm so glad it stopped raining. The nerve of the sun coming out after all this. Boy, whoever owns this place is going to have a mess to clean up. Does your head hurt?"

"*Ya,*" he croaked out. "*Yer* chattering's not helping."

"You need a doctor," she said, ignoring his words.

"*Gut* idea. I'll call one right now."

"Very funny." But she could see he was out again. If he couldn't stay awake long enough to have a conversation, he couldn't walk back to his house, which was closer than the Yoders' was. She glanced at his head again. Several dots of blood had appeared on her *kapp*. Lord, what am I supposed to do? She closed her eyes and started to pray.

When Margaret opened her eyes, it was almost dark in the shed and Owen was resting his head in her lap. She put her palm in front of his nose and mouth and felt his exhaled breath. "Oh, thank God," she said. But how could she have fallen asleep? Her mind started to clear, and she remembered Owen groaning in pain. Her arm had already fallen asleep, and to ease their discomfort she had helped him lie down the best she could. She also remembered being tired as she prayed and tried to figure out what to do. Now that she was clearheaded, there was only one thing they could do.

"Owen?" she said.

"*Ya?*"

His voice was weak, but at least he was speaking. Thank you, Lord. "We can't stay here all night. We have to *geh* to the hospital." They would have to walk a good distance to get out of the woods, and once they made it to the main road, she would stop at the first house she saw. She was sure whoever lived there would let her use their phone. Better yet, she would ask them to call 911 for her. "Let's get you up and on your feet." She helped him sit up. "How's that?"

"I think I'm going to throw up." Then he held up his hand. "Wait. I'm okay now. I must have a concussion."

"How do you know?"

"The nausea. Nelson got walloped upside the head with a baseball bat during a game a few years ago." He flinched, and she wasn't sure if it was in sympathy for his brother or if he was still in that much pain. "One of his teammates was taking a practice swing and didn't see Nelson behind him. *Mei bruder* passed out, and when he woke up, he vomited on the way to the doctor's office." He flinched again and looked at her. "Sorry for that detail."

"That's all right." It was a good detail to know. "Do you remember anything else about his concussion?"

"He said it was like seeing stars, but I don't remember having that same sensation when I got knocked in the head. I think as soon as it happened, I lost consciousness."

"You did. But you've had some time to rest and you're awake now." She didn't want to push him, but they had to leave. "How are you feeling now?" she asked.

"Pretty sure I can stand up."

She would take it. "How can I help?"

"I need something to lean on."

Margaret moved closer to him just as the last speck of daylight disappeared. Great, now she couldn't see.

"Where . . . are your shoulders?" he asked, sounding weaker than he had a second before.

"Here." She reached out and felt his arm, then tucked herself underneath it.

"Maybe this isn't a *gut* idea." But as he spoke, he leaned against her. "I don't feel too steady. I don't want both of us falling down."

"That's not going to happen," she said firmly. "I won't let it. I'm small, but I'm mighty when I need to be."

"I believe you."

Margaret held on to his waist. "On the count of three. Ready?"

"*Ya*." His voice was faint, but he tightened his arm around her shoulders.

"One, two, three." They both stood at the same time, and Owen almost fell against her. She staggered a few steps, but they both remained upright.

"Margaret? You okay?"

"I'm the one who should be asking you that."

"Well, I still haven't tossed my cookies, so that's a *gut* sign." But he was literally using her as a crutch, and she knew if they lingered here any longer, they would never be able to leave. It was going to be a long walk in the dark, but they would walk at Owen's pace. Anything was better than getting stuck in the shed. *We'll make it, Owen. I promise you that.*

Chapter 11

Lester flipped on the switch in the middle of his flashlight as he stood in front of the woods. Bright light illuminated the trees in front of him. Here I go *again*. After his last trip to these woods, he was sure he would never return. But since overhearing Loren and Delilah's conversation earlier that day, he'd been on edge. It didn't help that a violent storm had come out of nowhere, extending his workday at the inn while he waited for the torrent of rain to pass.

Fixing the leak in Room 4 had been an easy job, and when he finished, he went downstairs to the lobby. He opened the front door and stood on the porch. Katharine wasn't there, of course. He was sure she had abandoned trimming the front bushes. As the rain fell in sheets in front of him, he could still see that she had done an excellent job with the few bushes she had finished. Maybe he would ask her to help him in the future. But right now he was stuck at the inn. His thirdhand car barely ran on a good day, and the nearly bald tires didn't fare well on slick roads. If he tried to drive right now, he had a more than slim chance of getting into some kind of accident. That was something he couldn't afford, for a number of reasons.

Finally, the storm relented, and he clocked out for the night and headed home. But instead of going to his house, he had driven over here. He still wasn't sure why he'd come. It wasn't like anything had changed since his last visit. There wasn't a surge of courage compelling him to face his past. But something made him drive to the woods, and he had no idea what it was.

Water drops pelted him as he moved forward. The rain had stopped, but the storm left behind a wisp of a breeze, enough to make the leaves flutter and shake off the residual rainwater. Despite the tension humming through him, he started to relax slightly. The woods had always been his refuge—that was one thing that hadn't changed. Perhaps his mind instinctively knew that coming here would help him, even if it was only for a short while. Anything was preferable to sitting in his small rental house and eating another bland-tasting TV dinner.

As he approached the cabin, he heard a loud rustling sound. He froze, listened again, then aimed his flashlight in the direction of the sound. All he saw were trees, bushes, logs, and limbs. When he didn't see anything, he headed deeper into the dense woods. Must have been a deer. These woods weren't the best for hunting, but every few seasons or so the deer would return.

He continued walking, unsure what he would do once he reached the shed. Could he force himself to go inside? The tension returned as he battled the thought in his mind. What would it accomplish anyway? More importantly, though, why couldn't he bring himself to do so?

He continued to waffle back and forth until the light from

his flashlight landed on a toppled tree. He froze. The tree had fallen on top of the shed and caved in one side, the side with the window. There was no doubt what caused the tree to plummet. He scowled. This was twice that a storm had taken out the shed. His decision to go inside had been made for him, and he should be happy about that. But for some reason, he wasn't.

"Help!"

The faint, desperate sound of a woman's voice reached his ears. He hurried to the shed and nearly gasped at what he saw. On the other side of the tree, a young man squinted at him as he pulled a small female closer to his body. Then Lester saw the bloody bandage on his head. Wait, that wasn't a bandage. The girl had used her prayer *kapp* to staunch the wound. Pretty ingenious. Then the full shock of what he was seeing hit him.

"Can you help us?" The girl squeaked.

Before he could answer, the young man's legs buckled. To her credit, the girl tried to keep him upright, but a second later both of them dropped to the ground.

Springing into action, Lester hurried to them. "Tell me what happened," he said, shining his light in the man's eyes. His pupils were okay, but he was pale.

"The tree fell on us." The rest of the details spilled out of the girl, and Lester fought not only to catch all of them but also to make sense of what she was saying. "We were looking for butternuts and then the storm happened and then the tree fell through the window and then it hit Owen and then he passed out. He's bleeding and he needs to see a doctor." Fear entered her eyes. "I'm sorry we trespassed, but he needs to go to the hospital."

Lester couldn't argue. The young man's head lolled forward until his chin touched his chest. "Is he unconscious?" Lester asked.

"Almost," Owen murmured before the girl could respond. "Seeing spots before my eyes."

That wasn't a good sign. "I'll take him to the hospital."

"I'm going too," she said.

"Well, I wouldn't leave you here alone in the dark. You should probably get your face looked at too." He'd been so focused on Owen's injury that he hadn't noticed she had a big scrape on her cheek. "But you're gonna have to move so I can help him. You can hold the flashlight and light our way."

She nodded and slipped out from underneath Owen's arm. Lester eased the kid up to his feet, hearing him inhale sharply in pain.

"Concussion," Owen said, sounding more alert now than he had been a second ago.

"Sure looks like it." It also looked like the kid had a bleeding cut under the makeshift bandage. The gash needed to be cleaned out, and he might have to get some stitches. Lester didn't envy him that experience.

The three of them made their way out of the destroyed shed, and Owen leaned against Lester while the girl led the way to his car. She jumped in the back seat with Owen as Lester sat behind the wheel and started the engine.

"How far is the hospital?" she asked.

"Twenty minutes, but I can make it in fifteen." He peeled out and headed in the direction of the Geauga Hospital.

"You're going to be okay, Owen," the girl said softly.

Lester glanced at them in the back seat. Owen was leaning against her, his eyes closed. Poor kid. He was going to be okay, but concussions and split skin brought along a world of hurt. Lester had knocked his noggin a time or two, and the headaches that ensued were brutal.

"What's your name, young lady?" he asked, not taking his eyes off the road as he sped to the hospital.

"Margaret."

"Well, Margaret, Owen's going to be fine."

"Thank you," she said in a small, but relieved voice. Which made him think he was right to encourage her. He didn't know the relationship between these two people—his first guess was that they were boyfriend and girlfriend, considering they were alone together in the shed—but either way, he could see she cared about him.

When he pulled up to the emergency room entrance at the hospital, he yanked the gearshift into park and turned to face the two young people. "Run inside and tell them what happened. I'll stay with Owen."

She nodded and checked on Owen again, who was now sitting more upright. Then she dashed out of the car.

The kid looked at him. "Who are you?" he asked, his voice sounding shaky.

Lester froze for a moment, then said, "A good Samaritan." He started to turn around and wait for the girl when he glanced out the passenger window and spied a wheelchair. "I'll be right back," he said, flinging open the door. He dashed to the wheelchair, which had Geauga Hospital stamped on it, grabbed the handles, and wheeled it over to the back seat of his car. He flung open the door. "Can you scoot over to the edge of the seat?" he asked. "Then I can help you into the chair."

Owen complied, and with Lester's assistance he was seated. Lester gripped the handles of the chair again and then pushed Owen to the front of the hospital. He paused at the door. He couldn't go inside. Although he doubted anyone would recognize him here, he couldn't take the risk. "Sorry, kid," he said, leaving Owen at the door. "Your friend will be back out in a minute." Awkwardly he patted Owen's slim shoulder, then dashed back to his car, jumped inside, and drove away.

As he headed back to Birch Creek, he did something he hadn't done in years. He prayed—not for himself but for the two young people. If he was a better man, he would have stayed with them, maybe kept the young lady company while she was in the waiting room. *But I'm not a good man.* He couldn't even pretend to be.

Margaret carefully cleaned the scrape on her face in the emergency room bathroom. She had refused the receptionist's offer for a doctor to see her. Her injury wasn't that serious. Her skin stung and the scraped skin looked bad, but now that she washed it off with soap and water, she was fine. Owen was the one she was worried about.

She went back to the ER waiting room, sat down in a chair, and waited. Her legs swung back and forth as her toes grazed the worn laminate floor. Now that she had a few minutes to think, she tried to process what had happened. The chances of a stranger showing up in the woods just when she and Owen needed help . . . that was a miracle. No one would convince her otherwise that God hadn't provided the man for them. She still didn't know his name, and she didn't understand why he had left Owen alone outside the hospital. When she came back with a nurse to get him, she saw him slumped in a chair. The car and the mysterious driver had disappeared.

She glanced at the clock, forgot about the stranger, and started to worry about Owen again. When the nurse had taken him back to the treatment area, she told Margaret that she could see him once the doctor said it was okay. After filling out an information form the best she could, she had asked if she could use the phone and called *Aenti* Mary. As she'd guessed, her aunt had been worried, and when Margaret explained what happened to Owen, she was horrified. "We will be there as soon as we can," she said. "I'll call Miriam right now."

She had no idea where this hospital was in comparison to her aunt's house, but she had been waiting half an hour already. Surely they had stabilized Owen by now. Unable to wait any longer, she went to the front window. "Can I see Owen?" she asked.

The silver-haired woman behind the counter looked at her through her brown-framed glasses. "His full name?"

"Owen Bontrager."

She clicked her computer mouse twice. "I'll go see how he's doing." Then she turned to Margaret. "Don't worry, honey, your boyfriend will be okay."

"Oh, he's not my . . . boyfriend." But the woman had already left.

Sighing, she stood there and waited again. At least the waiting room was empty, and she hoped that meant the doctor had already seen Owen and had taken care of his wound. Margaret decided right then and there she was going to dedicate more time to studying herbal medicine and first aid in general. She hoped she'd never go through something like this again, but if she did, she wanted to be prepared.

The woman returned. "You can go back in a few minutes. I'll call you up when it's time."

"Thank you." She turned and sat back down. Then she froze, finally remembering what had happened when the tree crashed through the window. He shielded her from it and had been willing to take the brunt of the impact if the tree had hit him. She'd been so focused on his injury and figuring out how to get out of the woods in the dark, she forgot what he'd done. *He saved me.* She shivered, then closed her eyes and prayed for the third time since their arrival. *Please, Lord, let him be okay.*

"Margaret?"

She opened her eyes and the receptionist motioned for her to go to a large wooden door to the right of her desk. Margaret stood and walked over, and when she heard the clicking sound of the receptionist unlocking the door, she opened it. A nurse appeared, her black hair pulled up in a fluffy bun with a colorful scarf wrapped around her head. She smiled, her plum lipstick complementing her dark skin. "Hi, I'm Bridget. I've been helping Dr. Caldwell take care of Mr. Bontrager. We x-rayed his skull and there isn't a fracture, just a serious concussion and a deep cut that the doctor will stitch up soon." She pointed to the hallway stretching out in front of them. "He's in Room 6 at the end of the hall and to the left. Don't worry, sweetie. Your brother is going to be okay."

Margaret opened her mouth to explain that Owen wasn't her brother, but she changed her mind. It didn't matter what the nurse or the receptionist thought. All Margaret cared about was seeing Owen. "Thank you," she said. Then she hurried down the hall to his room. His door was closed, and she gently knocked on it. "Owen?" she said, opening the door slightly. "Is it okay to come in?"

"*Ya.*"

She pushed on the heavy door and walked inside. He was lying on his back, a gauze bandage on his head, his eyes closed. For some reason tears formed in her eyes, and she wiped them away. Why was she crying? He was going to be all right, and she was all right. But she couldn't stop thinking that he wouldn't be hurt if he hadn't put himself in danger to save her.

"You can come closer," he said, sounding a little groggy. "I'm not going to bite."

She couldn't even laugh at his lame joke. Clasping her hands in front of her, she walked over to the side of his bed.

"That's better." He looked up at her through those amazing eyelashes of his, but his eyes weren't open all the way. He smiled. "They gave me some pain medicine. That stuff works great."

Relieved that he wasn't hurting as much, she smiled back.

"Guess I owe you a *kapp*." His eyes opened a little wider. "Clever *maedel*."

"Don't worry about that. I have another one."

To her surprise, he motioned for her to come closer. When

she did, he reached for the bottom of her braid, which was lying over her shoulder. She had yanked her *kapp* off so fast it pulled on her hair and loosened her braid. "So beautiful," he whispered, rubbing the lock between his fingers.

She stilled, knowing she should pull away from him. She'd never been on painkillers before, but from the glazed look in his eyes and the trauma he'd just gone through, she could tell he wasn't himself. But she wasn't 100 percent herself either right now, and being this close to Owen as he gently stroked her hair sparked something inside of her that she'd never felt for any other man. No man was as kind, smart, and brave as Owen Bontrager. She was sure of that. And more than anything right now, she wanted to show him how much she cared about him.

But that didn't mean she could take advantage of the situation. Owen was also forthright and honest. *And here I am enjoying his touch when he doesn't know what he's doing.* "Do you need anything?" she asked, trying to ignore her emotions. Better to focus on being a nursemaid than something else.

He glanced up at her, his hand lowering to her waist and resting lightly there. "*Nee.* I don't need anything else. Just you."

Drugs or not, the way he was looking at her and the yearning in his voice evaporated what little resolve she had left, and she moved closer to him. "Owen . . ." Unable to stop herself, she leaned over and kissed him. She only intended a light peck, simply to show her appreciation.

To her shock, he kissed her back, curling his arm around her waist and drawing her even closer to him. She dropped her pretense and responded to the most tender kiss she'd ever experienced.

"Excuse me," a male voice said from behind her.

Margaret jumped back from Owen, who still had his hand on her waist. His arm dropped to the side and he groaned in pain. "Sorry," she squeaked, taking a step back. She bumped into the monitor behind her. "Sorry," she said to the machine. Then she looked at the tall man in a white lab coat in front of her. "Sorry to you too." The person she really needed to apologize to was Owen, but she was too mortified to look at him again. "I'll go to the waiting room."

"Wait," Owen said weakly.

But she ignored him, something she should have done a few minutes ago. She couldn't help but touch her mouth as she hurried down the hallway, her cheeks aflame. Stopping a man in blue scrubs, she asked, "Where's the exit?"

"To the waiting room? It's right here." He pointed to the door a whole inch to her right, the only one on that side of the hallway. She nodded her thanks and burst through into the room. *Aenti* Mary, *Onkel* Freemont, Thomas, and Miriam were all seated near the door. They all looked at her at the same time.

"Oh, thank goodness you're all right." Her aunt rushed over to her and gave her a big hug. When she let go, Miriam caught Margaret up in another hug.

"How's Owen?" Miriam said, worry in her eyes as Thomas and Freemont talked to the receptionist at the counter.

"He's okay." *And a good kisser.* Good grief, she was a lost cause. Gathering her wits, she said, "He's getting stitches."

Thomas appeared next to his wife. "They said we can *geh* see him, Miriam." She looked at Margaret and *Aenti* Mary. Then the two of them went to Owen's room.

Once they were gone, *Aenti* Mary turned to her, *Onkel* Freemont now at her side. Mary searched her face. "Did the doctor take a look at this?" she said, gesturing to the scrape on Margaret's cheek.

She shook her head. "It's not that bad. I took care of it."

But Mary didn't look convinced. "I can't believe the doctor didn't look at you. What if something else is wrong?"

"*Aenti*, I'm fine. I promise." She wasn't, though. Not after kissing Owen. She kicked herself for appreciating his kiss when she had clearly taken advantage of him. If he hadn't been out of it, she was sure he would have thought she was crazy. He probably would have been right. She certainly felt a little like she had lost her mind right now. *And possibly* mei *heart.*

Onkel Freemont put his hand on his wife's shoulder. "She's okay, Mary." Then he turned to Margaret, his expression implacable. "We need you to tell us everything that happened. And I mean everything."

She nodded, prepared to tell him about everything—the shed, the tree falling through the window, Owen protecting her, the stranger who brought them here. She would reveal all, except for one thing. She would never, ever tell anyone about her amazing kiss with Owen.

"The nurse said you were brother and sister." The doctor smirked as he pulled over a stool next to a tall silver table on wheels laden with a full syringe, various medical tools, and a packet of what Owen assumed was thread.

Owen turned his head to the side so the doctor could access the wound. He'd had stitches before, but not on his scalp. When the nurse first offered to ask the doctor for pain medication, he'd refused, despite the pounding in his head and the soreness from her cleaning the glass and dirt out of the cut. He figured he could handle the numbing shot the doc would give him before he started stitching. But after a stern look from the nurse, he relented. Now he was glad he did, because the idea of anyone stitching on his head made him nauseated again. "We're not brother and sister," he said firmly.

"That's obvious."

Owen could see the doctor out of the corner of his eye, and the smirk was gone from the man's face. Now he was all business. He picked up the syringe. "I'll give you some numbing medicine, although you probably won't feel the pinch of the needle. That painkiller we gave you should be kicking in right now."

He didn't bother to tell him that it already had. True to the doctor's word, he never felt the needle. Instead he closed his eyes, his mind filled with Margaret, the feel of her soft hair, the loveliness of her face, and of course that incredible kiss. His brain might be fuzzy from the drugs, but they hadn't started really messing with him until a minute or so ago. He'd been completely lucid when Margaret came into the room. When he touched her hair. When he put his hand on her tiny waist. *When I kissed her back*.

Guilt cut through the fog, and he felt like a jerk. He'd clearly seen the worry in her eyes, but he couldn't resist her when she was so close to him. Her chestnut hair had felt as soft as it looked, and he thought for a split second that getting slammed in the head by a tree limb had been worth it. Then there was the kiss. He couldn't figure out if he had started it or she had, but the memory of it was crystal clear.

"Mr. Bontrager?"

"Mm-hmm," he murmured.

"I can't tell if you're moaning or groaning. Do you need more pain medication? I can get you some if you're still hurting."

His eyes flew open. "I'm fine." He wasn't, though. Not by any stretch. Even in his dazed state he knew he would have to talk to Margaret about what had happened and admit that despite being aware she had zero feelings for him, he had knowingly kissed her. The more he thought about it, the more he realized that he must have been the one to kiss her first and she'd only kissed him back because he was injured.

As his brain grew fuzzier, he tried harder to concentrate. Their conversation would have to happen some other time. Right now, he just wanted to get out of here and go home.

The door opened and a nurse poked her head inside the room. "Mr. Bontrager's parents are here," she said to the doctor. "Can they come in?"

"Sure," the doctor replied. "We're almost finished here."

Suddenly *Mamm* appeared next to him, making sure she was out of the doctor's way. "How are you, Owen?"

Owen glanced up at his mother. She was stoic, as he expected her to be in front of strangers, but he could tell she was worried. Wanting to put her at ease, he mumbled, "I'm fine. Can't feel a thing."

"He's on pain medication," the doctor said.

Feeling a tug on his scalp but no pain, Owen mumbled, "It's good stuff."

He heard his father chuckle from behind. "This isn't exactly what we expected when we told you to take a vacation."

"Uh-huh." His eyes closed, sleepiness overcame him.

"All done," the doctor said.

But Owen was nearly out. Had he really kissed Margaret, or did he imagine it? Wait, he thought she had kissed him. Had she? Now he wasn't so sure. He wouldn't do anything as foolish as kiss her. And even if he did, she wouldn't kiss him back.

Or would she?

After Margaret finished telling her aunt and uncle about what happened during the storm, she blew out a relieved breath. There. Everything was out in the open now. Almost everything. Even though it hadn't been easy to admit that she and Owen were trespassing on someone else's property—and not just one time—she was glad she told them. Owen's father said he thought the property wasn't owned by anyone, but someone had put the shed there. And since she and Owen hadn't, they didn't have the right to use it. She could see that clearly now. "We knew we shouldn't have been there," she added.

"You're right." Her uncle frowned. "Why did you keep going back?"

"It was an easy place to meet." She crossed her ankles, trying to still her swinging legs. "The shed made a *gut* landmark. I'm sorry, *Onkel* and *Aenti*. I really am."

"The important thing is that you're both okay," *Aenti* Mary said. "In hindsight, it's *gut* you had shelter. I was so worried about you and Owen when that storm came up. We had a few large limbs fall down around our house. We haven't had that strong of a storm all season long."

"Do you remember the name of the road by the woods?" *Onkel* Freemont asked.

"Baxter," she said.

Her aunt and uncle exchanged a glance, but she couldn't tell what they were thinking.

"Do you know who owns it?" Margaret asked.

His lips thinned. "Possibly." Then his expression relaxed. "It's okay," *Onkel* Freemont said. "You both did the right thing. It could have been worse for you if you had tried to walk home in the storm. The lightning was intense."

At least she had done something right.

The door that led to the waiting room opened and Thomas and Miriam walked in. "We're meeting Owen at the other exit," Thomas explained as they approached. "They have to wheel him out when they discharge him. *Gut* thing because that pain medicine is doing a number on him."

Her conscience pricked her again, and she stared at her hands, unable to face Owen's parents. She said a silent little prayer of hope that he didn't tell them about the kiss. Normally she wouldn't expect him to speak about something so personal, but who knew what he would say while under the influence. She listened as the four of them talked about the separate taxis they'd taken and how they would talk more tomorrow.

"Give Owen our best," *Onkel* Freemont said.

Thomas nodded. "Will do." A pause. "Margaret?"

She looked up at him.

"*Danki* for being there for *mei sohn*. I don't know what would have happened if you weren't."

Miriam nodded, her eyes watery. Then the two of them hurried out the door to talk to their taxi driver.

Margaret was grateful that they hadn't stated the obvious—if they hadn't been where they weren't supposed to be, Owen wouldn't have been injured at all.

Her uncle stood, pushing up his glasses. Her aunt had told Margaret he'd just gotten them three months ago. "Let's get out of here."

"You must be hungry," *Aenti* Mary said as they headed for the emergency room exit. "I can fix you something to eat when we get home."

But food was far from Margaret's mind right now, and she didn't anticipate her appetite improving on the ride home.

She followed her aunt and uncle outside. When she saw another pair of headlights in front of the emergency room, she turned, stunned to see Owen being brought out in a wheelchair at the same time they were leaving. Talk about bad timing. Or good timing, considering she could see he was all right.

Then he turned his head and looked at her. They were a good distance away and it was impossible to see his expression even under the bright lights of the parking lot. Still, she couldn't just leave without acknowledging him, especially after he'd sacrificed himself to keep her safe. But when she waved at him, he looked away without waving back. Then his father helped him into the taxi.

That bruised her ego a bit. *Nee*, it's not *mei* ego that's hurt. She tried to tell herself not to take his rebuff so personally. He was in pain, on medication, and probably dealing with some shock from the concussion.

Or he was realizing that she had taken advantage of him, and he was angry? If he was, she wouldn't blame him. She would be upset if someone had kissed her when she was vulnerable. She had no right to do what she'd done. Not to such a great guy like Owen. Or to any guy, for that matter. Other than Nina and her cousins, he was the only friend she had in Birch Creek, and she had ruined everything between them because she couldn't control her emotions. She was exactly what her mother said she was— thoughtless, impulsive, and unable to follow rules and guidelines. She and Owen had set the parameters of their friendship, and she had trampled all over them tonight.

Whatever was left of her and Owen's relationship now, she didn't know. The only thing she was sure of was that it would never be the same. And she only had herself to blame.

Chapter 12

Lester pulled his car off the interstate and drove to the gas station near the exit. He got out of his car, his knees and back stiff. Once he dropped those Amish kids off at the ER the other night, he drove back home, packed his bags, and took off.

Now he was near Georgia, and he not only needed gas and food but he also needed to rest. His car was riding on fumes, but as soon as he filled up his tank, he would find a cheap motel nearby and sack out for the rest of the day, and hopefully the night too.

He leaned against his car as the gas pump emptied into the tank and he shoved his hands through his thinning hair. Guilt, a feeling he had ignored during his youth but was more than acquainted with in his older years, slammed into him. He shouldn't have just dropped those kids off at the hospital and ran. He didn't recognize them, so obviously they hadn't been to Stoll's Inn while he was there. And speaking of the inn, he'd up and quit without even giving Loren a call that he was leaving. So not only had he abandoned a bleeding kid and his companion, he'd also left the Stolls, who had been nothing but good to him, without a handyman. But even with the guilt and the knowledge that he was in the wrong, he hadn't hesitated to leave Birch Creek. Clearly, he wasn't ready to face his past. He wasn't sure he ever would be.

But abandoning Owen and Margaret wasn't the only reason he was fleeing. It wasn't even the main one. The conversation he'd overheard between Loren and Delilah still nagged at him. It was a fact that he was afraid of owning up to what he had done years ago, but there was a slight ray of hope he had held on to all these years. *She would be loyal.* Now he doubted even that, the one sure thing he'd always clung to. But did he have a right to demand her loyalty? Or to even want it?

The pump abruptly stopped, and Lester flinched. He was a bundle of nerves, and he wouldn't fully settle down anytime soon. Although he hadn't eaten all day, the idea of food made his stomach turn sour, so instead of getting a bite to eat at the convenience store he hopped into his car and sped out of the parking lot. He'd find a motel room later. Right now, he needed to put as many miles between himself and Birch Creek as he could. Then he might be able to take an easy breath. But that wasn't going to happen until he was much farther away.

"You have all the interesting adventures." Nina picked up a carrot from the plate in front of them and cut off the soft, fuzzy green top.

Margaret scowled. "I'll take less adventure from now on," she said, slicing the carrot on the cutting board in front of her into neat coin-shaped pieces. She had arrived at Nina's an hour ago, and she and her friend were cutting the carrots Ira brought home from the Yoders' farm the day before. Once they were all prepped, they would be canned and put up for the winter.

Two days had passed since Owen was hit by the tree. Her aunt and uncle hadn't brought up the incident again, and her renewed fear that he might make them confess in front of the church had been eased. Her aunt had said that *Onkel* Freemont was reasonable, and she was finding that out firsthand. There was still a chance *Aenti* Carolyn might mention it to *Mamm*, but Margaret was starting to doubt that. She had more than one reason to be grateful—her aunt and uncle weren't angry with her, they had given them mercy regarding the trespassing, and she and Owen were okay. At least she was physically. She wasn't sure about Owen since she had avoided seeing him since that night at the hospital.

She whacked an extra thick carrot with her knife. She was finding out a lot about herself during her time in Birch Creek, and one of those things was that she was a coward. She told herself she was too embarrassed to face his parents since they had been caught alone together in the woods and she didn't want them to think lowly of her. Then again, if they knew her past, their bad impression of her would be warranted.

That almost made her feel worse than she did about kissing him at the hospital. He had to still be upset with her. He wasn't the kind of guy who kissed girls just for fun, she was sure of that. Then again, she was assuming the kiss was as big a deal for him as it was for her. Ach, she was so confused. But either way, she'd find the courage to face him eventually and to apologize.

Nina took a peeler and scraped it against the side of the carrot. If she had any idea of Margaret's inner battle, she didn't let on.

"Don't get me wrong, I'm so grateful you and Owen are okay. Having a tree nearly fall on you—that had to be scary."

"*Ya*, it was." She had said many prayers of thanks over the past two days that she and Owen escaped serious injury, thanks to his quick thinking.

"I still can't believe that property belonged to Emmanuel Troyer."

Margaret nodded. Yesterday *Onkel* Freemont had announced that the land was deeded to Emmanuel, to everyone's surprise except for her aunt and uncle. She assumed Ira told Nina about it. "Did you know him?"

Nina shook her head. "Ira told me about him. He also told me Seth was the one who rebuilt the shed. He found it a few years ago and kept returning to it to see if anyone had come back to it. When no one did, he decided to rebuild the shed and make it into a wood-carving workshop. Last year they abandoned it and made a workshop at their house instead. It was more convenient that way."

That all made sense. Seth and Martha created beautiful wood-carvings as a side business and sold them at Ivy's shop. Margaret had seen them at the store on her last visit to Birch Creek. That the shed had been used as a woodshop explained the sawdust that covered everything.

Owen and I weren't the only trespassers. She certainly wasn't going to point that out to her aunt and uncle. But she felt a little better knowing her cousin had done something similar, even going as far as rebuilding the shed. He did a good job, Margaret had to admit, and it was a shame it had been destroyed again.

"Ira doesn't talk about Emmanuel much. In fact, no one

around here does." Nina handed her the peeled carrot. "I've seen everyone go quiet in the room when his name is mentioned."

She wasn't surprised to hear that, remembering her aunt's refusal to talk about him, too, along with her uncle saying nothing else after he'd told them Emmanuel owned the property. "Does anyone know where he is?"

She shook her head. "Not a clue. From what I understand, the only person who wants him back is Rhoda." Nina paused, and when she continued not to say anything, Margaret looked at her, then grew concerned at her sudden gray pallor. Before she could say anything, Nina shot up from the table and ran off.

Margaret started to go after her, then stayed in her seat. Morning sickness. That had to be it. She went to the kitchen sink and filled up a glass of water, then set it on the table where Nina had been sitting. The water would be ready for her friend when she needed it. Then she went back to slicing carrots.

As usual when she was alone, her mind strayed back to Owen. Was he still hurting? She hoped not. She had read up about herbs that helped with wound pain and found a recipe for a salve that involved ingredients *Aenti* Mary already had—ginger, cayenne pepper, turmeric, beeswax, and olive oil. She made a small jar of it last night and this morning she asked her aunt to take it with her the next time she visited the Bontragers.

"Why don't you *geh*?" *Aenti* Mary had asked while she and Margaret washed the breakfast dishes.

"I have plans to see Nina today." Margaret kept her head down as she dried a coffee mug.

"The Bontragers don't live that far from Ira and Nina. You could drop it off on your way home."

Margaret stilled, the dish towel she was using still inside the cup. There was no point in discussing the subject further because she knew if she did, her aunt would ask why she was reticent about seeing Owen. And that was a conversation she didn't want to have.

Nina walked back into the room, looking pale but at least she wasn't the color of concrete anymore. She plopped down on the chair. "Remember when I said I didn't have morning sickness? I now have morning sickness."

"When did it start?"

"Yesterday." She put her hand over her stomach. "Right as I was fixing Ira some bacon and eggs before he left for work." Her lips twisted. "I shouldn't think about that right now."

"So, you told him the news after you left my aunt's last week," Margaret said, smiling. "How did he react?"

"Well, I didn't tell him right away. He fell asleep on the way home and I had to take the reins from him. When we got back to the house he went straight to bed. He was still so exhausted I didn't want to keep him from having a good night's sleep."

"I'm sure he wouldn't have minded."

"Maybe not, but I was tired too. But I did tell him the next morning." She smiled, as if she were savoring the memory. "He's apprehensive, like I am. But he's also excited too."

"Are you feeling all right other than the morning sickness?"

"*Ya.* I feel different this time. I don't know if I'm being optimistic, or if things really are different with this *boppli.*"

"I'll pray that they will be." She was glad that Nina and Ira had talked to each other. She also had to hand it to her cousin—he hadn't given a single hint about Nina's pregnancy. She would follow suit.

For the next hour they prepped the carrots, but when Nina had to race to the bathroom three times, Margaret told her to lie on the couch. "I'll finish up here," she said. "The lids and jars are already sanitized."

"*Danki*." Nina's expression was both weary and grateful, and the fact that she didn't argue with Margaret made it clear she needed rest, and probably a few saltines and water to settle her stomach.

For the next several hours Margaret focused on the carrots. When she was finished and the jars were sitting on a large cutting board, and the kitchen was cleaned up, she checked on Nina, who was still sleeping. She thought about waking her up, then decided against it. She went back into the kitchen and found a pencil and a notepad.

Nina,
   The carrots are ready to be put away once they cool. I didn't want to wake you. I'll talk to you soon.
   Margaret

She placed the note on the table, picked up her bag off the counter, and left the house. She was at the edge of Nina's driveway when she paused. To the left was home, to the right was Owen. The small jar in her purse started to feel like a brick. Of course Miriam would be keeping her son comfortable. He probably wouldn't need any pain salve—or Margaret's help. She started to walk toward the Yoders' house.

But when she was only a few feet away she groaned. She couldn't resist the urge to check on Owen, and he was only a brisk walk from Nina's house. Turning on her heel, she followed her conscience and headed to see him. "I'm just checking on a friend," she mumbled as she kept walking. "Giving him something to relieve his pain. We are friends, aren't we?"

That kiss was miles away from friendly.

She had to face up to what she had done and apologize to him if he was angry. She also needed to stop talking to herself. Getting caught up in the moment was expected considering what they'd been through. She was making mountains out of ant hills, or whatever the saying was. *I made a mistake, and I have to apologize. Then things will be back to normal.* Or so she hoped.

Owen was losing his mind.

He'd expected his forced vacation to be dull, and it had been anything but. He could have done without the concussion and the stitches, along with the pain that accompanied both, but overall, he hadn't been as bored as he thought he would be, thanks to Margaret. But he hadn't seen her in two days, and not only was that driving him crazy, he had also discovered what it was like to be truly bored.

Mamm, of course, wouldn't let him do anything other than take care of his personal business. At least during his vacation he'd been able to fix his own plate, pour his own drink, and get his own books to read. Now she wouldn't even let him do that. The morning after the storm, he made the mistake of mentioning to her that he felt dizzy, which was a side effect of his pain medication. That had sent her into overprotective mode, and she hadn't let up since.

When she said he probably shouldn't go outside for a few days, he thought she was overdoing it. Then he thought about it, and realized she was right. He wasn't the type of person who could sit on the porch and watch the world go by without sneaking off to do something, and when he had been clearheaded enough to read his discharge instructions, he found out he wasn't supposed to do anything anyway, including reading. That had been a big disappointment.

So he took a few wakeful naps during the day, which didn't help him with his sleep at night. Today he decided not to take any more medication. He didn't like the way it made him feel—tired, groggy, and thick-minded. It also somehow interfered with his sleep. Instead he took regular aspirin.

Now he was sitting on the couch, a fresh bandage on his head thanks to *Mamm*, and with nothing to do. He closed his eyes and of course thought about Margaret. Or more specifically, their imaginary kiss. He couldn't get it out of his mind. It had felt that real. That was another reason he had to get off the pain pills— they were making him believe something that never happened. It was bad enough he had touched her hair. He was guilty of that, which was probably why she hadn't come by to see him. His jaw tensed. Margaret Yoder had exited his life as quickly as she had entered it. That shouldn't affect him as much as it did. *But it does.*

A knock sounded on the door and his eyes flew open. He waited for *Mamm* to appear and answer it because if he did, he'd get an earful from her for not obeying her orders to rest. Never mind he was twenty-three years old and could handle himself. *Yeah, I handled myself real well in the emergency room.* After a few minutes, his mother didn't show. As he rose from the couch to answer the door, he wondered where she was. Maybe she had gone outside to the garden or had taken jugs of lemonade out to his father and brothers, something she did occasionally when they were working in the fields all day.

He opened the door, then froze. The last person he'd expected to see standing there was Margaret Yoder. He also realized she was the only person he wanted to see. "Hey," he said, the word catching in his throat. So much for sounding casual. He coughed. "Hi, Margaret."

"Hi, Owen." She took a step back, her gaze darting everywhere but on him. "I, uh, wanted to see how you were doing."

"I'm okay, all things considered." He tried to meet her gaze. "How are you?"

"Oh, I'm great. Just canned some carrots with Nina." She tapped her foot and stared at the doorjamb. "Pickled some eggs with *Aenti* Mary yesterday. You know, the usual."

He nodded, his gut twisting. Here he'd been thinking about her almost nonstop and she was pickling eggs. Fantastic. But hadn't he expected that? He had no right to hope that she had given him an inkling of a thought. And yet, she was here. That had to mean something, right? "Do you want to come in?" he asked.

Her eyebrows shot up, as if his offer surprised her. "Sure," she said, now directly looking at him. "If you're up for visitors, that is."

"I wouldn't have invited you in if I wasn't." He smiled. How could someone be so pretty and cute at the same time? *Settle down.*

"I wanted to thank you," she said as she walked into the house.

He shut the door and turned around, looking puzzled. "For what?"

"For saving *mei* life. If that tree had landed on me . . ." She shook her head. "Anyway, *danki* for sacrificing yourself."

"You're welcome, but I wouldn't call it a sacrifice."

"And you're being modest." She looked up at him. "Does your head still hurt? I have something that might help if it does."

"A little." More than a little, but he wasn't about to tell her that. He motioned for her to sit down on the couch, and when she did, he sat beside her—but not as close as he wanted. "What did you bring?"

She dug in her purse and brought out a small jar with a gold lid. "Ginger salve. I made it myself."

It touched him that she would go to so much trouble to make a pain reliever for him. Maybe she wasn't as upset with him as he thought. Or maybe he'd imagined touching her hair just like he'd dreamed he kissed her. Other than acting slightly strange when he opened the door, things seemed to be returning to normal between them. Whew.

"It works better when it's warm, though." She handed the jar to him. "You can set it out in the sun for a couple of hours or heat it up on the stove on the lowest temperature for ten minutes or so."

"What's in it?" He listened as she named the ingredients. "Do I have to use it warm?"

She shook her head. "*Nee.* It works fine as it is. The warmth just makes it more soothing."

As if his head had a mind of its own, a sharp pain shot through the wound. He tried not to wince but failed. "Sorry," he said. "Sometimes I get a stabbing pain in *mei* head."

"Do you need some now?" She took the jar from his hands. "I could put some on for you."

His pulse started to race. Now how could he turn down an offer like that?

Chapter 13

*A*s soon as the words were out of her mouth, she wanted to disappear. Not because she didn't want to help Owen. She very much wanted to. But then she thought about how she would have to touch him . . . and her thoughts were anything but medical.

But she was being stupid. He was in pain and she had something that might help him. Who cared if she had to touch him again? She was the one who was making a big deal out of something innocent. And since he hadn't answered her, maybe he would refuse her offer and all her mental gymnastics were for nothing.

"That would be great," he said. "I'm sure your salve would work better than the aspirin I'm taking. What should I do?"

"Face me." She inched closer to him on the sofa. Her breath quickened. *Get a grip.*

"All right."

She tried to take the lid off the jar, but her fingers fumbled.

"Guess I screwed it on too tight," she said, forcing out an ungainly laugh that sounded more like an angry duck call.

"I'll open it." He took the jar from her and with one easy twist, the cap came loose. Then he handed it back to her.

"*Danki*." Desperate to take her mind off of being this close to him, she asked, "How many stitches did you get?"

"Ten."

"I didn't think it would be that many." She scooped out a tiny dollop of the salve with her index finger. "I knew the cut had to be deep because you were bleeding so much, but I couldn't tell how long it was."

"It was hard to see in the dark," he said. "*Mei* hair was in the way too. And I had your *kapp* on *mei* head. That was smart thinking, Margaret."

His compliment pleased her. "I wasn't sure what else to do, and suddenly it popped into *mei* head that I could use *mei kapp* to stop the bleeding."

"You did exactly the right thing."

And you always say exactly the right thing. Right now she had to make sure she didn't do the wrong thing because she was relieved they were back to normal with each other, or as normal as they could be with him having a big bandage on the side of his head, and she didn't want to do or say anything to change that. Focusing on her ministration, she said, "The directions said to dab this on the temples for a headache."

"I definitely have one." He grinned slightly. "Dab away."

After hesitating for a moment, she gently rubbed the salve into his temple, focusing on that part of his face and not his gorgeous eyes. Even his hair was nice, and she only had to move her hand a millimeter or two and she could run her fingers through it.

"I can smell the ginger," he said.

Oh, thank goodness he started talking. She needed the distraction. "Is it helping?"

"Definitely."

Against her will, she glanced at the rest of his face and saw that his eyes were closed. He looked relaxed, and because of that she was able to loosen up. Obviously he didn't remember the kiss. If he had, he would have said something by now. She could finally let it go. She continued to rub his temple, then scooped out a little more salve and started on the other temple, grateful she was helping him. When she finished, she set the jar on the coffee table near the couch.

"*Danki.*" He opened his eyes a little, then settled back against the couch and closed them again.

She waited a minute before speaking. "Owen?" When he didn't respond, she realized he had fallen asleep.

Smiling, she put the lid back on the jar. Then she looked at him again. She couldn't resist taking the moment to observe him while they were so close. How could she care so much about someone she'd only known for a week? She'd been around enough losers for a lifetime, a few of them she had known for years, and she'd never, ever felt the strength of emotion she was experiencing now.

It wasn't just physical attraction, although there was plenty of that now. Ironic, because when she first saw him at the bus station, she hadn't thought he was attractive at all. Now she could barely take her eyes off his face as she noticed new details—the dark, but faint, stubble on his chin and upper lip, the small freckle above his left eyebrow, and the fact his hair wasn't just dark but had thin threads of amber woven through it from being out in the sun. She could gaze at him all day, and at that moment she didn't care that it was wrong, or that he didn't feel the same way about her. She didn't care about anything except that he was out of danger and she wanted to take care of him.

Then he turned his head toward her, his eyes halfway open. He smiled, revealing those cute overlapping teeth, and she couldn't breathe. She started to lean toward him. *Stop!* Had she completely taken leave of her senses? She was doing the exact same thing she had done at the hospital, even after vowing to behave herself. But when she was around Owen, she couldn't think or act straight. *But I have to. I don't want to lose his friendship.* She started to back away—

"Don't," he said, his voice low and husky. He grabbed her hand, gently but firmly. "Don't pull away."

She did as she was told, locking her gaze with his and trying to figure out what he was thinking. The way he was looking at her right now was similar to how he had in the hospital . . . only with more intensity. So much so, she felt it clear down to the tips of her toes. "Did you take your pain pills today?" she asked, striving for a light tone. He hadn't been acting woozy or out of it, but that was the only explanation for what was going on between them right now.

"*Nee*," he said firmly. "I haven't had one since yesterday."

"I hear the side effects can last a long time."

"Not that long." His eyes were still half-lidded, but he hadn't looked away from her for even a split second. "And before you point out I have a concussion, I want you to know I'm fully in control of *mei* faculties."

Oh my. There went all her excuses. She searched for another reason why there was such electricity between them, but she came up short. Which meant there was only one other alternative. Could he—

"Owen, your snack is ready." Miriam sailed into the room, carrying a small plate of sliced apples. She halted when she saw them sitting together on the couch. Close together. "Oh," she said, her eyes filled with surprise. "I didn't realize you were here, Margaret. I've been outside gathering rhubarb . . ." Her eyes flashed to Owen, confusion entering them.

He was sitting up straighter now, not looking at either his mother or Margaret. The tops of his ears were bright red. Great, she'd embarrassed him. Not what a *gut* Amish woman would do. In fact, nothing she had done had been appropriate by her mother's standards. Her stomach lurched. She'd made such a big deal to Owen about how she wasn't interested in romance, and now all she could think about was romancing him. If she couldn't even stick to her own standards, how was she going to meet anyone else's?

Owen fought not to roll his eyes in frustration. His mother's timing was the worst. He wasn't even hungry right now. The tops of his ears heated, something that happened when he was exasperated. One thing he didn't want to do was embarrass Margaret, so he tried to be as casual as possible. "*Danki, Mamm,*" he said, looking at her. "You can put the snack on the coffee table."

Mamm did, but he saw her glance at Margaret again. From his mother's neutral expression, he couldn't tell what she was thinking. But he also knew *Mamm* well enough to know that an invitation to stay for supper was forthcoming. She invited anyone who came over to stay for a meal. That would be a disaster for him and Margaret. His brothers would jump at the chance to embarrass him, her, or possibly both of them in a lame quest to be funny. He didn't want to put her through that.

But he also didn't want her to leave either.

He looked at his mother again. Please don't ask her to stay . . . please don't ask her to stay . . .

"Would you like stay for supper, Margaret?" *Mamm* asked.

Owen inwardly groaned. Then he held his breath. What would she say? Now he was leaning toward her saying yes. He could handle his brothers. Extending his time with Margaret would be worth a little teasing.

"*Danki*, but I have to get back home." She picked up her bag off the floor and stood.

His heart sank.

"Are you sure? Thomas and I haven't had a chance to thank you for taking care of Owen." She glanced at him, warmth shining in her blue eyes before she turned back to Margaret. "We're so grateful to you."

"You don't have to thank me," Margaret said. "I realize we weren't supposed to be there in the first place, but I'm glad he wasn't alone."

He willed her to look at him, but she kept her gaze on *Mamm*.

"Maybe another time then," *Mamm* said. "Did you walk here? I can get one of the *buwe* to drive you home."

"I don't mind the walk. It's not that far anyway, and I wouldn't want to put anyone to any trouble."

"It wouldn't be any trouble. I'm sure any one of *mei sohns* would love to get out of farmwork for a little while." She lifted her brow at Owen. "Except for this one. But he won't be going back to work for several days, according to the doctor. Rest and relaxation, that's the cure for his concussion." She turned back to Margaret. "You're welcome to come back and visit anytime," she said with a smile. Then she returned to the kitchen.

Owen started to get up from the couch, but Margaret shook her head. "I can let myself out." She started for the door, then paused. "See you later." She opened the door and walked out.

But would they see each other again? Other than church, they wouldn't be in the same place at the same time. There would be no more foraging, at least not for him for a long while. Once his concussion healed, he would be back to the farmwork. There was still more work to do at the end of the harvest, on top of the normal duties and chores—taking care of the animals, cutting and splitting firewood for the winter, preparing the land and gardens for their winter nap, among so many other things. He would be busy, like he always was. And even if he made the time, he wasn't sure she even wanted to be alone with him again, despite what they had experienced before his mother's untimely entrance. Or what he thought they had experienced.

There were sparks between them. He'd seen them in her eyes, along with something else he wasn't sure of. Concern? Doubt? If that was the case, he could see why she would feel hesitant, considering the way he had been so adamant about things being platonic between them.

But they weren't anymore. He had seen the attraction in her eyes. Felt it in his heart. He couldn't blame that on medication or a concussion.

He rubbed his temple, which activated the ginger scent of the salve. The concoction had worked—he didn't have a headache anymore. He looked at the jar on the table, touched that she had made it for him to ease his pain. She didn't have to go to the trouble, but he wasn't surprised she had. Her thoughtfulness was one of many things he was attracted to.

Then an idea occurred to him. He couldn't just accept a gift like this without reciprocating in kind. She had also sacrificed her *kapp* to staunch the bleeding from his head, so he needed to replace it. He smiled, feeling much better than he had a few minutes ago. He wasn't sure exactly how he was going to manage it, but he would definitely be seeing Margaret Yoder again.

Chapter 14

When Margaret returned home from Owen's, her mind and heart were a jumbled mess. She spent the entire walk home thinking about what had just happened between them. The situation with him was different from any other she had ever faced, and she realized she was out of her depth. The superficial relationships she'd had with other men weren't relationships at all. A real relationship was about connection. Respect. Companionship. The things she had with Owen. Her problem was that she wanted more than that with him, and he didn't. Despite the look she saw in his eyes, he didn't insist that she stay for supper when his mother extended the invitation.

By the time she reached the Yoders, she concluded that whatever she thought she saw simply reflected her own wishful thinking. She also concluded that she needed some time away from him. Two days hadn't been enough obviously. And it wasn't like she didn't have plenty of things to keep her occupied. She still needed to go to Ivy's store, and she also wanted to see Rhoda Troyer and talk to her about herbal medicine. There were other places to explore around Birch Creek too. Hopefully more nature walks alone would help her clear her head—and her heart. Then maybe the next time she saw Owen again, her inner conflict about their friendship would have resolved itself.

But just the thought of not seeing him saddened her. Even though she knew it was the right thing to do.

As she turned into her aunt and uncle's driveway, she heard a ringing sound coming from the phone shanty a few feet away. She decided to answer it so none of the Yoders had to rush to the shanty before the caller hung up. When she got to the phone, she picked it up. "Yoder residence."

"Mary? Is that you?" *Mamm*'s voice clanged in her ear.

Margaret's spirits, which were already precarious enough, took a nosedive. "*Nee, Mamm.* It's me."

"I should have known. You don't have as nice a voice as Mary."

Ouch. She could already tell this conversation was going to go swimmingly.

"You're the one I want to talk to anyway."

Dread pooled in her stomach. "Why do you want to talk to me?"

"Because I'm your mother, of course."

Despite the insult, did her mother actually miss her? She didn't think it was possible, which was why she hadn't called or written her since she arrived in Birch Creek. That, and she hadn't thought of her home much, except in the negative. But Margaret had heard that absence makes the heart grow fonder. A tiny spark of joy lit in her heart.

"Have you found a husband yet?"

The spark died. "I've only been here a week, *Mamm.*"

"And that town is full of bachelors looking for wives, *ya*? Are you saying you haven't been able to gain even one eager man's attention?"

Owen suddenly came to mind. But he definitely wasn't eager for anything related to marriage, and her mother wouldn't care that she'd found a friend. "The advertisement is misleading," she said, hoping *Mamm* would understand the situation. "There are single men here, but they're not all looking for wives."

"The trip was a waste of time then."

"*Nee*. I've helped *Aenti* Mary with the harvest, and I've learned a lot about herbal medicine and foraging—"

"I just hope you haven't caused Mary and Freemont any trouble." *Mamm*'s tone was laced with enough censure to make a hardened criminal fold. "Or been a bother to them."

"I haven't," she replied in a small voice, feeling like a child instead of a woman of twenty.

"I've been writing to a friend in Kentucky," she said. "She has a son who is looking for a wife. I will tell her that you'll be visiting soon."

"*Mamm*! You can't do that." She gripped the phone. "I don't want to leave Birch Creek."

"There's *nee* reason for you to stay there anymore."

"But I'm visiting family. And friends." There was Nina of course. And she thought of Owen again, even though things were complicated with him.

"Since you can't find someone to marry in Birch Creek or here at home, then you have to look elsewhere."

It was as if her mother wasn't listening to her at all. Then again, when had she? "*Mamm*—"

"I expect you home by Monday. At that time, we will make arrangements for you to visit Ada and her son."

"But I haven't finished *mei* visit here."

"Yes, Margaret. You have." *Click.*

Margaret stared at the phone in her trembling hand. She slowly put the receiver back in the cradle as her mother's words slammed into her again. Any hope that *Mamm* would forget or change her mind about Margaret finding a husband disappeared. Her mother would never give up. That much was clear.

Unless . . . Owen and I got married.

"*Nee!*" How could she even think about something so awful? Not that being married to Owen would be awful. Actually, she was certain it would be nice. More than nice . . .

She squeezed her eyes shut. She couldn't marry Owen because she didn't love him, and he didn't love her. Bottom line. And she refused to marry someone she didn't love, no matter what *Mamm* or anyone else said. Marrying Owen was out of the question.

There was nothing else she could do but go back home. She couldn't rebel against her mother and still face God. There was even a commandment in the Bible that said children were to honor their parents. If she didn't do what her mother wanted, she would be going against her and against God. She couldn't do that.

Lester flipped on the light and stared at the pad of paper and box of envelopes he'd purchased at the discount store across the street from the hotel. He hadn't been able to sleep tonight. Make that the last several nights, and he was certainly counting. It was three in the morning, and soon he would have to go to work at the very same discount store he'd made the stationery purchase. The stocking job didn't pay as much as Stoll's Inn had, but it was enough to rent this hotel room by the week.

He sat down at the desk and ran his hand through his unkempt hair. In about two hours, the members of the Birch Creek community would be rising to get ready for church. There was a time when he did the same, sometimes even earlier. Ever since he left, he had tried not to think about Ohio, or the past. He should never have gone back there in the first place. Now he knew the legacy he had left behind, and it shamed him to his core. He thought at some point he would have been able to reveal himself to his family, but now he was sure he couldn't. Not only because he was a coward—something he couldn't deny. But also because they would be better off without him. He could see that now.

He picked up the pen stamped with the hotel name and began to write. An hour later he had three letters in front of him. He stuffed each of them in an envelope and wrote the recipient's name on the front. He wouldn't mail them right away. Maybe he wouldn't mail them at all. But he had to get his thoughts and feelings out somehow. If he didn't, he would for sure lose his mind.

He grabbed the letters and put them in the bottom of his duffel bag, along with the rest of his sole possessions. Time for a new start. Again. But this time he wasn't going to look back at the past. He would continue to move forward. From now on, he would permanently be Lester Smith.

From this point on, Emmanuel Troyer no longer existed.

The next morning, as Margaret rode with her aunt and uncle to the Chupps, she tried to put on a pleasant face for them and for the rest of the community that she would see in a short while. All but Owen. She was determined to avoid him and to hurry home after the service. The Yoders lived a decent walking distance from the Chupps, but her aunt and uncle had decided to take their buggy. Once she returned to the Yoders' she would arrange to go back to Salt Creek. Then she would pack her suitcase and tell her aunt and uncle she was leaving.

A heaviness settled on her heart as *Onkel* Freemont turned into the Chupps' driveway. Judah was there to hitch the horse to the post near the barn where the service would take place in a little more than an hour. She stayed near the buggy while her uncle and aunt headed toward the barn, *Onkel* Freemont stopping to talk to Timothy Glick, the minister who would deliver the sermon this morning. Judah and Malachi, who was Phoebe and Jalon's son, dashed to the barn where Margaret guessed they were setting up the pews for the service. Usually she would go to the kitchen of whoever was hosting the service and ask if the ladies needed any help with anything. But not today. She was already internally withdrawing herself from this community, and by the time she left she wouldn't be too upset about leaving everyone behind. *I hope.*

She walked over to the other side of the barn as people started arriving, some in buggies and some on foot, everyone dressed in their Sunday best and eager to see each other and worship together. She pretended to be studying the wildflowers and plants in the ankle-high grass surrounding that side of the barn, which led to a large fenced-in field of corn that had been picked over.

If she focused, she would probably find at least a few flowers or even a pretty weed that she could press into the encyclopedia one last time. But it was all she could do to resist seeking out Nina or Martha or her cousins. For the first time in her life, she didn't want to be part of a group. She needed to be alone.

"Margaret?"

She turned around and saw Elam, Owen's little brother, standing behind her. Surprised, she said, "*Gute morgen*, Elam."

He nodded, then held out a folded piece of notebook paper. "I'm supposed to give you this."

Margaret took the paper, opened it up, and read the contents.

Meet me by the fiddleheads after service.

Gripping the paper, she looked at Elam. "Tell him I can't."

Elam leveled his gaze at her. "He's not gonna like that answer."

"How do you know?" She bent over, but not too far. Elam was eight, but the top of his head nearly reached her shoulder. "Did you read this?" she asked, holding up the note.

"Ah, *nee?*" Then he nodded. "Please don't tell Owen I read it. He'll be mad at me."

She hesitated, letting him squirm for a moment. Later she would have a discussion with him about not being so nosy. *What am I thinking?* There wouldn't be any later. After today she wouldn't see Elam, or Owen, for a long time, if ever. "I won't say a word."

Relief crossed his face. "I'll tell him you'll be there."

"Wait—" But Elam had already dashed off.

Margaret looked at the note again. She wasn't surprised that

Owen's penmanship was neater than hers, the letters small and evenly spaced. She folded the note, keeping her resolve. It wasn't her fault Elam ran off before she could stop him. She wasn't about to make a scene flagging him down. Eventually he would get tired of waiting for her and realize she wasn't going to show up. Why did he want to see her anyway?

She pushed the thought aside. It didn't matter why. Not anymore. She was going back home, and there was nothing anyone could do to stop her. Not even Owen Bontrager.

As he waited for Elam to return, Owen tried to focus on the conversation Zeb and Zeke were having in front of him. The past twenty-four hours had been torture. On one hand, he'd decided to give her the new *kapp* he asked *Mamm* to make after Margaret left the day before. On the other hand, he couldn't figure out the best time to see her. He'd finally decided not to wait another day, and he wrote her a note. Where was Elam anyway? How long did it take to deliver a piece of paper?

Finally, his little brother showed up, and after telling Zeb and Zeke he would see them at the service, he took Elam aside. "What did she say?"

Elam bit his bottom lip, and for a moment Owen panicked. Was she refusing to meet him? If so, why?

Then Elam blurted, "She said yes."

He grinned, then ruffled his brother's already wild hair.

"Hey. Stop messing with *mei* hair." Elam tried to smooth the wayward locks down but failed. "Can I *geh* now?"

"*Ya*, you can *geh*." After his brother ran off, he turned to go to the barn. Service would be starting soon, and he hoped he could concentrate. But he knew it would be the longest three hours of his life.

Owen slid into an empty space next to Jesse on the men's side. The Bontrager brothers still took up an entire pew even without Devon, Zeb, and Zeke. The twins were sitting with Christian Ropp and Levi Stoll, and Jesse scooted over to give Owen room just as the service started.

As everyone began to sing hymns, Owen tried to focus on the worship, resisting the urge to seek out Margaret, who always sat with her aunt, her cousins Ivy and Karen, his mother, and his sister, Phoebe. He was grateful she had been spared any gossip about what happened in the woods, thanks to Freemont instructing everyone from the pulpit not to discuss the subject.

He tried the best he could to pay attention to the service, but he had trouble thinking about anything else but Margaret. Even though he knew she didn't feel the same about him that he did about her, he was happy to have the chance to spend some time alone with her. Finally. Although he tried, he couldn't stop grinning.

After the service was over and it was time for lunch, Rhoda scooped a spoonful of fresh fruit cocktail onto Malachi Chupp's plate, then dished out consecutive servings to the boys he usually hung out with—Judah Yoder and Nelson and Jesse Bontrager. She smiled as they continued down the line while the other ladies who were helping serve filled their plates with tuna salad and chicken salad sandwiches, cubes of various cheeses, pickles, homemade potato chips, and brownies and cookies for dessert. They were the last to be fed of the families who had stayed after the service. She looked around at all the people gathered at the tables the Chupps had set up outside. The district was over twice the size it had been when Emmanuel left. If it kept growing, they would have to split the district into two separate ones, each with its own bishop.

Emmanuel would have never stood for that.

She cut off the thought and stared at the almost empty bowl of fruit cocktail. After telling her sons she had finally accepted that he wasn't coming back, it was as if a ten-ton weight had lifted from her shoulders. She didn't have to measure every thought or decision she made—or that Freemont made—against what Emmanuel would have done. The habit wouldn't disappear overnight, but she could stop the thoughts when they came to her. She smiled again. After years of living under his oppression, then refusing to give up the thought that he had left Birch Creek for good, she was finally able to breathe easier. There were no more secrets to cover up, nothing tethering her to Emmanuel anymore. He might still be alive, but he wasn't returning home. She knew that in her heart . . . and God forgive her, she was glad.

"Hi, Rhoda."

She looked at Loren, who was standing in front of her, his plate in his hand. "Hi," she said, trying not to glance away. Her ever-present shame had always kept her from looking people in the eye. That was going to change starting now. "Fruit cocktail?"

"Please." He held out his plate and peered over it. "Any cherries left? Those are the best part of the cocktail."

"I think so too." She fished out a few extra cherries for him, then filled the large spoon with pineapple and peach chunks, along with two grapes, and ladled it onto his plate.

"*Danki*," he said before moving down the line. The other women had filled their plates and were seated and eating, leaving whatever food was left to anyone who wanted seconds. Loren placed a chicken sandwich on his plate.

"Loren?"

He turned to her, his hand hovering over the tuna salad sandwiches. "*Ya?*"

"I found a few more cherries," she said, meeting his gaze.

Grinning, he walked over. "I'll take them."

She gave them to him, and as he finished getting the rest of his lunch, her mood became slightly tempered by reality. Emmanuel might be gone, but if he was still alive, she was still married to him. She couldn't contemplate getting a divorce, but she also couldn't deny she found Loren attractive. She'd been lonely in her marriage, and she was still lonely now. *But I'm also free.* And that was something she could live with.

Chapter 15

*O*wen looked up at the cloudless sky. When he had arrived here where the fiddleheads grew near his house, the sun was directly above him. Now it had moved enough that he figured he'd been waiting on Margaret for over an hour. Frowning, he brushed his toe against one of the fiddleheads that had already started to bloom and looked down at the plastic bucket he was holding. Inside was the *kapp*. Surely she hadn't forgotten they were supposed to meet. Maybe she was just running late, even though she'd always been on time before. *Or she's standing me up.*

He shook his head, squinting at the sky again. A cool autumn breeze shot through his white shirt, and he adjusted his black church hat. He'd removed the bandage earlier that morning, and the stitches and bald patch were a sight to behold, and not a good one. The stitches would be removed next week. Maybe Margaret could go with him while he had them removed. It would give him a good excuse to hold her hand.

He walked into the road and searched in the direction of the Chupps, thinking she might have been detained by someone after church. Nina possibly. The two of them were good friends. But he didn't see a trace of her anywhere.

Turning around, he walked back to the patch of fiddleheads, the bucket swinging in his hand. He had chosen this place knowing that everyone would still be at church, and they would have some time alone. In a way he thought of this little patch of fiddleheads as their special place now, replacing the shed in the woods that he was sure neither of them would ever go back to. He would wait a little longer, and then he'd go to the Yoders'. Panic suddenly rose within him. Had something happened to her? Maybe he shouldn't wait. He started walking toward the Yoders' when he heard Elam calling to him.

"What?" he said over his shoulder, slowing down his steps.

Elam rushed to him, his little chest heaving when he arrived.

"What are you doing home? I thought you were staying at church."

"Ezra decided to *geh* home, and I came with him." He paused. "I'm sorry, Owen."

Owen faced him and frowned. "For what?"

"I didn't tell you the truth." Elam ran his toe over the gravel at the edge of the row.

Now he was completely confused. "About what?"

"Margaret. She said she wasn't coming."

Panic changed to apprehension. "But you told me she was."

"I know. I thought she'd change her mind. *Mamm* said you two like each other—"

"Hold on." Owen held up his hand. "When did she say this?"

"Last night after you went to bed, while we were eating dessert." Elam smirked. "She said you're mooning over her."

He lifted his brow. That did not sound right. "Mooning or swooning?"

"Maybe swooning. I can't remember. Anyway, like I said, I thought she'd change her mind. *Mamm*'s always telling *Daed* that it's a woman's right to do that."

Owen would have laughed if he weren't so upset. She really wasn't coming. For some reason she didn't want to see him. Then again, why would she? For the first time he realized he must remind her of that horrible night, and although she hadn't been injured, she'd seen him get his head split open. He couldn't deny that he'd had one nightmare about that night already. Why hadn't he thought of this before?

"I'm sorry I lied," Elam said, now looking solemn. "And I'm sorry Margaret doesn't like you." He turned away and started walking toward their house.

His brother's words were a punch of reality to his gut, even though Elam didn't mean them to be. But he was right. Margaret didn't like him, at least not the way he wished she did. His heart started to ache. The first woman he'd ever been interested in was rejecting him. No, he was more than interested in her. He had fallen hard for her.

He pressed the heel of his hand against his forehead. *Stupid, stupid.* He should have never let his feelings overcome common sense. His imagination had already gotten the best of him when he'd dreamed he and Margaret had kissed in the emergency room. That hadn't been true, and neither was his hope that she returned his feelings. She probably thought he was crazy, asking her to meet him here.

There was nothing else he could do but go back home and

stare at the walls and try to heal as fast as he could. Then he would throw himself into work more than ever before. He'd make sure he was so busy that he would barely have time to think about anything else, and when it was time to fall asleep, he would crash as soon as he got into bed. And if his mother ever mentioned dating again, he would tell her to mind her own business. Owen was through with romance . . . before it had even begun. How pathetic.

He started walking toward the house, the soles of his shoes dragging against the asphalt and gravel. He wasn't in any hurry to go back home, but he couldn't stay in the fiddlehead patch any longer. Once he was able to, he would mow the patch down, then throw some weed killer on it for good measure.

"Owen?"

His heart skipped a beat. He turned around to see Margaret standing behind him.

Margaret's emotions were spinning faster than a merry-go-round. As soon as the service was over, she told *Aenti* Mary that she wasn't staying for lunch. Her aunt had given her a questioning look, but fortunately hadn't pried. Then Margaret left the Chupps and started walking, spending the past hour or so mentally zigzagging from thinking she should go back to the Yoders, to feeling guilty over standing Owen up. She also had a few choice thoughts for little Elam, who had put her in this predicament. Ultimately, she couldn't ignore her conscience any longer, and she headed to see Owen.

"Hi," Owen said, walking to her. "Elam told me you weren't coming."

"He did?" She could have avoided an hour of angst altogether.

"Eventually, *ya*. He told me you said you were going to meet me, and then he ended up telling me the truth." He grimaced. "I really dislike lying."

Her stomach sank. She tried not to look at him, but she couldn't help it. How could she have ever thought he wasn't handsome? Or that she could never be attracted to him?

"I brought you something." He handed her an ice-cream bucket. "It's a new *kapp*."

She already knew that. The plastic container was the perfect size to keep the *kapp* stiff and to retain its shape. She took the container from him and opened it up, then pulled out a beautiful brand-new white *kapp*.

"I asked *Mamm* to make you one, and she's very particular about her sewing," he explained. "Even our work pants have perfectly even stitches. I'd match them up against any machine-made pants."

The stitching was flawless. A lump formed in Margaret's throat. "You didn't have to do this," she said, keeping her focus on the *kapp*.

"Of course I did." The tension she'd seen on his face when she arrived had disappeared, replaced by that half-smile she was starting to adore so much. But she had to remain strong. She had to tell him she was leaving. She had to—

Her stomach suddenly growled. Loudly.

He chuckled. "Hungry, *ya*? We can *geh* inside the house and

I can make you a sandwich. *Mamm* finally relented and lets me fix *mei* own lunch every once in a while. I make a mean PB&J."

She wanted to take him up on his offer more than anything. Even if he gave her crackers and water, she'd be happy. But she couldn't. "I'm going back to Salt Creek tomorrow, Owen."

Shock crossed his features. "What?"

"I have to *geh* back home."

"But I thought you were staying with *yer aenti* and *onkel* for three weeks? It's only been a little over one."

"I know."

Owen rubbed the back of his neck. "Did something happen? Are *yer* parents all right?"

She nodded. "They're fine." She should leave the explanation at that, but she couldn't. He deserved to know the real reason. "*Mamm* wants me to meet her friend's *sohn*. He lives in Kentucky. I'm going home for a day, and then I'm going there to meet him."

"Oh."

"She called yesterday. She asked me how *mei* search for a husband is going. I had to tell her the truth . . . I hadn't found anyone to marry."

"She expected you to find someone in a week?"

"I told her *nee* one here was looking for a wife."

"But you said you weren't looking for a husband." His voice was tight.

"I'm not. But she's not going to give up on marrying me off. Since nobody here wants to get married, there's *nee* reason for me to stay." Margaret looked into his eyes. "There isn't, is there?"

He averted his gaze and didn't say anything.

"Who knows?" she said, forcing a light tone. "This guy in Kentucky could be *mei* perfect match." Her heart squeezed as she said the words. "He might change *mei* mind about getting married."

"*Ya,*" he muttered. "He might."

She waited for him to say something else. When he didn't, there was nothing left for her to do except leave. "Bye, Owen," she said.

"Bye, Margaret."

Tears welling in her eyes, she hurried back to Mary's.

Owen couldn't move. He was numb from head to toe as he watched her walk away. She was leaving. She was walking out of his life as fast as she had entered it. That had been expected, though. He knew her visit was less than a month. She was shortening the timeline—or more accurately, her mother was forcing her to. But if Margaret really wanted to stay, she would have told her no and stayed. *I didn't give her a reason to.*

He took off his hat, letting the air cool his head. What was he supposed to do? Beg her to stay? Tell her he cared about her after only one week? For a moment he considered offering to marry her to get her mother off her back. But that wasn't right. He wouldn't trap her, or himself, into marriage. Neither one of them would settle for that.

A lump formed in his throat and he yanked on the neck of his collarless shirt. Then he took a deep breath. He would get over this. He was going on light farm duty tomorrow, and soon he'd have the go-ahead to be on a regular schedule. Life would go back to normal, at least for him.

Margaret disappeared from his view. The lump hardened and he could barely swallow. He didn't like the idea that she was going to Kentucky to meet another man. But she was a grown adult, and he didn't have the right to stop her. Besides, maybe it was God's will that she meet this man. Even marry him. Who was he to stand in the way of the Lord's plan?

Owen dragged his feet as he went back to the house. When he walked inside, he passed Elam and Ezra eating a cold lunch in the kitchen.

"Where's Margaret?" Elam asked around a mouthful of pimento cheese sandwich.

He didn't answer him or look at either of his brothers. Instead he went upstairs and tossed his hat on the floor, then flopped on his bed. Pain that surpassed any headache he'd ever had gripped his heart. Eventually he'd have to move past this . . . he just had no idea how.

That evening after supper, Margaret opened the encyclopedia that she had used to press the flowers she'd found on her foraging expeditions with Owen. She started turning pages in the encyclopedia to the center of the book. When she saw them, she choked back a sigh.

Aenti Mary came into the kitchen and looked over her shoulder. "Those are lovely. Are you going to put them in a frame?"

Margaret paused, then shook her head. "You can keep them," she said.

Aenti Mary gave her an odd look and walked to the gas-powered refrigerator. "Warm milk? I thought I'd add a little bit of honey this time."

"*Ya, danki.*"

Aenti Mary pulled out a carton of milk. Then she walked to the stove and took a small saucepan out of the lower cabinet next to it. For a few minutes, the only sound in the kitchen was the quiet simmering of milk heating. When the milk was hot enough, her aunt turned off the heat and started pouring the beverage into the two mugs sitting on the counter. "Have you talked to Doris recently?" she asked.

She still hadn't told her aunt that she was leaving in the morning, but she couldn't put it off any longer. "*Ya.*"

"How is she doing?"

"All right."

Aenti Mary set the pan back on the stove, then picked up the mugs. She sat down at the table and gave Margaret her milk. "Are you okay? You've been quiet today."

She nodded, even though it wasn't the truth. She spooned some of the golden honey into her mug, but it didn't look appetizing. Now she wished she hadn't put her aunt to the trouble of making the milk.

"We haven't had much time to talk lately, have we?" *Aenti* Mary continued. "We've all been so busy and tired from the harvest. I'm glad you're here to help. With Ivy working so many hours at the store, it's nice to have an extra pair of hands."

Margaret nodded, still not saying anything. Her heart

squeezed as she thought about how much she had enjoyed working with her cousins the other day. Even Nina joined them, telling her she had found a remedy for her morning sickness—peppermint candies. Nina shared her recipe for mock Cheez Whiz, a cheese sauce Margaret had never tasted but all the women had insisted was exceptionally good. Martha also shared a recipe that had been in her family for generations—tapioca pears. Margaret couldn't wait to try those. As she did every year, Karen made corn relish, which was always delicious, and her aunt made her specialty, rhubarb punch. Margaret participated by preparing beet jam, a staple at her family's table. There had been lots of work, but also lots of fun and laughter, two things she rarely experienced around her mother and sisters.

"I just want to make sure you're all right. What you and Owen went through was traumatic."

"I know. But I wasn't the one who got hurt."

"*Ya*, but someone you care about was."

Her gaze flew to her aunt.

"You do have feelings for Owen, *ya*?"

"I . . ." She didn't want to reveal what she'd been trying to hide from herself, but she also hated the idea of lying to her aunt, who had always been good to her. "I do. But he doesn't have any for me."

"How do you know?"

Margaret touched the raised lettering on the old book's cover, debating if she should tell her aunt why she was so sure of Owen's feelings—or rather his lack of.

"I'm sorry," *Aenti* Mary said. "I shouldn't pry. Karen and Ivy didn't appreciate when I did that either."

"It's nice to know you care." Her thumb pressed down on the letter *a* in the middle of the book.

"Of course I do." After a pause, she said, "I'm probably overstepping *mei* bounds here, but I want you to know that I understand that your *mutter* isn't easy to get along with."

That was a surprise. "I thought you two were close."

"We are, but that doesn't mean I don't see her foibles. And I'm sure she sees mine. I remember when she and John got together. I thought they were either a perfect match or they were setting themselves up for a lifetime of trouble because they were so different. When they had June, Ruth, and Wanda, I couldn't believe they were all born with the same personality as Doris. Then you came along and broke the mold."

Margaret leaned her chin on the heel of her hand, fascinated by her aunt's revelation. "No one was happy about that."

"I disagree," *Aenti* Mary said. "Your parents love you. They just don't understand you."

She sat back in her chair, stunned that someone actually grasped what she had been struggling with for so long. But she couldn't lay all the blame at her parents' feet. "I haven't made it easy on them."

"Now on that point I agree." Her expression turned kind. "But you've changed. I can tell. So can Freemont. Doris will figure it out, too, eventually."

"What if she doesn't?" She revealed her biggest fear. "What if she still thinks I'm a failure?"

Aenti Mary arched her brow. "You're not a failure, Margaret. We're all guilty of sin and we all struggle, including *yer mamm*. You need to have a talk with her and hash this out, though, if she's making you feel this horrible. Why don't you call her back tomorrow?"

"I already talked to her." She explained her phone call with *Mamm* to her aunt, who looked stunned. When she told her about going to Kentucky, *Aenti* Mary plopped down her mug of warm milk.

"What about you and Owen?"

Why was her aunt still insisting there was something between them? "He's not interested in me, *Aenti*. I know that for a fact." Once she told her aunt about her and Owen's first meeting, she sat back in her chair.

"Then you haven't changed *yer* mind at all about him?"

The memory of kissing him at the emergency room suddenly came to mind. "*Ya*," she whispered. "I have."

"Don't you think if your feelings have changed, his possibly could have too?"

She thought about the kiss again. He had kissed her back, but now she knew it was because he was under the influence of painkillers. If the kiss had been real, he would have asked her to stay in Birch Creek. "*Nee*," she said emphatically. "They haven't. And I believe that's for the best."

"All right." *Aenti* Mary touched her arm. "I wish you didn't have to leave tomorrow, but I understand why you have to. Once Doris gets something in her head, it's almost impossible to convince her to change her mind." Her expression became stern. "However, don't let her talk you into doing anything you don't want to do. She's *yer mamm*, but *yer* an adult. You know *yer* own mind, feelings, and heart."

Margaret let the words sink in as *Aenti* Mary took the mug

to the sink, quickly washed it, then set it in the dish drainer to dry. "Would you mind turning off the lamp when you *geh* to bed?" she asked. "Freemont has already turned in and I want to join him. His eyes were bothering him a little bit tonight. We might have to *geh* back to the doctor to get new eye drops for his glaucoma."

Margaret nodded, making a note to pray for her uncle. She hadn't known he had glaucoma until *Aenti* Mary told her the second day she was there. It wasn't common knowledge, but she said she trusted Margaret with the secret.

She walked over to Margaret and put her hand on her shoulder. "I'm going to miss you so much," she said, her voice sounding thick. "What time are you leaving?"

"Early morning. I'm catching the first bus out."

"I can ride with you to the station then," she said, giving her a watery smile. "The men can fend for breakfast on their own for once."

Margaret managed to smile back. "I'd like that."

After her aunt left, Margaret looked at the encyclopedia again. She was tempted to take the flower home with her but decided against it. Instead she got up and turned out the lamp, then went upstairs. She needed to purge her mind and heart of Owen, and that wouldn't happen if she had a memento of him. The memories were going to be painful enough.

Chapter 16

On Monday afternoon, Margaret was back in Salt Creek. She stepped out of the back of the taxi and waited for the driver to open the trunk. He handed her suitcase to her and she paid him his fare. As the car left the driveway, she faced her house. Dread pooled in her stomach. She didn't want to be here. But *Aenti* Mary was right. She had to work things out with her mother. If she didn't, she wouldn't be able to be her own person, faults and all. And she would never get over her past and her failures if she continued to let her mother control her life.

Still, she was disappointed. *Mamm* had demanded she be here, and she couldn't even bother to meet her outside. Neither had her father, but she could excuse him due to work. She figured he was back in the field somewhere, probably cutting off the last ears of corn for the season with her brothers-in law. How different this arrival was from when she had visited Birch Creek. *Aenti* Mary had been so excited to see her, running out of the house and giving her a huge hug. She had even sent Owen to come get her at the bus station so Margaret wouldn't have to ride back all by herself.

Owen. She had to stop thinking about him. While she had no intention of marrying Ada's son or anyone else, that didn't mean there was a future for the two of them. He had let her go too easily for that, and that should have been enough to quash her feelings for him. But it wasn't, and she couldn't fool herself into believing it was. Hopefully . . . eventually . . . she would be able to let go of him.

A cold wind kicked up, the first seriously chilly sign of fall, and her jacket was still in her luggage. The brisk air pulled her out of her reverie, and she gripped the handle of her suitcase and marched to the house. Whatever the outcome of her conversation with *Mamm*, Margaret was going to have her say.

When she opened the door and walked inside, she yelled, "I'm home!" She paused, waiting for a response. There wasn't one. Good grief, had her mother forgotten that she was coming home today? That didn't seem likely since *Mamm* was the one who wanted her here in the first place. She set down her suitcase and headed for the kitchen, the most obvious place to look for her mother. But when she got there, the room was empty. Was she even home?

She was about to go upstairs when the outside kitchen door opened. *Mamm* strolled into the room. "I just got off the phone with Ada," she said as she walked over to the pantry and took a jar of spaghetti sauce off the middle shelf, along with a package of noodles. "She's expecting you on Wednesday."

No hello? No, "I'm glad you're back"? "*Mamm*, I just got here. I haven't even taken *mei* suitcase to *mei* room yet."

"I wouldn't bother unpacking." *Mamm* placed the sauce and noodles on the counter next to the stove. "You'll just have to re-pack it tomorrow night."

Anger stirred within Margaret. "I'm not going."

Mamm pulled out a pot and started filling it with water. "Samson will meet you at the bus station."

"I said I'm not going."

"She said he has bright-red hair and is on the hefty side. He also has a pockmarked face. I told her you weren't picky."

Margaret balled her fists. She felt bad that he had to deal with acne scars—that couldn't be easy—and she had learned enough about herself to know that if she cared about him, a small flaw wouldn't matter. But none of that was the point. She stormed over to her mother and tapped her on the shoulder. It took everything she had not to poke her. "Aren't you listening to me? I said I'm not going to Ada's. I'm not going to meet Samson, and I'm not getting married . . . to anyone!"

Her mother shut off the tap, but she didn't pick up the pot. Instead she turned to Margaret, her expression tranquil. Too tranquil. A storm was brewing underneath her calm demeanor. Margaret had experienced enough of those. "You will do as you're told," *Mamm* said in an even tone.

She crossed her arms over her chest. "Not this time."

"Now you listen to me, Margaret—"

"*Nee*, you listen to me for once! I know I've been rebellious. I know I've done wrong. I haven't been a *gut* daughter but I'm trying to make up for that. I'm trying to be like June and Ruth and Wanda. But it doesn't matter what I do. It's never *gut* enough. I'm never *gut* enough." Tears filled her eyes. "Why do you want to get rid of me?"

"Because I'm tired of worrying about you!" *Mamm*'s face turned red. "Your *schwesters* were always well-behaved—"

"I know, I know." Her head pounded, but she wasn't leaving

this kitchen until she got through to her mother. "I'm not them. I'm not you. I'm me. Why can't you love *me*?"

Mamm slowly turned and faced the sink. "We're having spaghetti for supper tonight." She lifted the pot out of the basin and set it on the stove. "*Geh* out and tell *yer vatter*. He's in the barn."

Margaret went numb. She waited for her mother to say something else, but *Mamm* continued to adjust the gas burner under the pot, not even looking at her.

Her worst fear was confirmed—her mother didn't love her. Couldn't love her because she wasn't the daughter she wanted.

Turning on her heel, she did what *Mamm* told her. But as she walked to the barn, her heart began to break. She'd always held out hope that *Mamm* loved her deep down. Now she knew it was a false hope. By the time she got to the barn, the tears started flowing again.

Her father was sitting on a chair repairing one of the horse's harnesses. She tried to control her emotions. All she had to do was tell him what was for supper. She could do that without breaking down. "*Mamm*—" she said, her mouth sticky and dry at the same time. "*M-mamm* . . ."

"Margaret?" *Daed* put the harness down and went to her. "What's wrong with *yer mamm*?"

Where do I start? "*N-nix*. W-we're having . . . h-having . . ." She started to sob, then turned around and covered her face. Her father didn't say anything. She didn't even know if he was still in the barn. He probably ran off to check on *Mamm*. Never mind that she was the one breaking into pieces next to a pile of hay bales.

Then she felt a tentative touch on her shoulder. "Margaret?"

Her hands fell from her face. She had never heard her father speak so tenderly, not even to *Mamm*. She turned around, and when she saw the worry and concern on his craggy face, she fell against him and started crying all over again.

"It's all right." He patted her back once, then twice. "Whatever's wrong, it will be all right."

Once she finished crying, she stepped away. "*Mamm* is fine," she managed to finally say. She sniffed and wiped her eyes with the back of her hand. "We're having spaghetti tonight."

"All this hubbub was over spaghetti?"

Margaret shook her head. "I asked her why she doesn't love me."

Daed went still. "You did?"

She nodded.

"And what did *yer mamm* say?"

Several tears slid down her face. "That we're having spaghetti for supper."

Her father shook his head. Then he went into the tack room and reappeared with a chair and placed it next to his. When he sat down, he patted the seat next to him. "Let's talk."

Stunned, she sat in the chair. But instead of talking, her father picked at his fingernails, the nail beds dark with dirt from working the land all day. After a few minutes, he finally spoke.

"*Yer mamm* has a certain way she likes things." He jabbed at the cuticle on his thumb. "She wanted to marry a farmer, so she married a farmer. She wanted only three children—she got three children. She wanted all girls—she got all girls."

"Pretty sure you had something to do with that," Margaret mumbled.

"Very little, according to *yer mamm*."

Margaret's head jerked up at that. "What?"

Daed sighed. "When I met *yer mamm*, I thought we were a *gut* match. I was a little on the wild side—"

"Wait a minute." She turned until she was almost facing him. "You were wild?"

"A little. Not much. Just some sneaking out during *rumspringa*."

"Really?" Margaret couldn't believe what she was hearing. She'd never imagined her father had a rebellious streak.

"Really. But at twenty-two I was ready to settle down. I met *yer mamm* and she was as straightlaced as a woman gets. Not just in temperament, but in her daily life. Everything is on a schedule, and we don't deviate from it."

"*Nee*, we don't."

"She's organized, intelligent, and disciplined. She was also very pretty back in the day. You take after her in that department." He smiled slightly, then became serious again. "But years of having to be in control of everything have taken its toll on her. When we were younger, it was easier to deal with. I just let her have her way, and everything was fine. Then you came along."

"The fourth child." The unwanted one.

"*Ya*." His voice grew soft. "The spitting image of *yer mamm*'s face . . . but obviously the rest is from me."

Margaret was in shock. She had no idea her father had noticed much about her. But some of what he was saying was making sense.

"I was so excited the day you were born. *Yer schwesters* were so tied to *yer mutter* that I felt left out . . . even more than I was feeling left out to begin with." He paused and looked way. "Maybe I shouldn't be telling you all this."

"*Daed*," she said. "It's okay. I want to hear it."

"I figured you'd be *mei* special one. But *yer mamm* had her specific way of being a mother, and she wasn't going to deviate from that. She was the parent. I was the provider. End of story. But I had hope that things might change, especially as you grew older. You liked to fish and play in the dirt. Remember the time I took you to Catnip Pond?"

She had forgotten all about Catnip Pond, other than remembering that she thought the name was funny. "A little."

"You were only three, but you were a natural with a fishing pole in *yer* hands." He stared straight ahead, silent for a few seconds as if he were lost in the memory. "But girls weren't supposed to fish—"

"Or get dirty."

He nodded. "It got to the point where I had to back down. I didn't want *yer mamm* and I to get into a tug-of-war match over you, so I stepped aside. I can see now that was a mistake."

Margaret looked down at her lap. "She wants me to *geh* to Kentucky and meet her friend's *sohn*."

"I didn't know that." He rubbed his chin.

"She didn't tell you that's why I came home?"

He shook his head. "We haven't talked much since you've been gone. Less than before, which I didn't think was possible."

"Oh, *Daed*." She'd had no idea how bad her parents' marriage was.

He gave her a bitter smile. "It's okay, Meggy."

Her heart melted. "You haven't called me that since I was little."

"*Yer mutter* doesn't like it, so I stopped. I know this is hard for you to understand. But I love *yer mamm*. I really do. She makes it hard sometimes, and I'm starting to see that letting her get her way all the time wasn't the best thing for anyone. Especially for you." His eyes became watery. "Can you forgive me, Meggy? Forgive me for not standing up for you?"

She threw her arms around him. "*Ya, Daed.* I do."

When they parted, her father's face turned resolute. "Things are going to change around here. First off, you don't have to *geh* to Kentucky if you don't want to. Secondly, you don't have to get married if you don't want to."

Margaret grinned. "But I'll be twenty-one soon."

He rolled his eyes. "That deadline is going out the window. I never did get it in the first place. But that's *yer mutter* for you."

She'd never been so relieved. But her relief was suddenly tempered. "Do you think *Mamm* loves me?"

Daed paused. "In her own way, *ya.* If she didn't, she wouldn't be working so hard to get you a husband."

"She says she's tired of worrying about me."

He looked surprised. "I can't believe she admitted that," he said. "But it's true. Try as we might, we both worry about you." He smirked. "Especially when you used to sneak out of the house two or three times a week."

Her eyes widened. "You knew? Does *Mamm* know?"

"Only that one time. Otherwise, *nee.* She has *nee* idea you snuck out before."

"How did you know?"

"*Yer mei* daughter, remember?"

She laughed and hugged him again. "I love you, *Daed.*"

His arms tightened around her. "I love you too."

"Why did Margaret leave?"

Owen stopped hoeing around the pumpkin plants and glared at Elam. Then he tempered his expression. Little Elam didn't understand the complexities of relationships. Owen didn't understand them himself. He began hoeing again. Many of the plants had started to sprout small pumpkins. Many of the plants had pumpkins that were ready to harvest and sell, while there were still plenty of smaller pumpkins left on the vines. Once they ripened, they would be sold in November. "She had to *geh* back home."

Elam, who was holding a smaller hoe, leaned against it. "Why?"

"Are you trying to get out of work again?"

"*Nee.*" Elam jabbed the hoe at the dirt twice. "See? I'm working. I just want to know why she left all of the sudden. I thought you two liked each other."

"We do." Make that did. "We're just friends, Elam. She's not tied to me or Birch Creek." That answer seemed to satisfy his brother, and they went back to tackling the weeds in silence.

After a few minutes Elam piped up again. "Do you always look at *yer* friends the way you looked at Margaret?"

"What way?"

"Like you want to marry them."

Owen almost dropped his hoe. "Did Jesse tell you that?" He turned to Elam, expecting to see a smirk on his face. But his brother was serious.

Elam shook his head. "*Mamm* said Jesse's not allowed to say anything about you or Margaret in the same sentence, or he'll get grounded."

Danki, Mamm. "Then what makes you think I look like I want to get married?"

"Because you and Margaret act like *Mamm* and *Daed* when they look at each other. But mostly you've been a grouch since she left, and you get even crabbier when someone mentions her."

He hadn't mentioned her lately. Margaret had been gone for three weeks. Three long, painful weeks. Good grief, he missed her. More than he ever thought he would. Even throwing himself into work wasn't keeping her from his mind, and he worked harder than ever now. He fell into bed every night, his body exhausted but his mind racing. Had she gone to Kentucky to see Samson? Were they courting? Had she fallen in love? *Does she ever think about me?* He couldn't stop thinking about her.

"Owen?"

He turned to his brother. "What?" he snapped.

"Are you in love with Margaret?"

He hesitated. No, he couldn't possibly be in love with her. Not after only knowing her a week, even though he felt like he'd known her forever. But love meant marriage, and he wasn't ready for that. She wasn't either, even though she had left to go meet the guy her mother had set her up with. His teeth clenched until his jaw ached.

"Do you love her, Owen?"

Looking down at his brother, he was going to tell him the truth. Love took time to grow. Mistakes were made when people took risks, and when they didn't think things through. Marriage was for life and wasn't to be taken lightly. There was absolutely, positively no way he could have changed his mind about marriage in a week or could have fallen in love with Margaret in that short of a time. Right?

Did he love Margaret? He shook his head. "*Ya.*" *Wait, what?*

Elam's brow furrowed. "Huh? *Yer* shaking *yer* head but you said *ya.* Which is it?"

Owen's eyes widened and he started to smile. "I love her, Elam."

His brother grinned. "Then you're going to *geh* get her and bring her back to Birch Creek?"

His smile faded. "It's not that easy. She doesn't love me."

"How do you know?"

"Because she left."

"Did you ask her to stay?"

Doggone it, his eight-year-old brother was smarter than he was. "*Nee,* I didn't."

"Then I don't blame her for leaving." Elam pushed a clod of dirt away from one of the larger pumpkins. "You can be a *dumm-kopf* sometimes."

Owen stared out into the pasture. But he wasn't looking at the cows nibbling the Timothy grass, or the horses in the adjacent corral doing the same thing. His heart slammed into his chest. He loved Margaret, and he had let her go without even telling her. Fear and anticipation flowed through him. She might reject him. She probably would, and he would be miserable. But he was miserable right now. He had to take the risk. He had to tell her he loved her, and let God sort out the rest.

"Finish up here, Elam," Owen said, dropping the hoe on the ground and darting toward the house.

"Are you going to see Margaret?" Elam yelled out.

He turned around and jogged backward. "*Ya.* I'm going to see her." *If it's not too late. Dear Lord, I pray it isn't.*

Chapter 17

Despite her talk with *Daed*, not much had changed between Margaret and her mother. Her father must have told *Mamm* that she didn't have to go to Kentucky, because during the three weeks she had been home since returning to Birch Creek, she hadn't brought up the subject again. *Mamm* had been spending more time with Margaret's sisters, leaving Margaret home alone for most of the day. But she didn't mind. She fixed lunch for her father and brothers-in-law. Jonah, Wanda's husband, had even complimented her on the yumasetti she had made yesterday.

In addition to cooking, she also spent her time reading books about herbal medicine she checked out of the library. She had seen foraging books near the shelf where the herbal medicine books were, but she avoided them. She wasn't sure she would ever forage again.

The most important thing she did, other than rebuild her relationship with her father, was to donate all her English clothing and items to the local thrift shop. When she had handed over the plastic bin with the single outfit, pair of shoes, and some leftover makeup she had forgotten about and found in the back of her bottom dresser drawer, she had finally closed the door on her English life.

This afternoon she was preparing alfalfa tea for her father. She had noticed he was rubbing his knuckles often during supper, and that in the evenings he was moving slower. Alfalfa tea was supposed to help with arthritis, along with sitting in a tub with one-and-a-half cups of apple cider vinegar for fifteen minutes every night. *Daed* was going to try the remedy tonight and she wanted to have everything ready for him. She had also made several jars of the ginger salve to give to her sisters and their families, and one especially for *Mamm*. She wasn't sure if her mother would accept it, and Margaret was keeping her expectations low. But it would be there for *Mamm* if or when she wanted it.

Using a mortar and pestle, she finished grinding the last of the alfalfa leaves and put them in a small glass jar similar to the ones she used for the salve. After cleaning up the kitchen, she slipped on her navy-blue sweater and went outside. Nearly every leaf from the surrounding trees had fallen to the ground, but the evergreens kept their needles and color. She sighed. Moments like this, when she was outside and alone, were when she missed Owen the most. She hadn't been able to stop thinking of him since she'd left Birch Creek. No, she wasn't just thinking about him. She was yearning for him. But it was pointless. Eventually she would forget about him, but it would take a long time and a lot of help from God.

Margaret sat down on the bottom porch step and leaned her elbows on her knees. She closed her eyes and felt the cool air on her cheeks, heard the sound of the cows lowing in the pasture, smelled the musty scent of dry, crunchy leaves. Her heart started to calm, but only a little. Still, she would take it.

Her eyes opened as she heard the sound of a car pulling into her gravel driveway. She didn't recognize the gray sedan. Her heart started to hum. Several times she had hoped Owen would show up out of the blue and ask her to come back to Birch Creek. Then she would tell him what she should have said before she left—that she loved him. She stood as the car came to a stop. Had her dream come true? Was God giving her a second chance?

The door opened, and her heart jumped to her throat.

"Hey, Margaret." A tall, well-muscled man with a cocky grin strode toward her.

Her stomach clenched. Dylan. She hurried up the three porch steps, then gripped the railing post. What was he doing here?

"Long time no see." He stopped at the bottom step and looked up at her. Then, as usual, he looked her up and down. "Still looking good."

Blech. He might be handsome on the outside, but he was a grimy jerk on the inside. And he didn't come close to comparing to Owen. She would have to take a shower after he left, and if she had anything to say about it, it would be soon. "What happened to your fancy sports car?"

"Totaled it." He shrugged and gestured to the car behind him. "That's a rental. I'll get another one. I haven't decided if I want a BMW or a Porsche."

Dylan's parents, who had a lot of money, had bought him that red sports car and were no doubt going to purchase him a new one. *I'm so thankful I'm out of the English world.* "Get in your rental and leave, Dylan. We don't have anything to talk about."

"Sure we do." He climbed to the second step. "We left things hanging between us."

"No, we didn't. And you can stay right there. Don't come any closer."

An annoyed look crossed his face. "You're acting like I'm going to hurt you." His expression changed. Now he was slick Dylan, the guy she had fallen so hard for. "Remember all the good times we had? All the fun?" He was on the middle step now.

"All I have to do is scream and my dad and brothers will be here."

"Don't be so dramatic, Margaret. I'm just here to ask you on a date." One foot landed on the top step. He was now only a foot or two away. "I've missed you."

"I don't miss you." She stepped back. "I've got a new life now, Dylan. I'm not interested in a date or anything else with you. You need to leave now."

Before she could move again, he darted toward her. She ran to the end of the porch, which was hidden behind a large evergreen bush. That had been a mistake. Now he had her cornered, and there was nowhere to go. Dylan was a jerk, but she'd never been afraid of him until now. He was acting different, as if he were under the influence of something. "Have you been drinking?" she asked.

"Nah. I've just been thinking about us a lot lately. We have unfinished business."

But she wasn't convinced he hadn't drunk something earlier in the day. Or worse, taken something illegal. "No, we don't. Like I said—"

"You left me." His eyes turned stormy.

"I joined my church." She lifted her chin. He was mad because she broke up with him? "I explained that to you already."

"You don't miss me at all?"

"No. I don't. I moved on, Dylan. I thought you had too."

He stepped back. "Oh, trust me, I have moved on, little Amish girl." He looked down at her. "You think you're really something, don't you? Playing Little Miss Innocent after everything we've done together."

Shame filled her. Her chin dipped. "I don't think I'm innocent. But I am forgiven." She looked him in the eyes again. "This is the last time I'm telling you. Leave. Now."

He scoffed. "I'll leave when I'm ready."

"She said leave!"

Margaret looked behind Dylan and her heart leapt. *Owen!*

When Owen's taxi pulled behind the gray sedan, he had been practicing what to say to Margaret when he saw her. Then he caught sight of her and a big guy in the corner of her front porch. A flash of jealousy hit him for a split second. Then he realized she was in trouble. He didn't hesitate. He threw the cab fare at the driver. "Put *mei* suitcase in the driveway." He scurried out of the car and ran to the porch.

Now the big guy was facing him. And he was big. Muscles strained at the cuffs of his short-sleeved shirt and broad chest. Obviously the attire was to show off his physique since the weather was too cold not to have a jacket on. The guy was several inches taller and a lot heavier than Owen. But he wasn't worried about that. He glanced at Margaret, seeing her white face and worried eyes. That was who he was concerned about. And he needed to get rid of this pest so he could see if she was all right.

"Leave," he repeated, making sure the man knew he meant business.

"Now a little Amish boy is telling me what to do?" Dylan shook his head. "Go ahead. Make me."

"Don't be a jerk."

"A jerk, huh?"

But as Dylan charged toward Owen, Owen moved in close. He put his leg beside Dylan's, grabbed him by the shoulders, and pushed him down, sweeping his leg behind Dylan's ankles at the same time. He landed hard on his back.

"*Oof.*" Dylan didn't move for a second, then he shook his head. He looked up at Owen, his fists clenching.

Owen didn't move. He didn't say a word. He stared Dylan down, as if daring him to try to make a run at him again.

"Not worth it." Dylan got up and sneered at Owen, then at Margaret. "She's not worth it."

That did it. Anger burst inside him, and he lost his senses. Owen started toward him, but Margaret suddenly blocked his way. "Don't," she said in *Deitsch*, putting her hands on his chest. "Let him *geh*."

Her sweet voice and calming touch brought him back to reality. He nodded as Dylan rushed off to his car. As he got in, Margaret said, "He shouldn't be driving. I think he's under the influence."

"Where's your phone? We can call the police and report him." He looked at Dylan's front license plate. "I got the number."

A few minutes later, Margaret was in the phone shanty, calling the police. She reported Dylan, and the officer said they had a squad car nearby. "Thank you," she said before hanging up. She walked outside the shanty and looked up at Owen. "The police are going to find him," she said.

"*Gut*." He looked at her. "How are you doing?"

"I'm fine." She smiled. "Looks like you saved me again. Although I could have handled him."

Owen looked dubious. "How?"

She explained that her father and brothers-in-law weren't that far away. "I would have been all right."

"Then you didn't need me?" Hurt, he moved away from her. He didn't regret coming here when he did—which had to be God's timing—because Margaret had clearly been in trouble, no matter what she said. But if she didn't need him, even in a situation like that . . .

Doubt crept in his mind, and suddenly all his courage evaporated. "Well, uh, I guess I better get going back home," he said. He sounded stupid, as if home were only across the street and not more than two hours away by bus.

Her brow furrowed. "You just got here. Why are you here, Owen?"

"I, uh . . ." This was it. She'd given him the opening he needed to reveal what was on his heart. And he was stumbling. If Elam and Jesse and the rest of his brothers were here, they would tease him without mercy.

But none of this was funny. And if he didn't tell her now, he probably never would. But something else was also nagging at him and asking the question would give him a few seconds to regain his nerve. "Who was that guy?"

She paled, then looked down at her feet. "Dylan," she said. "My ex-boyfriend."

—❧—

Margaret's hands trembled, but that was nothing compared to the shakiness going on inside her. The shock in Owen's eyes when she told him she used to date Dylan pierced her core.

"You dated him?" Owen still looked stunned.

If he was reacting this way about dating, he would be outright offended if he knew what else she had done with him. This wasn't the first time she wished she hadn't made the choices she did. But she had never been filled with this much deep regret before. Her throat tightened, and she could feel the tears welling in her eyes. Oh *nee*. This was the last thing she needed to do—break down in front of him. But she was so sure he would reject her outright if she told him the truth about her past. And if she told him how she really felt about him, she would have to be honest about what she had done. Either way, he wouldn't want to have anything to do with her. Like her mother constantly said, she wasn't a *gut* girl, despite telling Dylan she was forgiven.

"Margaret?" Instantly he was at her side, and he put his arm around her shoulders.

She wondered if he realized what he was doing. Then again, this was Owen. Kind, smart, handsome Owen. Even if he did care for her, she didn't deserve him. The tears came down faster. When he led her to the swing at the other end of the porch, she didn't protest.

"What's wrong?" he asked after they had both sat down. He

no longer had his arm around her shoulders, but he was sitting close to her.

By now she couldn't stop the tears from flowing. "Everything's wrong," she blurted, and to her horror she couldn't stop herself from talking. "*Mamm*'s barely speaking to me and you had to deal with Dylan and I'm not a *gut* Amish girl. Woman. Whatever."

"Dylan wasn't a problem."

But Margaret heard the edge in his voice. "*Ya*, he is. And I was stupid for going out with him and dumb for—" She covered her mouth.

Owen stilled. "Dumb for what?"

"Do I have to spell it out for you?" She crossed her arms over her chest. "I didn't just dabble in the English world during *rumspringa*. I embraced it, wholeheartedly. There wasn't a thing I didn't try . . . or do." She covered her face with her hands, unable to look at him. "I got too close with Dylan. And playing with fire is just as bad as the act itself."

The sounds of the lowing cows, peaceful before, made her flinch. The silence grew between her and Owen. This was it. She steeled herself for his rejection. Why would he even want to be friends with her at this point?

When he didn't say anything, she finally lowered her arms, still unable to face him. She sniffed, wiping her cheeks with the heel of her hand. "I'm not who you think I am," she said, staring at her feet that couldn't reach the porch boards. "I'm not an innocent and *gut* Amish girl."

"Why do you keep saying that?" Owen asked in a quiet voice.

"What?"

"That you're not *gut*."

"Because it's true." Then she told him everything. About her relationship with her mother and sisters. How she had never reached their standards. She even revealed her recent conversation with her father. Talking about him settled her some but not much. At least she and *Daed* had a solid relationship now. "I realized when I turned eighteen I didn't want to live a wild life," she continued. "I wasn't happy, and there was something missing. I knew I needed to *geh* back to God and to confess what I'd done and then join the church."

"And you thought that would make *yer mamm* happy."

"I didn't do it for her," she said. Then she nodded. "But I thought it would help." Finally, she got the courage to turn to him. "I'm sorry," she whispered.

"For what?" He reached over and brushed a tear from her cheek. "Not being perfect?"

"I'm not even close."

"Let me tell you what I see. From the first time we met, I saw that you were honest. You were up front about not wanting to get married." He paused, and she thought she saw his Adam's apple bob up and down, but he kept on talking. "Then as we got to know each other, I saw that you were kind and thoughtful. You even brought water and muffins the day of the storm, and I hadn't even thought about bringing anything other than *mei* book. I saw that you love nature, and you love learning and adventure. All those things are *gut* to me."

"Really?"

"Really." He reached into his pocket and handed her a white handkerchief.

"What about Dylan?"

Owen shrugged. "You're not going to see him again, are you?"

She scrunched her nose. "Never."

"Then he's forgotten."

For the first time, she felt every bit of tension drain from her body. The shame was still there, but just admitting what she had done, even minus the details—which would always stay between her and God—was making her feel better. Then again, she shouldn't be surprised. Owen always made her feel good. Still, she didn't know why he was here, and whatever the reason was, he sure didn't expect to be met by her weird ex-boyfriend and a walk down her mistake-filled memory lane. "I'm sorry I dumped all that on you," she said.

"Stop apologizing." He looked at her. "We're . . . friends, *ya*?"

She pressed her teeth against her lip. *Oh boy.* How was she supposed to answer him? *With the truth.* She took a deep breath. "*Nee*, Owen. We're not friends."

Owen couldn't believe he'd been metaphorically punched in the gut. This time the pain reached his heart, and it hurt more than he could have imagined. It was one thing for him to try to accept that she didn't care about him, but for her to say they weren't even friends? He'd gotten the sense that she had just shared her deepest secret with him, and he had to admit he wasn't happy hearing about Dylan. But why would she share something so personal if they weren't friends of some sort? *But I don't want to be friends either. I want more.*

Suddenly the emotions he had tried to keep buried came to the surface. "You know what? I don't think we're friends either."

Her mouth dropped open. "What?"

"I came here because . . ." If she could be honest with him, he would be honest with her, even if she didn't feel the same way. "I know we both made it clear that neither of us was looking for romance—"

"Owen—"

"And I meant what I said at the time." Even though they were sitting next to each other, he couldn't help but move another few inches closer to her. "But not anymore. Margaret, I care about you," he said emphatically. There. It was out in the open.

She tilted her head and looked up at him. "In what way?"

He hadn't expected her to ask him that. Now what was he supposed to say? He figured she would know what he meant. "In, uh, a not-friendly way." Was that a smile twitching on her lips?

"I see."

"Do you? Because I want to make it clear as crystal." And just so she didn't have any doubts about what he meant this time, he said, "I really, really care about you."

Her beautiful eyes grew wide, as if what he was saying finally sank in. "You do?"

He nodded, as sure about his feelings in that moment as he was about his faith in God. "*Ya*, I do. I know we had an agreement—"

"Never mind the agreement." She put her hand behind his head and gently tugged his mouth to hers and kissed him.

Oh, this was nice. It was also familiar, as if they'd kissed before . . .

He broke the kiss. "I did kiss you!" he exclaimed. "At the hospital."

Her face turned red. "You remember that?"

He pressed his palm against his forehead. "I can't believe you didn't slap me upside the head."

"Wait a minute." She frowned. "You think you kissed me?"

"I actually thought I imagined it." He instinctively touched his mouth, then dropped his hand to the side. "I wasn't exactly in *mei* right mind at the hospital, and even though the painkillers kicked in a bit later, I started to question everything about my time there."

"Oh boy." Margaret leaned back. "You didn't kiss me. I kissed you." She wrung her hands together. "I knew I shouldn't have, but I couldn't help myself."

He had to keep himself from laughing. This was wonderful. She had actually kissed him. Twice now. His heart was singing. "Like you couldn't help yourself a minute ago?"

"I've always been a little forward." She shook her head. "Make that a lot forward."

"I kind of like that about you."

"But I told you about *mei* past. And about the kiss at the hospital." Confusion crossed her features. "I figured you'd be running for the hills by now."

"If you haven't noticed, the land is pretty flat around here. Let's get back to what's important. Margaret, there are a lot of things about you I like."

"Even now that you know the real me?"

"I've always known the real you." He ran the back of his

fingers over her cheek. "Our pasts don't define us. It's what we do with our lives after we've learned our lessons."

"I can't imagine you having any lessons to learn," she said.

"Oh, there's plenty. I've learned there's more to life than work, for one thing."

"That hardly compares to all the mistakes I've made."

"Who's keeping track? I'm not." He smiled. "I care about the woman you are now. Shall I *geh* through your list of virtues again?"

"You didn't mention how pretty I am."

How could he have forgotten to tell her that? She was the most beautiful woman he'd ever seen, and he would tell her so every day for the rest of her life—

"*Danki.*" Her eyes sparkled with delight. "You didn't mention it, which means you see the real me. That's means everything."

He put his arm around her shoulders, and she leaned against him. With a push of his foot, the rocker moved back and forth. He closed his eyes. This was heaven.

"Owen?"

"*Ya?*"

"How did you learn how to take Dylan down?"

Chuckling, he said, "I have ten *bruders*, remember? I know every wrestling move possible."

She laughed and snuggled against him.

A few moments later he spoke. "Margaret?"

"*Ya?*"

"Come back to Birch Creek with me. I'm not talking about getting married or anything." *Not yet.* But he knew in his heart it would be an eventuality. "There's lots of foraging left to do there. And in the winter we can tap the maple trees and make syrup. *Daed* has a sleigh, and I'm sure he'll let me borrow it. I can show you more of Birch Creek."

She lifted her head and looked at him. "What about work?"

"There are more important things in life," he said, gazing into her eyes. "Like you."

Her smile captured his heart. "Like us."

Epilogue

*M*argaret waited at the end of the Yoders' driveway for Owen to pick her up. She wondered if she'd ever stop feeling excited every time the two of them had a chance to spend time alone together. He didn't tell her where he was taking her today, but she didn't care. She loved surprises, and she loved him. Snow covered the ground and flurries surrounded her, but her coat—and her thoughts about Owen—kept her warm.

Then her thoughts shifted to the phone call she'd had with *Mamm* last night. After telling her two months ago that she was returning to Birch Creek indefinitely, her mother had been furious, enough to actually yell at her. But Margaret stood her ground and left with Owen the next day, with her father's approval. Since then they had talked infrequently on the phone, and Margaret had initiated most of the calls. But yesterday her *mamm* had actually called her, and even though the conversation was still strained, she hoped one day her mother's heart would soften.

Owen pulled his sleigh into the Yoders' driveway and brought the horse to a halt. She climbed inside and gave him a quick kiss on the cheek, not caring if anyone saw them. It wasn't exactly a secret that they were together, and that didn't bother her in the least. She was tired of keeping secrets. By the pleased look on his face, he didn't mind if anyone saw them either.

"I've got something to give you before we *geh*." He reached under his seat and pulled out a rectangular-shaped package wrapped in plain brown paper and handed it to her. "This is for you."

She grinned. "Ooh, a present. But it's not Christmas yet."

"Think of it as an early Christmas gift. *Geh* ahead and open it."

Carefully she unwrapped the paper. She loved getting presents, even the ones her family gave her, although those were always practical, such as socks, underclothes, or a hairbrush. Even as a child she had wanted a game or a toy or even a book, but her *mamm* insisted that the ones her sisters had handed down to her were good enough. Long ago she gave up on getting anything silly or fun from her. As she pulled back the paper, she saw that it was an old book on herbs, plants, and their uses.

"Ezra and I went to visit Ivy last week at her shop," he said as she gingerly opened the cover. "I saw this in the window and thought of you. It's from the 1800s."

"This is incredible." The book had that old musty smell to it, and she thought it was wonderful. The pictures were hand drawn and somewhat faded, but still lovely to look at. Next to each picture was a detailed explanation about each plant and its uses. She could spend hours poring over this valuable volume. Her head jerked up. "I hope it wasn't too expensive."

He smirked. "That's for me to know." Then his expression turned serious. "Do you like it?"

"I love it." She closed the cover and set it on her lap. "*Danki,* Owen. This is the best gift anyone's given me."

"I have one other thing for you," he said, then reached behind the seat of his buggy.

Before she could say anything else, he grabbed her around the waist and pulled her onto his lap. Then he kissed her.

She leaned her head against his shoulder. "I wish I could stay here forever," she said, snuggling against him.

"Why don't you?"

When she met his gaze, she saw he was serious. "Are you asking me to marry you?"

"*Ya.* I'm asking you to marry me."

She pulled back and smirked at him. "Are you sure? I wouldn't want you to make a mistake or anything—"

He stopped her with another kiss. Then he touched his nose to hers. "Just say *ya*, okay?"

"*Ya.*" She kissed him, and when she broke the kiss, she saw that a snowflake had landed on one of his long eyelashes. She brushed it away with her glove-covered hand. "I love you, Owen."

"I love you too." He grabbed the reins of the sleigh and drove off for their ride, and she stayed tucked in his embrace. She was ready for their afternoon ride, and their future together.

Rhoda knocked on Cevilla's front door. Unlike the last time she was here several months ago, she wasn't nervous or unsettled.

She had thought about this, prayed about it, and had even tried to talk herself out of it. But she was tired of living in limbo, of not having a sense of closure.

Then there was Loren. While they made sure not to spend too much time together, there was a spark between them. One afternoon a month ago she had seen him by chance at the discount store in Barton, and they had gotten coffee together. He talked about his late wife, and although she said little about Emmanuel, she did reveal that it was difficult losing a spouse. He was a caring, kind man, and she could easily fall for him . . . but she wasn't free to do so.

She resisted knocking on the door again, knowing Cevilla needed extra time to answer. That didn't keep her from tapping her toe on the elderly woman's porch as snow floated down behind her.

Finally, the door opened. "Rhoda, what a surprise." Cevilla smiled, adjusting her glasses on her face. "Come in. Come in."

Rhoda followed her into the too-warm living room.

"Can I take your coat? How about some tea?" Cevilla shut the door.

"I won't be here long."

"Oh?"

She turned and faced Cevilla. "Does Richard still know how to contact that private investigator?"

Cevilla nodded. "I'm sure he does."

Relief flowed through her. "*Gut*. I need to know if Emmanuel is alive . . . or dead."

Acknowledgments

I'm so fortunate to have by my side as I wrote Margaret and Owen's story my longtime editor, Becky Monds, and my longtime agent, Natasha Kern. Thank you both for your expertise and encouragement. I say this after every book I write, but I mean it from the heart. A big thank-you to Karli Jackson and Laura Wheeler for their editorial wisdom and help.

As always, a huge thank-you to you, dear reader. I hope you enjoyed Margaret and Owen's story. I loved writing about this fun, but sometimes clueless, couple. I'd love to hear what you thought about their story! You can email me using the contact page on my website: www.kathleenfuller.com.

Discussion Questions

1. Rhoda believes she deserves to be lonely because she didn't stand up to her husband. Do you agree with her? Why or why not?
2. Early in the story, Owen has difficulty with balance in his life because he works too hard. What advice would you give someone who struggles with the same problem?
3. Owen tells Margaret that "all of us need to work on our pride." Do you agree with his statement, and if so, what are some ways we can be more humble?
4. Margaret thinks a real relationship is about connection, respect, and companionship. What other characteristics would you add to this list?
5. Owen believes marriage is for life and isn't to be taken lightly. Why do you think he believes this? How would you explain this belief to someone else?
6. The Amish like to use herbal medicines and remedies.

Are there any herbal recipes that you use, or that have been passed down through your family?

7. Owen tells Margaret, "Our pasts don't define us. It's what we do with our lives after we've learned our lessons." Discuss a time when this was true in your life.

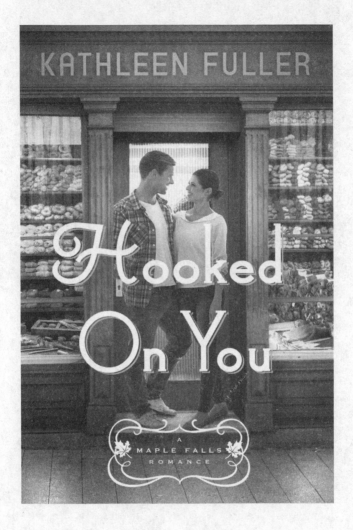

KATHLEEN FULLER

Hooked
On You

A MAPLE FALLS
ROMANCE

*Welcome to Maple Falls, where everyone
knows your name* and *your business.*

Available in print, ebook, and audio

Chapter 1

A riot of colors, textures, and fibers filled the canvas in front of Riley McAllister. She tilted her head to the right. To the left. Then, with careful precision and pointed tweezers, she started to apply a hair-thin golden thread to the narrow bead of glue on the peacock feather in the center, the final touch to a project that had taken over three months to complete.

"Riley! Your Mimi called!"

Riley flinched and the tweezers pierced through the canvas, marring the multilayered feather. She started to mutter a curse but bit her tongue. She couldn't afford foul language, not when she had almost zero dollars in her bank account. Besides, she was determined to win the cash in the cuss jar at the end of the month. There had to be over three hundred dollars in it already.

"Oops, my bad."

She turned around and glared at her roommate. Melody had entered her bedroom—art studio—living room in the apartment they shared, a silver headband pushing back her short, curly black hair. Then Melody's words hit her. The torn canvas and gold thread forgotten, she jumped up from her chair. *Mimi.*

"Is she okay?" Riley asked, panicked.

"She's fine, but she sounds a bit cranky. She said she must have called five times before I answered." Melody took a sip of coffee out of her brand-new *Probably Wine* mug. The purchase was courtesy of her winning the cuss jar bounty last month. "You really should put your phone on vibrate at least. It's a good thing I saw it light up on the kitchen counter."

Dread filled Riley. "What did she say?" Her grandmother was no spring chicken, and as the years passed, she worried the next call would be *the one*. She grabbed her cell out of Melody's hand.

"For you to call her. You're welcome, by the way." Melody scowled. "Geez, calm down. She's not at death's door, if that's what you're worried about."

Riley turned her back to Melody and tapped Mimi's number on the phone screen. "How would you know?"

"Because she said, 'Tell Riley I'm not at death's door.'"

Riley turned back around as she put the phone to her ear, relief flooding her. "I'm sorry. You know how I get when she calls."

"You get crazy," Melody said with a grin. At Riley's pointed look, she added, "Crazy with worry, I mean."

True. She tended to expect the worst when Mimi called, despite telling herself she was being ridiculous. But she couldn't help it. *If anything ever happened to Mimi . . .* She drew in a deep breath as her grandmother answered.

"Hi." Riley forced a cheerful tone. "I'm sorry I missed your—" She looked at her roommate.

Five, Melody mouthed, holding up her hand.

"Five calls." Riley winced. "Is everything okay?"

"Oh yes, sugar. Just the usual goin' on here." Mimi's lilting Southern drawl filled Riley's ear, triggering the tiniest spark of homesickness, which always surprised her. After nine years of living in New York City, she should be over it, but every time she heard Mimi's voice, it came back again. Riley's life in Maple Falls had been a big disappointment, but that wasn't Mimi's fault.

"The *usual* required five calls in a row?"

"If you had picked up the phone, there only would have been one."

"You could have left a message, you know." Riley plopped onto the pull-out sofa that was also her bed.

"I could have, but then I wouldn't have heard Melody's sweet voice. She's a peach."

Riley smiled and glanced at Melody, spying her friend's frown as she inspected the ruined canvas. Her stomach lurched. With some time and precision, the artwork could be fixed. Still, Riley would always know it was imperfect. She had planned to put it in her show next week, but that was impossible now. The work was too flawed to display in public.

"Riley? You still with me, hon?"

"Yes, sorry." She turned away from the canvas and focused on her grandmother, her prior concern rising to the surface. "How are you? Is everything all right?"

"I called because I haven't heard from you in three weeks. According to your social media, you've been a busy young lady." She sniffed. "Apparently too busy to call your decrepit old grandmother."

"You're *not* decrepit." Erma McAllister was far from feeble, but she was seventy-two, and Riley didn't like thinking about her getting older. She also didn't want to point out that her social media wasn't exactly a reflection of her life. She kept it going with carefully curated pictures of her works in progress, hoping to catch the eye of someone in the art business. A far-flung idea, but it didn't take much effort to post a picture and write a caption. "You're also too classy for guilt trips."

"It was worth a shot." Mimi sighed. "I guess I better get to the point. I need you to come home. ASAP."

Riley pressed her hand against her chest, feeling her heart rate speeding up. "Why? Are you sick? Are you in the hospital?"

"No, I'm not sick . . . or in the hospital. At least not anymore."

Riley sat up. "You were in the hospital and you didn't tell me?"

"There wasn't time. I broke my leg—"

"You broke your leg?" Her voice choked in her throat, and Melody rushed to sit down next to her. "When? How?"

"If I can get a word in edgewise, I'll tell you."

Mimi's quiet, composed tone immediately calmed Riley, as it had for so many years. After an unstable childhood, she'd moved in with her grandmother when she was thirteen. Mimi had been her rock ever since. "I'm listening."

"Put her on speaker," Melody said.

Riley tapped the screen. "You're on speaker now. Melody wants to know what's going on too."

"Oh, hello again, sugar. As I was saying, I broke my leg when I slid into third base last Sunday."

Riley and Melody stared at each other.

"What?" Riley finally said.

"You see, the young man playing third was blocking the

base, so I had to slide. Myrtle hit a lousy outside pitch straight to the first baseman, who clearly should have been riding the bench instead of playing the infield. He flubbed the ball, and I thought I'd made it to third, until everyone started yelling at me to go back to second. I was already committed, so down I went. I was safe, by the way."

"Is she serious?" Melody whispered.

Rolling her eyes, Riley nodded. Softball was one of her grandmother's favorite sports, and she had dragged Riley to many a community game until Riley was seventeen. Then the community games had stopped.

"Mimi, you shouldn't have been playing softball in the first place."

"I don't need a lecture from you, young lady," Mimi grumbled. "I need you to come home and take over Knots and Tangles while I convalesce."

"Oh no," Riley said, getting up from the couch. She shook her head. "I'm not falling for this again."

"Falling for what?"

Her grandmother sounded so innocent Riley almost believed her. "Like I've said a million times before, I'm not moving back to Maple Falls, and I'm definitely not taking over the yarn shop for you." She walked over to the painting and scowled at the hole in the canvas. "I am impressed, though. You spun a good yarn, pun intended."

"I'm not spinnin' anything." Mimi's tone was sharp. "It's the truth. Myrtle and I joined the new church softball team a few weeks ago, and we just had our second game. Now I'm out for the season, so stop what you're doing and get back here. Pronto."

Riley spun around and met Melody's stunned gaze. Her grandmother rarely used a commanding tone with her, and not once since Riley moved away had she been insistent about her returning to Maple Falls. Until now. While she had asked Riley to visit around the holidays, she never pressured her and even visited New York a few times. She understood how important Riley's career was to her and had always supported it 100 percent. Riley was banking that she still did.

"Mimi, I'm sorry you broke your leg—"

"Thank you. Now, about your return—"

"And I would love to come help you." Which she would, if it didn't mean going back to Arkansas. "But I can't exactly drop everything here at the last minute. I have a jo—" She hadn't told Mimi she was working part-time for a food delivery service. She had to pay her bills somehow, since her art wasn't making any money. "I, um, have a show coming up." At least that part was true. *Mostly*.

"Oh?" Excitement entered her voice. "I didn't know that. Where is it so I can tell everyone about my famous granddaughter?"

She wouldn't exactly be bragging about her one and only granddaughter, the supposed artistic rage of New York City, if she knew her art show was at the local flea market. It wasn't even a show, really. Just a place to sell some of her work so she could make her part of the rent. Telling herself it was an art show made it easier to swallow.

"The details aren't worked out yet."

"So it's something you can postpone? Sugar, you know I wouldn't ask you to come if I wasn't desperate. Myrtle's going on a three-week cruise again, so I can't count on her."

Guilt hammered Riley, but she stood fast. "What about one of the other Bosom Buddies?" she asked, referring to the small group of ladies that met weekly at the yarn shop for coffee, knitting or crocheting, and copious amounts of gossip.

"I suppose one or two of them could help," Mimi muttered. "But they're *awfully* busy."

Riley pressed her fingertip against her temple, feeling her pulse throb. She had vowed not to return to Maple Falls until she made it big in New York—or at least could say she wasn't living from hand to mouth, and she was barely doing that. She knew the Bosom Buddies wouldn't hesitate to help her grandmother if Mimi asked. Most of the seven women had been friends since grade school, except for two who had been folded into the group over the years.

"I . . ."

She turned and looked at Melody, whose thin brown arms were crossed over her chest, her dark eyes peering over bright-green square glasses. Riley knew that reproving look, and she didn't like being on the receiving end of it.

In truth she didn't need Melody to prod her. Riley couldn't refuse the woman who had practically raised her after her mother abandoned Riley for God knew where. If Mimi needed her, Riley would be there—just like Mimi had always been there for her.

"I'll get the next flight out," Riley said, holding back a sigh. The expense would almost max out her one credit card, but she'd worry about that later.

"Oh, Riley, thank you! Thank you!" Mimi gushed. "I can't tell you how much this means to me. I know the shop will be in good hands with you while I recuperate. I won't keep you. Once you've made your reservation, text me your flight info, and I'll have someone pick you up from the airport."

"I'll just get an Uber," Riley said.

"Nonsense. The airport is over an hour away. That would cost way too much money. Don't you worry, sugar. I'll make all the arrangements to get you back home."

Home? Maple Falls had never felt like home.

"Love you, sweetie," Mimi added before Riley could say anything else. "Talk to you soon!"

She stared at the phone after Mimi hung up. A few seconds later, she glanced at Melody, who had sat back down on their lumpy, secondhand couch and was now grinning at her.

"I knew you wouldn't let her down."

Riley trudged over to the couch and sank onto it again, her phone still in her hand. She continued staring at the black screen. "I don't know about this."

"What's the big deal? You're taking care of Mimi, who means a lot to you."

"But that also means going back to Maple Falls."

"So? You're overdue for a visit home, Riley. I've been back to Minnesota three times this year alone. When was the last time you were in Arkansas?"

Nearly ten years ago, when she first moved to New York. She wasn't about to tell Melody that. The two of them had become good friends over the last two years since they became roommates. But there were things Riley didn't want to share with her—or anyone else, for that matter. Like her reasons for staying away from Maple Falls.

Shifting the subject, she said, "You're right. I need to focus on taking care of Mimi. That's what matters. I'll make sure she's following doctor's orders." She smirked as she set her phone on the coffee table. "She has a tendency to think she's invincible."

"No way." Melody chuckled. "Imagine that."

"I can't believe she slid into third base," Riley said. "Or that she is even playing softball at her age. Then again, Mimi has been in sports all her life. She and Myrtle were on the first girls' softball team in Maple Falls, and they were both excellent. She still plays tennis with Gwen too." Riley looked at her slightly pudgy tummy, the result of cheap food, a few too many glasses of wine alone in her apartment, and more than a little stress. She didn't doubt her grandmother was in better shape at seventy-two than Riley was right now.

"I had no idea Erma was so athletic," Melody said.

"I shouldn't be surprised she's on the team. Well, maybe a little because of her age. Whoever is coaching ought to be smacked upside the head for letting her do something so ridiculous."

"You think they could have stopped her?"

"They could have stalled her at second." Riley shook her head and turned to her friend. "Anyway, what's done is done. I'm heading back to Arkansas." A sour lump formed in her stomach at the thought. She would have to quit her job and cancel her upcoming "show." "Don't worry about rent, Melody. I'll still pay my share." *Somehow.*

Melody nodded. "Any idea how long you'll be gone?"

Riley shrugged. "Depends on how fast Mimi's leg heals, I guess. I'll be back as soon as I can, but it could be a while."

Nodding, Melody adjusted her headband, seemingly deep in

thought. After a pause, she said, "Would you mind subletting to Charlie?"

"The guy in your acting class?"

"Yeah. He's been couch surfing for the past two months after a bad experience with his last roommate. He's looking for a place to land until he can find something more permanent."

"Are you sure he's . . . safe?"

"That boy's practically got wholesome tattooed on his forehead. I kinda feel sorry for him. He's character actor material and not bad, but he's rough around the edges. I've gotten to know him pretty well over the past year. Trust me, he's safe." Melody gripped Riley's hand. "Thanks for caring, sis."

"Always." Riley held her hand tight, then let it go. She was so grateful for Melody's friendship. She had answered Riley's ad for a new roommate at the local university where she took theater classes. Friendship had never come easy to Riley, but Melody's easygoing and caring personality had eventually pulled her out of her shell.

She was also grateful to the unknown Charlie for taking over the rent for a little while. "Guess I better search online for a flight."

"And I've got to get ready for the exciting world of waitressing. Double shift today. Yay me." Melody got up from the couch and headed for the one bedroom in the apartment. When they first rented the place together, they agreed to change rooms every three months. The arrangement had worked out well, especially since neither of them was big on entertaining visitors. When she wasn't delivering food, Riley was focused on her art, while Melody, a social butterfly who liked being out and about, often spent time with her actor friends at various places around the city. The few times she dragged Riley out of the cave had been torture. Riley was used to being alone, and she liked it that way.

A few moments later, Melody emerged from the bedroom, dressed in the white T-shirt and black pants her job required. Her blue-and-orange-striped drawstring backpack was slung over her shoulders, and her lips glistened with plum lipstick that perfectly complemented her dark skin.

"See you tomorrow," she said, opening the apartment door. "Don't wait up."

Riley waved goodbye as Melody closed the door. She rose from the couch and turned the double locks into place, then glanced at her ruined art. She wasn't in the mood to try to fix it now. Instead, she walked over to the window and gazed at the view of the brick apartment building next door. Not much of a vista, but like every struggling artist trying to make it in the big city, she couldn't afford to be picky. Still, New York was her home.

The window was cracked open, letting in the buzz of city life. When she'd first arrived, she had been awed by the place. Too awed, to the point of culture shock. She wasn't used to the mix of cultures, but she had quickly grown to appreciate the diversity of the people living here. She'd never gotten used to the nightlife, but that was fine. Her focus wasn't on having fun. She was determined to break into the hip art scene that had eluded her for the past ten years.

She might be broke and in serious need of some vitamin D, not to mention shedding a few pounds, but at least she wasn't in Maple Falls. The only way she'd planned to return was after she had proven to herself and everyone else that she was different.

Successful. Responsible. And nothing like Tracey. Thanks to her grandmother not acting her age, Riley's plan was now in shambles.

Riley turned and stared at the ruined peacock feather and the golden threads she had painstakingly glued over thick, lifted curls of purple, blue, ochre, and green acrylic paint. Poking through the colorful swirls in what seemed like a random pattern but had taken hours to design were the glossy black-and-white magazine pictures of city life. The comfort of nature's colors clashing with the harshness of human constructs. She loved to explore opposite concepts in her art using unexpected materials—fabric, feathers, a variety of paints, anything with texture, and especially substances that on the surface were easily discarded things yet could be transformed into something beautiful.

A sigh escaped. There'd been a time when she thought her art was unique, and in the unsophisticated town of Maple Falls, it was. But not here. Mixed-media artists were everywhere, and getting herself noticed in a sea of aspiring creatives had been beyond difficult. But she wasn't going to give up. There wasn't time to fix the piece the way she wanted to, but she would tackle it when she returned. Right now she had to go take care of her grandmother, which meant working at Knots and Tangles again.

A car horn sounded below, jolting Riley's thoughts. She'd never imagined she'd be working there again. During her teen years she spent hours in her grandmother's yarn shop. Not only working but practicing her art in the all-purpose room in the back. The old yarn store had been her job and her haven. But even she could see that it was a fifty-year millstone around her grandmother's neck. Mimi needed to sell the store and retire. Riley had mentioned it to her over the years only to be instantly shut down.

Maple Falls was in decline when Riley moved away, and from little hints she gathered during conversations with Mimi, things hadn't improved.

Riley thought her grandmother not only needed to sell the store but also needed to put her large house on the market and move in with Myrtle. Or maybe Myrtle could move in with Mimi. Riley wasn't naive enough to think her grandmother would come to New York with her, but Mimi moving in with one of her good friends was a possibility. They were both widows, and paring down expenses would benefit them both. If there was something Riley was an expert at, it was pinching her pennies.

While her brain knew retirement and consolidation were in Mimi's best interest, the thought of the store being in someone else's hands pinched at her heart. She shoved the feeling away, as she normally did when she grew sentimental. It was time her grandmother embraced change. This visit was a prime opportunity for Riley to convince her of that.

She felt an unexpected spark of hope. She had a plan now— help Mimi heal and convince her to sell her shop and the house. All three tasks wouldn't be easy, but she was determined. Once her grandmother unchained herself from the past, Riley could too— and when she left Maple Falls this time, it would be for good.

She crossed the small living room, opened her ancient laptop, and started to search for a flight. As she surfed, another thought popped into her mind. But no—she didn't have to worry about running into *him*. Like her, he'd moved on from Maple Falls. Still, remembering the crush she'd had on him in high school—one he had no idea about—caused a tiny flutter in her stomach. Talk about silly. She hadn't given him a single thought since she left

Maple Falls. Okay, maybe one . . . or fifty thoughts since she'd left, but not any recently. And there was no reason for her to think about Hayden Price again now. She put him out of her mind and booked her flight to Arkansas.

———

"Erma Jean McAllister, you need Jesus."

Erma set her cell phone on the counter and looked at her friend of close to sixty-five years. She tapped her chest with two fingers. "I have Jesus. Right in here."

"Then you need a double portion." Myrtle Benson straightened the business cards on the counter next to the small antique cash register that was just for show. A working adding machine from the eighties was right next to it. "Good thing we have evening service tonight."

Erma wheeled herself from behind the counter, trying not to knock down a display of knitting needles with her outstretched, plaster-covered leg. She was proud that her little store, Knots and Tangles, was one of the original businesses in Maple Falls and at one time had the most yarn and fiber art supplies within a one-hundred-fifty-mile radius. Her mother owned the shop before Erma, and her grandmother had started the business. A woman entrepreneur was almost unheard of back then. Erma had worked here since she was twelve, and very little of the shop had changed since then. The place was full to the brim, and that was the way she liked it.

Her wheelchair, however, did not. "What are you prattling on about?" she said.

Myrtle sighed. "That phone call you just made to Riley. Land sakes, woman, you know I can cancel my trip anytime."

"And let you disappoint Jorge?"

"His name is Javier. And I'm sure he's long gone from the ship anyway. You know those jobs can be temporary."

Erma caught the dreamy look in Myrtle's eyes, the same one she'd had when she came home from her cruise eight months ago after meeting Jorge, er, Javier, the silver-haired—and silver-tongued, apparently—maître d' at one of the fancy restaurants on the cruise ship. Erma couldn't remember the name of the place, but she did remember how Myrtle wouldn't stop talking about the food—and the *service*.

"You've been looking forward to this trip for so long."

"I haven't heard from him since my last letter." Myrtle stuck out her lower lip, covered in a soft pink lipstick that coordinated with her oversize handbag. "I might as well cancel."

"If you cancel, I'm going in your place."

"With a broken leg?"

Erma gave her a pointed look. "In a heartbeat."

"You might just do it too." Myrtle grimaced. "Fine. You win, as usual. But that still doesn't make it right that you acted like it was an emergency and Riley had to come right away."

"It *is* an emergency." She gestured to the overstuffed shelves and baskets in the store. "How am I supposed to maneuver around this place in this thing?" She slammed her hands on the wheelchair armrests, which jolted the chair and made her leg twinge. Uh-oh, that was more than a twinge. "I need a pain pill."

"Right away." Myrtle rushed to get a glass of water from the bathroom sink in the back, then handed it and a pill to Erma. "Bea has already told you she can help out."

Erma swallowed the pill, then leaned back in the wheelchair. Bea was Erma's closest friend, but Myrtle came in second. She was grateful for their offers of help, but she needed to refuse them this time. "It's high time Riley came home for a visit. Nine years is too long."

"So you took advantage of your injury to get her back here." Myrtle gave her a reproving look. "You know why she left."

Erma lifted her chin. "She can have an art career here."

"That's not what I'm talking about."

She knew exactly what Myrtle was referring to—her no-good daughter who hadn't returned since she disappeared fifteen years ago. Riley still carried the burden of that rejection, even if she stuffed it down behind a facade of small-town girl turned big-city artist. "I just want her home, Myrtle. Is that too much to ask?"

Her friend's blue eyes softened, the creases in the corners deepening. "It might be."

Erma didn't want to hear that.

The bell over the door chimed, and both women turned to see Hayden Price walk into the store. If Erma were fifty years younger and hadn't known not only Hayden's parents but also his grandparents and great-grandparents, she wouldn't mind taking a crack at the handsome young man. As it was, she could still appreciate his fine form, which looked even better in a baseball uniform. He wasn't as winsome as her Gus had been in his day, but he was definitely easy on the eyes. *I might be old, but I ain't dead.*

"Hi, Hayden," Myrtle said, casually patting the back of her short gray hair. "What brings you by?"

Erma smirked. Seemed like she wasn't the only senior woman who thought Hayden was the bee's knees.

"I came to check on our center fielder." Hayden walked over to Erma and crouched in front of her. "How's the leg?"

"Tolerable."

"She just took a pain pill," Myrtle blurted.

Erma shot her an annoyed look. "Don't you have a cruise to pack for?"

"I guess I do." She grabbed her pink purse, which looked big enough to house half the contents of the yarn store, and headed for the door. "*Hasta la*, um, whatever."

"You might want to brush up on your Spanish for Jorge," Erma called out.

"It's Javier!" The door shut behind her.

Hayden chuckled. "You two are a mess."

"Sugar, you have no idea."

He stood, still smiling, a shock of his thick blond hair falling over his forehead. Then all traces of humor disappeared. "I'm sorry about what happened."

She waved him off. "Not your fault."

"I was the third base coach. And I'm the head coach. I should have told you to stay on second."

"I wouldn't have listened to you anyway." She looked up at him, smiling as she remembered the split second before her leg ended up going in a direction God never intended. "Did you hear the crowd cheering?"

"They were yelling at you to go back."

"But I was already committed—"

He held up his hand. "Let's not go down that road again. I

came by to take you to lunch if you're so inclined. Today's special at the Sunshine Diner is liver and onions."

"Ugh, who likes that?"

"I do." He looked slightly offended.

"You're too young for old people food." Erma tried to move toward him and knocked over a display of T-shirt yarn. "Oh, for goodness' sake."

"I'll fix it."

She watched as he made a valiant attempt to put all the skeins of yarn in the cube she'd knocked over. They had been neatly stacked—one of the few displays that was—but now they were being haphazardly squished into the space.

"There," he said, cramming the last skein of yarn into the box. "No harm done. So, are we on for lunch? I only have forty-five minutes, and then I have to get back to the store."

Erma was about to tell him she wasn't hungry when an idea jumped into her mind. *Erma Jean, you're a genius.* "I'm not all that hungry, but there is something you can do for me."

"Name it."

She wished there were a way to convince him not to feel guilty over what happened. Truth be told, she should have known better than to attempt that slide. The accident brought home the fact that she wasn't as fit as she used to be, which was another reason she wanted Riley back. Although she'd never admit it out loud, Myrtle was right—she was taking advantage of her accident to coax Riley back to the fold. She was worried about her granddaughter. The child had always been a loner, and that tendency hadn't changed since her big move to New York. Riley needed fresh air and companionship. And potential companionship was standing right in front of Erma, wrapped up in a charming and attractive package.

"I need you to pick up someone from the airport for me," she told Hayden. "Either tonight or tomorrow, if you're free."

"Just so happens I am." He grinned. "All you need to do is let me know when."

"I'll send you a text." As the creator and coach of the newly minted church softball team, he had given all the players his cell phone number. For years Erma had been resistant to texting, preferring to pick up the phone and call whoever she wanted to talk to. But she acknowledged that sometimes it was convenient, especially if you wanted to avoid any unwelcome questions.

"That works." He put his hands into the cargo pockets of his shorts. "Are you sure you don't want anything to eat? I can bring you something if you don't feel like going to the diner."

"No, I'm fine."

"All right. Rain check then." He headed for the front of the store, then turned around and looked at her, smiling again— Hayden Price's typical expression. Not only was he handsome but he was unfailingly optimistic and had been since he was a young kid. The perfect contrast to her serious but sweeter than peaches-and-cream granddaughter. He waved at Erma, then left for the diner.

She smiled, steepling her fingers. Erma couldn't believe it—a broken leg might be just the thing she needed to help her granddaughter.

About the Author

With over a million copies sold, Kathleen Fuller is the author of several bestselling novels, including the Hearts of Middlefield novels, the Middlefield Family novels, the Amish of Birch Creek series, and the Amish Letters series as well as a middle-grade Amish series, the Mysteries of Middlefield.

Visit her online at KathleenFuller.com
Facebook: @WriterKathleenFuller
Twitter: @TheKatJam
Instagram: @kf_booksandhooks